Promise to Defend

PROMISE TO DEFEND

Rescue Ops Book 2

DIANA GARDIN

FOREVER
YOURS

New York Boston

Copyright © 2017 by Diana Gardin
Preview of *Mine to Save* copyright © 2017 by Diana Gardin

Cover design by Elizabeth Turner
Cover copyright © 2017 by Hachette Book Group, Inc.

Forever Yours
Hachette Book Group
1290 Avenue of the Americas, New York, NY 10104
forever-romance.com
twitter.com/foreverromance

First published as an ebook and as a print on demand: September 2017

Forever Yours is an imprint of Grand Central Publishing. The Forever Yours name and logo are trademarks of Hachette Book Group, Inc.

The publisher is not responsible for websites (or their content) that are not owned by the publisher.

The Hachette Speakers Bureau provides a wide range of authors for speaking events. To find out more, go to www.hachettespeakersbureau.com or call (866) 376-6591.

ISBNs: 978-1-4555-7155-0 (ebook), 978-1-4555-7156-7 (print on demand trade edition)

Acknowledgments

First of all, I'd like to thank my Lord and Savior Jesus Christ, who gave me the desire and skill to write. Through Him I can do all things!

My family is always there for me when I put down my computer and unplug from all things writing. I'm so thankful they're along for this ride with me.

Thank you to my agent, Stacey Donaghy. You are more than an agent: You are my friend, and I'm so very thankful to have found you. I am even more thankful that you're always on my side.

To my fabulous editor on *Promise to Defend*, Lexi Smail: Working with you is such an enlightening experience. Your thoughts and ideas on the world of NES are invaluable, and your expertise when it comes to how to make a story take off is something I could never trade. Thank you for everything!

To the team at Forever Romance: You are all such a well-oiled machine. From editing, to copyediting, to cover design, and all of the other inner workings I don't even get to see, you are all fabulous and I'm lucky to be a part of it all. Thank you for your efforts on my behalf!

To my favorite sounding board and the girl who's become one of my very best friends, Sybil Bartel: I don't know how it happened, but you're like the other half of my writing brain. You're there at all hours of the day and night whether I need to get an idea out, or I'm completely out of them. I only hope I help you as much as you help me! Love you, girl.

To the very best group of writers a girl could ever ask for, the NAC: Ara, Meredith, Kate, Bindu, Sophia, Laura, Missy, Jessica, Amanda, Jamie, Marie, and Marnee—you are my very best source of sanity. Without you, this business would have ended me long ago! Love y'all!

To blogger, publicist, and host extraordinaire, Tracy Comerford: Thank you for everything you do! You help spread the word about my books far and wide, and because of you I have an audience for these books I never would have found otherwise. Thank you for your never-ending support and patience.

To the Dolls—the best fan group a girl could ask for. Talking to you guys every day, sharing my fictional world with you, receiving your feedback, it all keeps me going! You all recharge me and refuel me when I need it, and your support and positivity makes this job so much more fun! Thank you all for being you!

To the bloggers who have supported me throughout this journey: There are too many of you to name, but you know who you are. You have read every single book, given me great reviews, and shared my work with as many people as you can. I couldn't do any of this without your help and your enthusiasm. A thousand thank-yous.

And last but never least, to the readers who find their way to Wilmington, North Carolina, to hang out with the sexy men of Night Eagle Security and the women who are strong enough to love them. I hope you fall in love with this world as much as I have, because without you I'd be nothing. <3

1

RONIN

The sky above me is deep purple, especially beautiful tonight with the generous dotting of stars. There are no clouds to block the glittering specks of light overhead, and I appreciate the view more than I usually would.

Tonight is a celebration of love, something I tend to avoid if I can.

The crisp North Carolina night hugs the wedding guests as they twirl around the dance floor or congregate at the tables, talking and laughing with one another like they don't have a care in the world. I spot the members of my team at Night Eagle Security gathered at one table, and my gaze roams over the group as they burst into raucous laughter.

They're enjoying their night. The thought almost makes me smile.

As Jeremy Teague's best man, I've enjoyed myself, too. Watching him fall in love with his high school sweetheart all over again has been fun. He never thought it would happen for him, thought he and Rayne were over a long time ago. When she strolled back into town with their eight-year-old son, Decker, in tow, Jeremy about lost his mind.

I was proud of the way he stepped right into that father role like it was easy. Like becoming a parent to a son you previously knew nothing about was a cakewalk. I knew it wasn't, but for him the choice was clear. He wanted that life with Rayne and Decker.

And now he has it.

My eyes find them, swaying on the dance floor. Rayne's head rests on Brains's—the nickname he earned as a gadgets guru on our private security team—shoulder while his hands wander up and down her back. It looks like they move as one unit, and I know that everything will be different now. She's his number one partner in life now, not me. And that's how it should be.

If I ever thought there was a chance I'd have that opportunity again myself, I'd take it.

But some people only get that kind of pure, unequaled love once in a lifetime.

I'd already had mine.

My gaze suddenly sweeps toward the sound of giggling, not far from the newlywed couple. I zero in on a flash of dark red hair pulled to the side, exposing a creamy expanse of graceful neck. Olive Alexander, Rayne's sister, twirls Decker around in a circle, and then ducks as he does the same for her. They're both grinning like mad and her dark, blue eyes sparkle in the moonlight. White, glowing paper lanterns all around the yard mingle with the twinkling lights strung from the trees, and the effect it has on Olive takes my fucking breath away.

I study the pair for a moment. Olive takes both of Decker's hands as the band launches into a lively tune and the silliness she gives him suits her. I've met Olive a handful of times, and even though her beauty always stunned me, I never took her for the laid-back, silly, hands-on-aunt type.

Apparently, I'd been wrong.

Two deep dimples appear in her cheeks as she drops her head back and laughs at something the kid did, and I find myself lost in a sea of thoughts. *How often does she smile like that? When will she be leaving to go back to Europe? Has she always had those goddamn dimples?*

"She's pretty." A soft, matter-of-fact voice reaches me, and I glance to the side and down to see that Sayward Diaz has crept up beside me.

I've only ever seen Sayward in a pair of jeans and sneakers with a hoodie at the Night Eagle office. Tonight, she chose to forgo her usual uniform and wear a simple turquoise dress that sweeps the ground at her feet, showing off the curves she apparently rocked underneath the jeans all this time.

"You look good tonight, Diaz." I catch her eye, making sure she knows I mean it.

Sayward shrugs. "Thanks. Everyone is supposed to dress up for a wedding, right? I bought this today." She fingers the soft material of her dress, and I bite back a smile.

Social graces aren't really Sayward's strong suit. As a consultant for Night Eagle Security, she's a legit computer hacker whose skills can't be beat by anyone. But she's easy to be around, and works her ass off, so I'd never complain about having her around.

I raise my bourbon to my lips and sip, appreciating the fiery path it burns down my throat. "Well…you're rocking the shit outta that dress. Not every woman could."

Now her eyes meet mine, like she's only just figured out that I'm complimenting her. A small smile works its way onto her lips. "Thanks, Swagger."

Lifting my chin at her in acknowledgment of my own NES nickname, I indicate the table where our friends are sitting. "Shall we?"

I hold out my arm, and she looks at it for a second like she's wondering what to do with it before she finally slips her hand through and lets me lead her toward the table. I pull out a chair for her beside Dare Conners's wife, Berkeley, and take the empty one opposite Grisham Abbot. His fiancée, Greta, grins at me.

"You taking all of this in, Ronin?" her sweet voice asks.

Shrugging, I down the rest of my drink and contemplate getting back up for a refill. "It was a good wedding."

Berkeley leans over Dare to peer at me. "The boys of NES are dropping like flies, Ronin. Don't tell me you'd never consider settling down again."

Dare stares at her. "His nickname is *Swagger*."

I roll my eyes. "You know that has nothing to do with women."

No, I earned my nickname for the confidence I carry when making a man scream like a crying baby at my mercy. My claim to fame? All the ways I can torture a man without actually killing him. Because in interrogation, the goal is always to make the prisoner talk. If he's dead, he can't talk. I have a magic touch in this area. Something I'm proud of? Maybe not. But afterward, I'm able to walk with my head high because what I've done furthers the greater good. And that's something I can live with when my head hits the pillow each night.

Grisham, or Ghost as we call his stealthy ass, snorts. "Definitely has nothing to do with women."

My team is aware that I already settled down once. It's just not something we talk about, and that's my choice. It seems like a lifetime ago, now, but my heart went into the ground at the same time that my wife did.

Game over.

"I don't think that whole happily-ever-after shit is for me." I keep my voice low as I answer Berkeley's question, averting my gaze.

Inside, my chest tightens, the feeling of my heart squeezing dangerously tight overwhelming me. The emotion, the grief and fury that I thought I recovered from a long time ago, resurfaces and threaten to pull me under.

Immediately, Berkeley's whiskey-colored eyes go all soft and gooey and her bottom lip disappears into her mouth. "You don't know that. Everyone deserves love, Ronin."

Shaking my head, I scan the ongoing party. If she thinks I deserve love, it's because she doesn't know the truth behind my story. I couldn't protect my wife the first time around. Pretty sure guys like me don't get a second shot. And I've accepted that.

I incline my head toward Brains and his brand-new wife, who are now standing beside a small table on the patio. Their faces are masks of utter concentration as they work together to guide a huge knife through a towering white cake. The crowd erupts in cheers when they succeed, and a photographer snaps their picture. I've never seen such a look of pure, unadulterated joy on my best friend's face. There's a peace about him he never had before.

I'm saved from having to answer Berkeley when Decker throws his little body into my side. "Uncle Ronin! You gonna eat cake?"

Looking at him, I'm pretty sure his cheeks might split open from the size of his smile. The kid just got everything every other child in the world wants. His mom and his dad together under one roof. Holding out my fist, he bumps it and then we blow it up.

"Cake? Heck yeah. We gotta have cake."

Decker nods, serious as a lethal injection. "Yeah. We gotta have cake."

Olive saunters up behind him, leaning low over his shoulder to kiss his cheek. She pauses there, her deep sapphire eyes meeting mine for a brief pause. I take the time to notice for the first time that there's a dusting of freckles, delicate and sparse, sprinkling her nose and cheeks. That, combined with the dimples, the huge, deep-set eyes, and the striking color of her hair, are enough to keep me locked in her stare.

Rising, she doesn't look away. "Hello, Ronin."

Olive's voice is a lot different from her sister's. Where Rayne has one of those throaty, sultry voices that screams sex appeal without even trying, Olive's voice is purer, sweeter. It makes me want to figure out all the ways I can dirty her up. I stand, holding Decker by the shoulders, and face her.

"Hey. Jeremy told me you'd be here for the wedding. How long you in town for?"

Her eyes go cloudy, and I zero in on her expression because something in it falters before she wraps it up tight and offers a strained smile. "Oh, um…I finished with the job in Paris a couple months ahead of schedule. My, uh, client…died. So, yeah. I'm back in Wilmington working out of our office here."

I know that Olive is an interior designer, and that the firm she works for has international clients. It's how she and Berkeley met, and how Rayne ended up working at Night Eagle when she arrived back in town. Beyond that, I don't know much of anything about Olive. There's something eating at her now, though. That much is obvious.

"I see." I nod, holding her gaze once more. But before I can get a read on her, she glances down at Decker.

"Ready for cake?"

He pumps his head up and down, turning toward me. "Let's go, Uncle Ronin."

Olive lifts her brows, her expression surprised. "He calls you Uncle Ronin?" she asks as we follow the little boy toward the patio.

I chuckle, rubbing the back of my neck with a hand. "Yeah. Brains's fault. I don't mind, though."

She frowns. "Brains?"

I smile down at her. The muscles it takes to do so feel unused, rusty. I've smiled at plenty of women before, just not women who affect me the way Olive seems to. "Nickname. We all have one."

She nods, understanding dawning across her face. "It's a military thing."

"Yep."

Walking onto the patio, Decker rushes straight into Rayne's arms, and Jeremy edges toward me. We both watch as Decker stands between Rayne and Olive, both women showering the eight-year-old with loving attention. When Olive brushes a lock of his hair off his forehead, my chest pulls tight.

The fuck? It's the sentimentality of this day, drawing me in and fucking with my head. That's all it can be.

"I'm a lucky bastard." Jeremy folds his arms, and when I glance at him, his eyes are locked on his family.

The family he never even knew he needed but is now willing to die to protect.

I watch them, too. My eyes keep straying to Olive, who looks so comfortable with Decker.

"You talked to her tonight?" Jeremy asks suddenly.

Glancing away from Olive, I find that he's staring directly at me. "Who? Olive?"

He nods, studying me. "Yeah."

Shaking my head, I look back at the two women and Decker. "Not really. Why?"

He turns away from the women, and I follow suit. Walking a few feet from the patio, he starts talking. "I don't know, man. She got into town last night. I picked her up from the airport, and she was…off. I mean, I don't know her that well. But she seems worried."

The protective instinct inside of me, the one that's lain dormant now for exactly seven years, lifts its head. "You ask her?"

He shakes his head slowly. "Didn't know how to. I mean, we knew each other back in high school because of Rayne, but we weren't close. And we certainly aren't best friends now. But she's my sister-in-law, and she means a lot to Rayne. I want to know what's going on with her. But I don't think she'd tell me if I asked."

"Why do you say that?"

He runs a hand through his long hair. "Olive is…capable. She likes to do everything herself. She likes to be in control. At least that's how Rayne tells it. I doubt she would respond well if she thought I was stepping in where I don't belong, or trying to help her when she thinks she's got it handled."

I nod. I get that. Every vibe I've ever gotten off of Olive tells me she's independent as fuck. She's always well put-together, she drives a nice car, she owns her own house. And she has a successful career. So if she were in trouble, she wouldn't necessarily ask for help.

"What do you need?" My tone cautious, I wait for Jeremy to roll out whatever it is he's asking.

"Rayne and Decker and I are going to Aruba for a couple of weeks. You know that. I just want you to keep an eye on her, Swagger. Make sure she's okay. Shit, make plans with her if you have to. I just need to know that you'll be there if she needs you. Obviously if need be, we can be on the first flight back to Wilmington."

I understood. Jeremy's all about family now that he has one, and he wants to protect Olive as a part of that family. As his best friend, I'm the first person he'd ask to make sure she's okay while he's away.

My eyes straying back to Olive as she takes a delicate bite of cake, I feel that the protective instinct inside of me is now fully awake. Even if Olive wants me nowhere near whatever problem she might be having, I'll be there. I'll step in whether she wants me to or not.

When her eyes meet mine, her fork freezes halfway to her mouth with her second bite and a strong current of something I can't understand pulls taut between us. When the cake finally makes it to her mouth, I watch, fascinated, as she chews. Then she swallows, her slender throat moving with the action. Her tongue darts out to lick the stray pieces of sugar from her lips and my dick stirs in my pants. I want to lick those plump lips. And where the hell does that desire come from?

Maybe getting to the bottom of whatever is bothering Olive Alexander won't be work, or just a favor for my best friend.

Maybe it'll be *fun.*

2

OLIVE

I lean back in my chair, tapping a pencil against my lips. The white decor of the office is usually soothing, the bright pops of yellow and blue dazzling my brain just enough to spur the creative juices that are nearly always flowing.

Work is the only place where I let my bubble of control deflate, because there's freedom in creativity I can't find anywhere else. Staring down at the sketch, my eyes drink in the bold lines mixing with the softer curves of a residential master bedroom. The measurements of the room are massive, the home a classic Victorian in downtown Wilmington. It's a nice change from the oceanic homes that serve as the bread and butter of the design house. Becoming a partner here six months ago was exactly according to my plan; I always knew I wanted to be a full partner at Eisengard Interiors—now Eisengard & Alexander Interiors—by age thirty, and I beat my own deadline by a year.

My life is on track. At least, it *was*.

My phone chimes from the top of the desk, and I pick it up. Irritation prickles me from the unexpected distraction. My coworkers, my partner Beth Eisengard and my friend Berkeley Conners, will both be in the office today, and my sister and her new husband are soaking up the sun in Aruba by now. So who's texting me?

Glancing at the screen, I exhale. *Of course. I should have known.*

Ken: Dinner tonight?

I've been on exactly four dates with Ken. We met at a client mixer that my firm hosts a few times a year. Ken Hart, a litigator for a prestigious law firm here in Wilmington, asked me to dinner that night after speaking with me for merely a few minutes. Flattered, I accepted.

Since then, Ken scheduled dates. They all took place before I left for Paris four months ago, and I had no idea if he'd want to continue seeing me when I returned. I texted him last night to let him know I was home, and apparently now I have my answer.

I hesitate, my mind wandering as my fingers absently hover over the keys. But instead of Ken, I picture tanned olive skin, dark hair just long enough on top for a woman to run her fingers through and shaved close on the sides, and the deepest, brightest pair of green eyes I've ever seen. A strong jaw covered in stubble, like he only shaves every few days and couldn't care less about it. Thick, corded biceps that flex with every small movement, and a rare smile that lights up an entire room whenever he uses it. His serious, intense expression, which normally graces his chiseled face, is the one that I usually see, and it's just as intriguing, if not more so, than his smile.

Ronin Shaw.

He's *not* my type.

Honestly, he's so far from my type it's almost laughable. Ronin Shaw is way too unpredictable, much too impenetrable, and…generally too much to handle. He's the kind of man you have a one-night stand with, not the kind of man you date. Not that he'd even be interested in that when it comes to me. Nor am I interested in one-night stands.

Remembering the phone in my hand and shaking my head to clear it, I send a quick text back to Ken. Date number five. This means I'll let him come inside after he drops me off from dinner. The thought doesn't send tingles of lust dancing along my skin the way it should. But then again, have I ever felt tingles of lust dancing along my skin?

Yes. But only when thoughts of a certain tall, dark, and gorgeous ex-soldier pop into my head.

Ignoring that thought, I press send.

Me: I'd love to. Pick me up from the office at five thirty.

I'll be in bed by ten. I slide my phone to the corner of my desk and frown. Usually after scheduling a date with Ken, I'm satisfied. Ken is the kind of man I've always pictured having by my side in the life I've built, and our dates have been going well. He's polite and well mannered, thoughtful, and controlled. Just the way I like my men.

But right now? I can't muster up an ounce of excitement for tonight.

Not, a big deal. When I see Ken, the way he makes me feel will rekindle. It'll be a great night.

Of course it will.

A knock on the doorway pulls me from my thoughts and I look up. The firm boasts a gigantic workspace, and we've separated the offices from the generous front lobby with glass partitions. There are no doors, something Beth thought would help the creativity flow freely around the place. I tend to agree, but today I'd really like a door to close and a solid wooden wall to hide behind while I try to figure out why the wrinkles in my life just keep getting bigger.

Instead, I plaster on a smile for my friend. "Hi, Berkeley."

She saunters into the office, looking like my perfect opposite in every single way. Berkeley is definitely a free spirit. Her creativity shines through every aspect of her being, and she's like a walking ray of sunshine. Wild, long blond hair she wears curly, and deep, soulful tawny eyes. Right now, her round, pretty face is looking at me with concern.

"Are you okay?"

Forcing my smile to grow, I nod. "Of course. Did you have fun at the wedding?"

She tilts her head to the side, her curls quivering as she studies me. I keep the smile pasted on my face, knowing I can fake it till I make it until the sun goes down if I need to.

Finally, she nods, but her clever eyes never stop assessing me. "It was beautiful and just the most romantic thing ever. I mean, seriously…a *surprise wedding*? Who does that?"

My smile turns softer and it's 100 percent real. "The guy who's been waiting a long time for a second chance with my sister, that's who."

Berkeley's lips pull into a dreamy grin. "Yeah."

We both fall silent for a minute, our minds most likely traveling in different directions. Berkeley's is probably on a train full of love stories, while I'm on a trip straight back to reality. I know that there's nothing in the world less possible to control than love. Which means I want no part of it. What I want is security, safety. Two things I need more than romance or happily-ever-after. Two things I can *control* without messy emotions getting in the way.

"Anyway." Berkeley perks up, her gaze brightening again. "I just wanted to say welcome back. I missed you."

She really is a sweetheart. Lacing my fingers together, I rest my chin on my propped hands. "I missed you, too, Berkeley. Happy to be home and back in the office."

One eyebrow arches as she regards me. "Really? Not missing the glamorous Parisian life? I know old Mrs. Dubois was a class act, and you spent a lot of time with her at the end."

The compassion in Berkeley's eyes takes me straight back there, to the rambling chateau at the edge of the city where Clara Dubois had made her home. I had no idea she was dying when I'd made the commitment to move to Paris for a few months in order to design the gorgeous estate, but she and I had become impossibly close during that time. Maybe it was the fact that I was estranged from my own righteous, intolerant parents, or maybe she saw something in me that mirrored her need to seize control in her own life. Either way, we'd clicked and the loss of her at the end of my time in Paris still aches.

For Berkeley, I shake my head. "Nope. I left Paris behind and am totally back in the swing of things here."

Berkeley shoves a thick chunk of her wild curls off of her face. "You're starting the new project on the boutique hotel in Wrightsville Beach today, right?"

Nodding, I glance down at the organized chaos of my desk. "And also the traditional Victorian inn downtown."

Berkeley's face lights up. "That one is close to Jeremy and Rayne's place."

I smile. "Yes, and I'm looking forward to both jobs. But the Victorian is going to be especially fun."

She nods knowingly. "Right up your alley." She turns, rapping her knuckles lightly on the glass beside the open doorway. "Let me know if you need anything."

Shaking my head, my gaze drifts back down to the sketch I'm working on. "Our assistant designer is going to help on both of these, so I'm all set. I know you have your own work to do."

It's true, even though Berkeley is five years my junior and not a partner in the firm, she's a capable and creative designer and often heads up her own projects these days. She nods, gives me a wave, and heads down the hall.

An hour after lunch, our design assistant Paisley and I climb out of my little silver BMW in front of the Whisper Hill Inn. I stare up at it, appreciating the eye-catching architecture. I'd taken on this project because, after my abrupt return from Paris, I wanted something to throw myself into at work. This project is daunting because it's not my usual style. It's going to be a challenge, and that's exactly what I need in my life right now.

A distraction.

Paisley catches her breath as she steps up beside me. "It's beautiful."

Nodding, I don't take my eyes off the old Victorian inn.

"It is. Now let's get to work."

By the time Paisley and I make it back to the office, it's after five.

"I'm glad we have three months to get this place done." It's the first thing Paisley has said since we left the hotel, and she sounds more than overwhelmed.

I offer her a smile. "First commercial project, right?"

She nods, biting her lip.

We'd hired Paisley as a design assistant just before I left for Europe. "You did great today, Paisley. You asked a lot of good questions about what the client wants, and we got a good feel for the essence of the building. Now comes the fun part. First thing in the morning we'll powwow, okay?"

We've stopped outside the glass that separates my office from the hall, and Paisley is staring inside. Following her awestruck gaze, my heart stutters to a near stop before I inhale and force it to begin beating again.

He's standing by the windows behind my desk, but even from the back I know exactly who it is. His gray long-sleeved thermal stretches tight across his broad shoulders and wide, muscular back. As we watch him, he reaches up absently to drag a hand through the messed-up locks on top of his head before allowing it to run down the shaved back and rests on his neck. I let my eyes travel south, past his narrow, trim waist, and they stop briefly on the perfect ass that fills out a pair of perfectly fitted jeans. No skinny jeans for Ronin Shaw. Hell, no. This guy…he's all-man. The fact that I'm usually attracted to men who shave every morning and wear tailored suits at all hours of the day makes it even more glaringly obvious that something about Ronin, whether I want to admit it or not, just *does it for me.*

As if he senses our heated gazes on his back, Ronin turns to face us, his big hand still gripping the back of his neck. His eyes skate over Paisley but then they fix to mine and stay there. His stare is so intensely focused as it sweeps down my body and back again, I feel like he's touched me intimately while standing ten feet away.

Paisley catches her breath next to me, and I glance at her before clearing my throat and entering the office. "Um, hi. Ronin?"

And that's it. Those are all the words I have. *Brilliant, Olive.* But seriously, why is he here? I didn't even know he knew where I worked.

"So," I say too loudly, turning toward my assistant. "Yeah, thanks, Paisley. See you in the morning."

She rips her eyes off of Ronin long enough to give me an approving smirk. "Yes, Ms. Alexander. See you in the morning. Have a good night."

She practically giggles as she heads down the hallway, and I close my eyes briefly to gather myself before focusing my attention on the man standing beside my desk.

I force my legs to work properly, noticing that they're feeling pretty rubbery and ineffective at the moment. I walk toward my desk, my laptop bag feeling suddenly very heavy on my shoulder. As I shrug it off, Ronin catches it and sets it gently on my desk.

"Thanks." My voice is a little bit breathless, and the way his eyes travel over my body again is making my skin feel heated. "Hey."

His lips twitch into an almost smile, but then I see a genuine smile light up his eyes. Ronin's eyes are extremely expressive, and as I stare into them I notice not for the first time that they're the most interesting shade of green I've ever seen. They're a super-light sage, with flecks of amber and gold swimming in the irises. Contrasted with his darkly tanned skin and his obviously exotic features, his face is almost a work of art. Strong jaw covered in scruff, chiseled cheekbones; dark, long lashes are the picture of perfection. But a forehead that's just a little bit too broad, and a nose that's just slightly crooked add notes of imperfection that complete the masterpiece in the most intriguing way I've ever encountered.

He swallows, and my eyes fall to the movement of his Adam's apple. That's when I know I've probably been staring at his face a little too long. *Thank God his shirt's on. There's no way I'd be able to tear my eyes from the muscles I know are under it.*

Inhaling, I try to focus. On the words. That need to be said.

"Hey. Busy day?" His voice is somehow rough like lava rocks and smooth like Brazilian coffee all at the same time. It rushes over me, leaving goose bumps on my skin.

Nodding, I round my desk and pick up a stack of papers for absolutely no reason. I shuffle them in my hands and place them back down again. *What is wrong with me?*

I know exactly what's wrong with me. Ronin Shaw is in my office, in my personal space. My personal space is off-limits, because his presence is far too large to be contained in here. "Can I help you with something, Ronin?"

One thick black eyebrow lifts, and his full lips draw into a slow smile. "Yeah. There's something I want to run by you. I came to take you to dinner."

My jaw goes slack as I stare at him. Remembering to close it, I suck in a deep breath and raise myself up to my full five foot seven. Add in the height from my heels and I'm on the taller side, but it doesn't matter when I'm still looking up at a man who's at least six three. "I can't."

His expression doesn't change. "Sure you can." He leans a hip on the side of my desk and just watches me while I attempt to give him a stern look.

I've perfected the look over the years. It works on absolutely everyone, informing them that I mean business and I'm not someone to be trifled with.

But Ronin just smirks through it, like my stern look doesn't affect him at all.

"No, I really can't, Ronin. I have plans."

That gets his attention. Three little lines appear in his forehead as his brows pull together, and his mouth screws to the side while he asses me with that serious gaze. "On a Monday night?"

A knock on the glass causes both our glances to dart toward

the doorway. Ken stands there, hesitating at the entrance as he takes in Ronin and me. I let out a sigh of relief, because Ken in my office makes perfect sense, whereas Ronin in my office does not.

Ken wanders in, pulling his platinum wristwatch in front of his face to check the time. He gives me a pointed look. "We have a reservation for six, Olive."

I thought I had perfected my stern look? Ken's makes mine look like puppy-dog-eyes. He stops a few feet in front of Ronin, who remains perched on the side of my desk. "Ken Hart. You are?"

Ronin glances at Ken's outstretched hand, which I can't help but notice is much smaller than Ronin's. Actually, every-thing about Ronin dwarfs Ken, now that they're side by side. And the differences between them are marked. From Ken's art-fully styled blond hair, to his gray pinstriped Thom Browne suit.

Ken is a fit, healthy guy. He's handsome. He's successful. But right now, as I evaluate him beside Ronin, all of that pales be-side the other man.

Finally, Ronin stands and grasps Ken's hand in his. "Ronin Shaw."

That's all he offers, and Ken's shrewd expression darkens slightly. He glances at me. "Ready to go?"

On the inside, I sigh. On the outside, I give Ken a faint smile. "Meet you in the lobby in just a minute."

He glances at his watch *again,* and then at Ronin. Dipping his chin at the other man before he exits, he disappears from the office in a cloud of expensive cologne.

I begin gathering my things.

Ronin chuckles, and I look over at him. "His actual name is Ken?"

Pausing, I stand up straight and rest my hands on my hips. "Why are you really here, Ronin?"

His hand returns to the back of his neck, gripping it tightly. His tone grows slightly chilly. "You know? I don't really know why. My friend married your sister, and I just thought I would check in on you while they're gone."

Staring at him, I narrow my eyes. "Are you serious right now? I'm a big girl, and I'm more than capable of taking care of myself."

I can hear that haughty tone in my voice, but I can't stop it. I don't know who Ronin Shaw thinks he is, but he's not my protector and I'm not his problem.

I have problems of my own to worry about. My thoughts stray and my stomach clenches.

"So, thanks for stopping by." I walk toward my corner cabinet and open the door, taking out my fall trench coat and putting it on. Grabbing hold of my laptop case and my purse, I give Ronin a pointed glance.

"Anything else?"

3

RONIN

Ken's prick face still scrolls through my brain as I watch her gather her things. When I don't answer her question, she shifts, and the shiny satin of her red blouse shimmers in the bright light of the office as she moves. When she turns away I watch her hips sway. The truth is that I memorized how the swell of her hips squeezed into the black pencil skirt the second I'd turned around and caught her watching me.

I know she's expecting me to leave, but something she said at the wedding is weighing on me. And hell, I did tell Jeremy I would look out for her.

"Olive." My voice is muted, quiet, so I don't startle her. "Did everything go okay…in Europe?"

She sucks in another breath before finally lifting her head and straightening. But the brief shuttered expression on her face was clear as day, and I shake my head in response before she even opens her mouth.

"Hey." My voice firms up just a little bit. Protectiveness

surges to the surface inside me, pushing me forward. "Tell me what happened."

The need to take control, to make her tell me what's wrong, is strong. But I force myself to stay put, to keep my distance, because the last thing I need in my life is someone to fix.

Not that I'd be any good at it, anyway.

But I can't deny the pull I'm feeling, the fact that I *want* to fix whatever it is that's making that pretty little mouth of hers frown. Something's churning up inside her, and I can't beat back the need I have to know exactly what it is.

She grabs a stack of paper off her desk, stuffs it into her laptop bag, and yanks her purse out from a drawer. Her arms full of her stuff, she rounds her desk and walks right into my space. Her eyes flash, and I take a second to appreciate the direct contrast they are to her creamy pale skin and her auburn hair.

Goddamn, the woman is fucking gorgeous.

"Has anyone ever told you you're one nosey, bossy brute of a man?" The stubborn set of her mouth causes her dimples to deepen as she takes a step toward me.

I slowly nod my head and a reluctant smile quirks my lips upward. "Maybe I've heard it a time or two."

She lifts her chin the slightest bit as a rush of color fills her cheeks, and I can't help it when my body reacts to her. Her closeness, the brush of her chest against mine, the wafting scent of peaches that rushes over me. I blink, taken completely off guard.

Shit. When's the last time a woman caught me off guard?

She makes a sound that's halfway between a snort and a groan before brushing past me and heading for the door.

"Olive."

She turns slowly, and when her eyes lift to mine there's something there I can't pinpoint. Interest? Curiosity? Longing?

I take two strides and am standing directly in front of her. This time, I've caught *her* off balance, which is exactly what I wanted to do. I'm not used to feeling so on edge, and there's a strong need inside me to see if I affect her the same way.

"After you're done doing whatever vanilla thing you're about to do with Ken, call me. I want to know you're home safe."

I scan her face. Her dark red hair is piled up on top of her head and there's not a single strand hanging around her face for me to tuck or stroke. Instead of touching her, I just let my eyes blaze a trail over her face, down her creamy throat dipping into the vee of her shirt where her top button lies undone. If I leaned over slightly, I'd probably be able to see what she's wearing underneath, but I can wait for that.

Wait for that? What the hell are you thinking, Ronin? This is one woman you won't be taking to bed. Too many complications.

Her cheeks flush, and I watch the stain spread down to her neck and chest. Her pupils dilate, and Olive can pretend all damn day like there's nothing between us, but her body can't tell a lie.

Her mouth moves a few times before she finds the words she's looking for. "I don't have your number."

I tilt my head to the side and smirk.

The diesel engine on my big, black Ram roars as I drive

through the darkened streets of Wilmington. I don't even have a destination, but it doesn't matter as my brain sprints through thoughts of Olive Alexander.

I admit, the main thought is the highlight reel of me bending her over that desk of hers and stroking every inch of her body while I pound into her, making her scream my name. And not in that controlled, managed voice either. But, unfortunately, I know it would be more than that with Olive. It's been seven years since I lost Elle, and I've been with other women since.

But I've never craved one. Not like this. But I get the sense Olive wouldn't be open to a one-night stand. And that's *all* I'm capable of.

The thing I'm really confused about though is my *need* to know what's going on in that head of hers. For me, with women, it's usually about sex. I get in and I get out, because it's just easier that way. Keeps shit simple. But with Olive? There's this need to know what makes her tick. No one can keep that kind of pent-up energy perfectly controlled, the way she does, forever. It's like she's juggling two too many balls in the air, and she's getting ready to drop the whole set.

I want to be there when she does. I have a feeling she's going to need someone around to help her catch them.

And then there's the fact that Jeremy asked me to look into what's going on with her while he's gone. He knew damn well she wouldn't want me "keeping an eye on her." She's way too strong and independent to want any part of that. And that's maybe the biggest turn-on of all.

But she's also sad. Or discontent. The look on her face when

I asked about Europe, the way her stance changed, her whole demeanor was different afterward. I've been trained to read people. I've been trained to hurt people.

But I've also been trained to protect people.

There are some people even you aren't able to protect. The thought forces its way into my brain unbidden, and I grip the steering wheel tighter as I try with everything I have to push those images out of my head. The thoughts that threaten to poison me with their potency every time I let them take over.

Not tonight.

I picture Olive, instead, and the thought puts a smile on my face.

I pull the truck into the parking lot of my favorite bar, The Oakes. It's not too far from my oceanfront condo. The bartender, Bennett Blacke, has become something like a friend, his military background bonding us.

As I walk in I notice that the bar is quiet on this Monday night and television is tuned to the football game that's about to kick off.

Bennett leans toward me, his expression friendly as his straw-colored hair falls over his forehead. As the manager of this place, he has free rein, and my first drink is always on him. More often than not, one drink is all I have, and in that case I leave him a generous tip to cover the drink and the gratuity.

Bennett takes one look at my face and lifts a brow. "Looks like a Jager kind of night."

Grinning, I shake my head and pull my phone from my pocket to shoot Olive a quick text.

Me: done with Ken yet?

There. Now she has my number. Up to her what she'll do with it. Chuckling, I leave the phone on the bar. "Just a beer tonight, man. I might have somewhere to be later."

Bennett's eyebrow lifts and his eyes twinkle with curiosity. "For real? You done gone and got a date?"

I shake my head, grabbing the neck of the beer bottle he passes me and putting it to my lips. "She's already on her date. She'll be calling me after."

Bennett throws his head back and laughs. "Then she's a smart chick."

I nod, sipping my beer as my thoughts flip back to a gorgeous redhead who holds herself so tall, who has a war going on behind her smile and a battle in her eyes.

Maybe she doesn't have to fight it alone. The more I allow myself to think about her, the clearer the picture becomes. Olive, underneath me in my bed? It's a good fucking picture. I like it way more than I should.

My phone buzzes on the bar top and I pick it up.

Olive: It's date number five, if you must know. That means Ken comes in tonight.

Why does that single line of text make me want to hurl my beer bottle at the wall? Or jump into my car and eat up the road until I'm pulling up in her driveway?

It's bullshit. I have no say who she does or doesn't sleep with. I barely know her. If she wants to have the most boring vanilla fuck in the world with Ken then who am I to stop her?

The truth hits me: to Olive, I'm no one. There's absolutely no reason for me to stop her. Or for her to think I would want her to stop.

Fuck.

I'm almost too lost in my thoughts to notice the *whoosh* of cold air that hits my back as the front door opens, or the way that Bennett stiffens in his stance behind the bar. But the laser-sharp focus in his eyes pulls me around to eye the newcomer walking in, and there's trouble written all over him.

The man glances at me before situating himself on a barstool two seats away. His hair is shaggy, curling around his neck in light brown waves, and his face is half-covered with a few days' dark shadow. It's hard to tell his age, but I'd guess by the way his eyes crinkle at the corners as he squints up at Bennett he's in his thirties. His casual dress doesn't suggests that anything's amiss; the worn jeans and flannel shirt combined with a warm vest just tell me he's prepared for the North Carolina chill clinging to the air.

Bennett stands with his arms folded, his eyes glued to the dude, though, and so I sit up and pay attention without making it obvious that I'm listening in.

"I'll take a beer." The man's voice is low and rough, and he lifts the brim of his trucker's hat to brush the hair off his forehead.

Bennett doesn't move. "What are you doing here, Mick?"

Mick pulls off his cap and runs a hand through his hair as

he sets it on the bar top. "It's none of your goddamn business what I'm doin' here. I said I want a beer."

Bennett's eyes narrow. "Does your dad know you're in his bar?"

That question gets Mick's attention, and he spreads both hands out along the bar and leans forward. "Just because you run this place for my old man doesn't mean what I do is any goddamn business of yours. Get. Me. A. Beer."

Bennett watches Mick for another minute, then shakes his head and tosses down the dish towel he'd been holding. I catch his eye as he reaches under the bar to grab a long-neck bottle, but he gives me the smallest shake of his head possible. He doesn't want me getting into it, and normally, I wouldn't. But Bennett has become a friend and if he's having trouble around the bar I want to know if there's any way I can help him out.

"I'll take another." I nod at Bennett, and Mick's eyes shift toward me. They're cool and calculating, an icy shade of blue that drives straight to the heart of a person without really trying.

I sip my beer, and so does Mick, but no one speaks again. I've never met the guy before tonight, but the way Bennett carries himself, mixed with the way Mick acts like he owns the place, I'm guessing that his presence is gonna be nothing but trouble for Bennett.

Finally, he turns to me and sticks out a hand. Without blinking, I shake it and wait for his introduction. "Mick."

His mouth twists into what's supposed to be a grin, but it seems like he's gotten it wrong so many times he can't figure out how to truly smile.

"Ronin Shaw. I'm a friend of Bennett's. You got business here tonight?"

An ominous shadow passes through the blue of Mick's eyes. It doesn't give me a good feeling in my gut, though. If anything, it makes me feel sick inside. But the flash is gone before I can comment on it, and Mick's shifty grin is back I place.

"You can call me the owner."

Bennett slams down the glass he's been cleaning. "Bullshit. Your father owns this place, Mick, not you."

Mick chuckles, a rusty sound coming from deep within his throat. "He didn't tell you? Thought you two were thick as thieves with all your old army connections and shit. Dad can't handle this place anymore. That's why he's handing over ownership to me. Expect some changes in the coming weeks, *Bennett*."

Bennett adopts a stance that suggests he could throttle over the bar top at any moment to plant a fist into Mick's face. "Whatever you're up to, Mick, just forget about it. It's not happening in this bar, and it's not happening to the good man who raised you." He points from his gaze to Mick's with two fingers. "I'll be watching you."

Mick slides his empty beer bottle forward and stands. "Ain't nothin' you can do to me, Blacke, that ain't already been done. So just get used to seeing my face. Because I own this bar now."

He pushes off his stool, aims one more curious glance in my direction before sneering at Bennett, and then walks out the front door.

Bennett sighs, and I glance at him. "What the hell was that about?"

He leans back against the wall, folding his arms across his chest and stares at the front doors. "That...is a fucking grenade just waiting to explode."

4

OLIVE

The five-star restaurant is fabulous, and as I sip my merlot, I eye Ken across the table. He's been talking to me for the past twenty minutes about a case he's currently working on. As a litigator in corporate law, he's always swamped with these boring-as-hell caseloads dealing with merging corporations and bickering CEOs. I can't stand hearing him talk about it, but out of consideration, I always listen. I know that everyone needs to unload about their day; I just wish Ken's baggage wasn't so *dull*.

As he prattles on about the clever way his client managed to conceal an entire account from the vying corporation, I allow my mind to wander. I wonder what I'd be doing if I'd left my office with Ronin instead of Ken. Which is ridiculous because I'm pretty sure that I'd bore Ronin Shaw out of his ever-loving mind. The way he expected me to just go out to dinner with him at a moment's notice, on a whim? The way he called whatever I'd be doing with Ken "vanilla"? My control issues aren't something a man like that has patience for. All control freaks get their start somewhere, and I've been this way since I was seventeen years old.

But it's clear to me that Ronin likes to be in control, too. And there's no way I'd give it up.

It'd take an act of God to change me, and as much as I'm shocked by my fantasies about Ronin's capable hands exploring my entire body, and that sensuous mouth doing the dirtiest things imaginable to the most intimate parts of me, I know that it'll never happen. He's off-limits for so many reasons. One of which being I wouldn't want to cause weirdness or uncomfortable scenes between us when we're around my sister and Jeremy. As far as I know, Ronin doesn't do relationships. And I don't do one-night stands. For me, there's no in between, regardless of how attracted to him I am.

But I can't help thinking: What if Ronin *had* taken me out tonight? What would we have done? I'm guessing this stuffy restaurant wouldn't have been at the top of his list. These are the kind of places I go out to, because these are the kinds of places the men I date take me. Men who are easy for me to read and predict. Men who can't get too deep inside my head, because that place is too messy for even me to be most of the time. I just want peace and quiet and men like Ken.

I'm pretty sure that peace and quiet isn't even in Ronin Shaw's vocabulary. Not that he's a loud and showy guy. He's laid-back and pensive most of the time, and you can tell that he's thought about every single thing that comes out of his mouth. He's a deep thinker. But thanks to his looks and the confident way he carries himself, Ronin always gets what he wants. He doesn't even have to try where women are concerned. Hell, I certainly have a weakness for him, even though I'm trying damn hard not to. And the last thing I'd want is his knowing eyes focused on me, figuring out all the things I have hidden inside. Like the reason for my drastic change of appearance during and after high school. And the reason I'd rather die than ever become that girl again.

Ronin's the kind of man who takes control. And that's simply not something I'm willing to give up, not ever.

"Olive?" Ken's irritation snaps me to attention, and I focus on his watery blue eyes. "Did you hear a word I've been saying?"

I nod, offering him a confident smile to reassure him. "Of course, Ken. I understand the accomplishment you must feel, now that the merger is finally under way."

He relaxes a little, satisfied that I've been listening, and nods with pompous pride. Why haven't I noticed before now just how irritated I am by his behavior? "That's right. Without my expertise, there's no way that deal would have gone through."

I sip my wine and offer him an understanding tip of the lips. "It's why you're up for making partner, right? No one is more qualified than you." *Stroke, stroke, stroke.*

He nods, sipping his own glass of chardonnay. "You're damn right. I'm going to run that place one day."

I try really, really hard not to roll my eyes. Ambition isn't anything to scoff at, and I'm sure that Ken will have top billing at his law office in the future. He works hard, and his career is the most important thing in his life.

It's why I'm with him. If the law and his job are at the top of his priorities list, trying to figure me out won't be. And I'm all good with that.

Our server brings our dinners. Ken tried to order for me, but I draw the line at that.

"I've already looked at the menu online and know exactly what I want to order," I'd told him sweetly.

He seemed a bit disgruntled, but as I cut a bite of my grilled chicken Caesar salad sans dressing and put it in my mouth, I'm thankful I ordered what I really like. Ken doesn't know me well enough to have a handle on my likes and dislikes.

After dinner, we climb into his sleek two-door luxury car and speed toward my home in the suburbs near Wrightsville Beach. It was the place where my sister Rayne had fled when she'd left Phoenix in a hurry. But since she's now happily living with her new husband and their family is complete, I have my house to myself. The way I like it.

Pulling into my driveway, my palms suddenly begin to sweat. Brushing them against my skirt, I jerk my head toward Ken as he shuts off the car and glances over at me. He leans back in his seat, perfectly at ease while inside my emotions are a jumbled mess.

I haven't had a lot of sexual partners, because, for me, it's just a part of dating. If I feel attracted enough to someone to take them to bed, I do, and I don't have any qualms about it. And up until tonight, I thought I had that with Ken. But now, instead of the blond-haired, blue-eyed man sitting across from me, as handsome as he is, I kept picturing another man in the driver's seat of a different car. Ken reaches across the console for my hand. "Walk you to the door?"

His voice was smooth, knowing. Apparently, he completely understood the five dates rule.

My insides tighten, my stomach clenching for reasons I can't identify. "Sure."

We both exit the car and stroll up my neat and tidy front walk. Arriving at my red front door, I stop and turn toward him. Ken leans in, his lips catching mine in a soft caress. I return the kiss, but my heart isn't in it. Leaning back, I plaster a bright smile.

"God, it's been an exhausting day. Did I tell you I started a new project at the oceanfront in addition to the Victorian I'm working on downtown? My feet are killing me." I send him a guilty smile, shifting on my feet. I could wear heels for twenty-four hours straight, but Ken doesn't need to know that.

Ken grins. "Then let's get you inside and prop those feet up." He reaches for the keys dangling from my fingers.

"Actually..." I hedge, causing him to lift his eyes toward mine again. "I think I'm going to call it a night here. But thank you so much for dinner, Ken. It was nice to see you again after being gone so long."

He schools his expression, not allowing his disappointment to bleed through his perfectly handsome features. "I understand. I'll see you tomorrow. We have those theater tickets."

No doubt that event will include dinner at a five-star restaurant.

The thrills.

I nod as I work the key into the door. "Thanks, Ken. Yes, I'll see you then." Pushing the front door open, I give him one last smile before slipping inside and closing the door behind me. The comforting darkness of my home greets me as I lean against the door and immediately pull off my black stilettos. I sigh as my back hits the wood and take a moment to mull over the events of the day. Of the week. Of the month, really.

I close my eyes, briefly remembering Clara, the old woman who'd become a mentor to me. I learned so much from her while designing her chateau, and even in her early seventies she was so vigorous and full of life. I had no idea that she was dying, and redesigning her beautiful home was one of the last things she would do. No idea that time spent in her home would be the last time I felt safe.

When my thoughts stray to the e-mail I received just before leaving to go to France, all traces of warmth leave me. I've been avoiding thinking about that message ever since I came back to Wilmington. But as I remember, I can feel the color draining from my face.

Inhaling, I open my eyes and reach for the light switch beside the door and flick it on. I blink, zeroing in on the scene in my front hallway, and then I blink again.

My hand flies to my throat where the scream is lodged.

5

RONIN

When my phone rings, a pleasantly surprised smile crosses my face. I've just walked in my front door, and I don't even bother to glance at the name of the incoming caller as I swipe my thumb across the screen.

"Hey, I—"

"Shaw."

The voice that interrupts me, although familiar, isn't the one I expect, and I shut my mouth. The pause must make him question whether or not I'm still on the line, because he tries again.

"Ronin?"

Finally, I clear my throat. "Uh, yeah. Watson?"

My muscles have cramped up, my mind going blank. The blood rushes in my veins, but I still feel sickeningly cold as I absorb the fact that the detective from my wife's unsolved homicide case is calling me out of the blue.

Hearing from him can mean only one thing. As that revelation sinks in, my breath hitches and the emotions I felt all those years ago when I lost Elle come surging back.

Bitter regret.

Anguish.

Rage. So much rage.

Lance Watson clears his throat. "I'm going to get straight to the point, Ronin. Something new has come up concerning your wife's case."

Standing rigid, stock-still, a rash of chills rush up my spine. "What's come up?"

Watson continues, like he can't get the words out fast enough. Having been on the force after returning from my final deployment, I remember how it feels to be working on something that suddenly snowballs, the rush of adrenaline that comes from discovering new evidence.

"There's been another murder. The details of the new homicide match the ones from Elle's case to a T, Ronin. This might be the break we've been waiting for."

There's no hesitation. I turn right back around, opening my front door and heading toward the elevator at the end of the hall. The one that will take me down to the parking garage and straight to my truck. "I'm coming in."

His tone takes on a note of warning. "I'll show you what we've got, because I know you. But you stay out of the way, got it?"

Grinding my teeth together, I remain silent. I'm not making any fucking promises. Not about this. "See you in a few."

The drive to the police station takes less time than it should. But tonight, red lights and speed limits are not stopping me from getting there fast.

Detective Lance Watson looks up as both of my hands land on top of his desk. Heavy brows furrow above dark brown eyes, and concern is written across his expression. Screwing his face up, he studies me. "Did you run every red light to get here?"

Ignoring him, I glance at the paperwork strewn across his desk. "Tell me about the new case."

Dropping down into a chair beside him, I watch closely as he pulls a folder toward us. Opening it, he removes several photos and sheets of papers. Sliding them my way, he leans back in his seat and taps a pen against his chin while I study them.

There's a stack of crime scene photos, and I flip through these first. The murdered woman lies sprawled out on a white tiled floor. She's flat on her back, her legs bent beneath her, her arms spread out beside her head. Her throat is cut; the amount of blood on her clothes and the floor around her is massive.

My stomach churns as the memories stir.

My mind flashes back to the day my world went dark. My gorgeous wife: long, black hair, heart-shaped face with perfect, full lips. Petite, lush body. All covered in blood, the life leaked completely out of her.

Revulsion rises in my throat, but I swallow it and tamp down my reaction. Glancing up at Watson to find him watching me with sympathy in his eyes, I push the photos aside and pick up the crime report.

Scanning it, I bypass the victim's name and personal details. That's not what I need to know right now. When I find what I'm looking for, I pause and read more closely.

Murder weapon: steak knife from the victim's own kitchen.

No sign of forced entry, which means the victim let her attacker in.

Partial boot print left near the victim.

There. This is where the similarities go from being coincidental to tying this case to Elle's. The killer had used the knife to scratch a note on the kitchen table. Four words that once meant the end of my world: **dead girls don't talk**.

"Son of a *bitch*!" Slamming the folder closed, I breathe deeply through my nose several times, attempting to exhale the fury so that I can focus.

"It's been seven years, but he finally reared his ugly head again, Ronin. We'll get him."

No. I'll get him.

Someone exits an office across the room and calls Watson's name. A superior, from the looks of him. Watson claps a hand on my shoulder as he walks by. "Be right back."

As soon as he's enclosed in the other room, I pull out my cell phone. Opening the case file, I snap a photo of the crime report and each photo. I'm sliding my phone back in my pocket just as the door opens and Watson returns.

Standing, I raise my chin in farewell. "Keep me posted."

He nods. "Will do, Ronin."

There's a determination in my step as I leave the police station and head for my truck that I haven't felt in a long time.

A brand-new fire burns in my blood: I'm going to be able to avenge my dead wife.

Hope blooms red.

As I settle in the driver's seat of the truck, my phone rings.

The dashboard lights up with the incoming call, and as Olive's name jumps out at me in blue, lighted letters, I frown. The jumble of emotions is making me feel exhausted. This night has been full of strange highs and lows, and I can't fully understand the reason behind the high I feel from seeing her name on my caller ID. Especially right now, at this moment.

It feels wrong.

Pressing the hands-free answer button on my steering wheel, I greet her. "Olive? Didn't expect to hear from you tonight." My tone is flat. The flirtatious banter I had with Olive earlier feels so long ago.

Like another lifetime.

My head rests back on the seat and I close my eyes.

"Ronin?"

Opening them again, I sit up straighter. Olive's voice is higher than normal, and there's a note of panic edging her words. "What's wrong, Olive?"

Without even thinking about it, I start the truck's big, growling engine.

"It's my...my house. Someone's been here?"

My blood chills for the second time tonight. "What do you mean, 'someone's been there'?"

A deep inhale on the other end of the line. "It's...someone broke in. I just walked in the door, and...there's *stuff everywhere*, Ronin. Not my stuff...I don't know how this happened." Her voice breaks on the last word.

Christ. "Olive, I'm on my way to you now. Get out of the house."

Her voice drops to a raspy whisper. "You think..." She

pauses, and I can hear her swallow. "They might still be here?"

I put the truck into drive and pull out of the police station parking lot. Trying to keep my voice even so she'll stay calm is tough. My pulse races, ramping up to match the speed of my driving. "I'm not sure, sweetheart. Just get out."

"I left my car at the office I rode with Ken. I was going to catch a ride with one of the girls to work in the morning." Her voice is breathier than I've ever heard it, and something in my chest squeezes painfully tight at the sound.

"Is he there with you?" At that moment, I really hope the dude walked her inside. But something tells me he didn't, or Olive wouldn't be on the phone with me.

"No."

Trying to instill urgency in my words without scaring her to death, I speak slowly. "Okay, Olive. Just get outside. If there's a neighbor you can hang out with until I get there, go there. I'm not far."

I picture her nodding as she answers. "Okay. I have a neighbor…Macy. I'll head to her house until you arrive. Um…thanks, Ronin. Should I call the police?"

"Is there any reason you wouldn't want to?" It's a question we ask our clients all the time. Our first priority is to protect them, and that can sometimes involve bending the law to work for the client, or for us.

"No."

Good. That makes this a lot less complicated. "Then call them. I'll see you in a few minutes."

When she ends the call, I stomp down hard on the gas

pedal. The need to get revenge for my wife is still lingering in my mind, but my immediate need is to make sure Olive is safe.

Jeremy asked me to look out for her while he's gone, but that's not the whole reason I'm running every red light to get to her. There's something about Olive that calls out to me whether I want to acknowledge it or not.

Pushing that thought down, I focus my attention on the road in front of me.

6

RONIN

I pull into Olive's driveway and study the house. It's dark and quiet, save for the soft porch light glowing beside the red front door. The front yard is immaculate, which shouldn't surprise me. It looks just like the woman: pristine, cool, and put-together.

Exiting the Ram, I let the door slam behind me.

"Ronin?"

Olive's voice calls out to me from the darkness, and I swing my gaze around the vicinity, looking for her. She approaches from the house next door. She's still wearing her clothes from earlier, the shiny red blouse and black pencil skirt, but her hair, usually pulled back, now tumbles down around her shoulders in a cascade of auburn. My chest contracts at the sight of her, but not only because of her obvious beauty. It's also because of the fear and apprehension apparent on her face.

"Hey." I greet her when she stops a few feet in front of me, her arms hugging her chest like she's cold.

I dip my head down so I can get a better look at her. "It's okay, Olive. Do you want me to go inside and check things out, or do you want to wait for the police?"

I study her face as she considers. "Let's go inside. It's my house, Ronin. I can't stand the fact that it's been violated."

An evident shiver rocks her thin frame, and instinctually I wrap my arm around her shoulder. I can't remember the last time I felt the need to hold a woman close, feel her heart beating against me just so I know she's safe.

I inhale the sweet scent of her hair. "Stay with me, then."

She nods and we cross the yard, step onto her front walkway and up onto the porch. Reaching down to a holster on my ankle, I pull out my 9 mm. I open the door and push so it swings silently open. There's a soft lamp shining on a table in the front hallway, and I suck in a quick breath.

The place is a perfect reflection of its owner, because it's damn near spotless. Except for the thick carpet of rose petals scattered across the floor. Roses, in every single color, litter every surface. They're everywhere; some are lying loose on tables or the floor, while petals cover absolutely everything. I can even fucking smell the thick, heavy sent as it settles in the air around us.

It's not romantic, it's over-the-top insane. Knowing Olive, seeing this when she walked in her front door must have crushed her. Turning from side to side with the gun out in front, I make my way down the hall. Entering the great room, open to the kitchen, I indicate to Olive that she should turn on the lights. She does, and her gasp echoes through my soul.

She's horrified to see everything that she owns covered in

petals, stems, and thorns. The room is in shambles. Her couch cushions have been covered in pink and white, trinkets and lamps coated with all kinds of floral debris. Whoever did this was clearly out of their mind. This was so far from normal I could hardly wrap my head around it, and it's not even my house or my stuff. I circle the entire space, noting that none of Olive's belongings have been messed with. Everything is still in its rightful place, just…embellished. With the goddamned flowers from hell. There isn't anyplace to hide, so after a wide sweep of the room I nudge Olive behind me and head for the stairs.

Her closeness burns into my back as we climb, sending an awareness blazing through my blood just because she's close. There's no sound except for the rapid rush of her breathing. We clear the top of the stairs, and I turn this way and that, brandishing my weapon in case of an intruder attack. But the landing is empty. We comb the rooms one by one. Olive stays in the hallway while I enter a room, sweep it from top to bottom, and declare it empty. Her master bedroom is last.

When she flicks on the light, the first thing I notice *isn't* the fact that the place is dripping in flowers. That's been the case throughout the entire house. The first thing I notice is how cold the room is. There's no sense of warmth, of belonging, of the love that a woman usually puts into a space. Her room is black and white, clinical with a single pop of red within a painting of a rose hanging over her bed.

Her king-size bed has a white upholstered headboard and a white down comforter.

But this room? It says nothing about the woman Olive is.

I'm quickly seeing that I'm going to have to peel back every layer of her one single piece at a time, because she's giving nothing away, even in her personal space.

"Oh, God." Olive's voice sounds like an echo, tiny and scared.

When I whirl around to face her, I see that she's crept closer to the bed and the naked look of desolation printed across her face has me eating up the distance between us in two strides and holstering my weapon.

"What is it?" I ask, trying to keep the hard edge out of my voice. But fuck if the fear in her eyes is making me want to hunt down whoever did this shit and make them feel every single ounce of terror they've put into her. And I'd *enjoy* it.

She lifts a finger, her hand shaking, and points toward the bed. I glance over my shoulder and notice the corsage sitting in the middle of her bed. Propped up against a small box and a bow, it reminds me of the flowers guy gave girls before prom.

I glance back at Olive, confusion riding me hard. "The corsage?"

She draws a shaky breath. "It's…" She trails off. Her eyes close, her lower lip trembling, and it feels like someone's heated up my blood past boiling as straight-up rage fills me.

"It's the same one…exactly the same." Her voice is a whisper, her eyes glazing over like she's gone somewhere far away.

Her lids peel back open and the look in her gaze almost wrecks me. I grab her shoulders with both hands, leaning in so I can see her eyes. Those eyes, so big in her face, so deeply blue and perfectly gorgeous, stare into mine. She's trembling, her entire body quaking so badly that I have to put my arms around her and pull her to my chest.

She stiffens for just a moment before relaxing into my embrace, and I rest my chin on top of her head. The feeling of her settling into my arms is indescribable. I take stock of the moment, summing up not just my body's reaction to her, but also my mind's. I'm about to ask her what she was talking about, what the corsage means, when the sound of sirens lifts from outside.

"You're okay, Red." I whisper the words, willing her to believe them. "There's no one here, and the police are pulling up outside now."

She pulls away slightly, and I feel her arms wind tentatively around my waist as she looks up at me. Damn, that feels…good. Really fucking good. "I'm not safe here, Ronin."

I catch her drift, and I shake my head slowly. There's no way I'm letting her stay here, not until we figure out exactly who broke into her place and why.

"You can stay at Jeremy's. I'm sure they won't mind."

She shakes her head slowly. "They're on their honeymoon and I don't have a key. More than that, this is their first family vacation with the three of them. If I call them and tell them what happened and ask to stay there, they'll come running back to check on me. I won't do that to them."

Blowing out a hard breath, I scrub a hand down my face and stare at her. She's right, no doubt. Jeremy and Rayne would be on the next flight out if they thought Olive was in danger. His words to me at the wedding ring soundly in my mind.

"Then you'll come home with me."

The words are out of my mouth before my brain can catch up, and her eyes go wide once they register. She steps back from me, her forehead wrinkling in an adorable little frown.

"I'm not staying with you. I'll call…Ken."

Her voice drops slightly with discomfort as she says the words, and I know right then and there that she doesn't want to call that prick any more than my name is Adam.

I step closer to her. Keeping my voice velvety soft, I focus all of my attention on her porcelain face. "You'll stay with me. If that sounded like a request, I'm sorry. It wasn't."

Her body goes stiff and rigid as she raises herself to her full height and her arms snap to her hips. I'm pretty sure she means to be forceful and assertive but to me it just comes across as pure sex. I want to know if she'll be that bossy and sure of herself when I lay her down on a bed.

Her defiance is addictive. The way she wants to call the shots even though she's obviously scared is amazing. On some subliminal level, it makes me want to be the man she doesn't see coming. The one who makes her *want* to listen to me.

With other women, when they find out that I'm ex-military, they can't wait to submit to the obvious dominance I can't help but display. Can't wait to let me "protect" them. But not Olive…she wants to keep control of the situation even though I'm standing right here telling her otherwise.

Her eyes flash as she assesses me. "Excuse me? I'm a grown woman, and I'll decide—"

She's cut off by the thundering knock on the front door downstairs.

I eye her with interested amusement, gesturing toward the bedroom doorway. "After you."

She spins and stalks out of the room and down the stairs, and I try really fucking hard not to chuckle as I follow. The disarray that meets us again on the way down sobers me enough to be completely serious by the time she opens the door and two officers from the WPD roll in.

Recognition flashes in one of their expressions. "Hey, Shaw. Got a call about a two-eleven." He scrunches his forehead, trying to figure out the reason for my presence.

I indicate Olive. "She's a friend of mine. This is Miss Alexander's home. When she came home to find it…*decorated*, she called me first."

The officer, a uniform named Briggs, nods in understanding. He turns kind eyes on Olive. "Miss? Can you give us a list of what was taken during the break-in?"

Olive leads the officers into the great room. "We've been through the entire house and I haven't noticed anything missing at all."

My mind flashes back to each room of the house. "Doesn't seem like this was a robbery."

She glances at me, murmuring her assent as Briggs begins jotting things down on his pad. We lead both officers through the home as they thoroughly check each room to assess what's wrong and take note of everything they see. When they're finished, we stand in the entryway once more.

"Miss Alexander." Briggs glances at her. "This was obviously personal. You have no idea who would have broken in just to leave you flowers?"

Her face drains of color, a helpless expression crossing her face as she glances around at the disarray in her home. "I...no."

Briggs nods. "Do you have another place to stay until we get this sorted out?"

Her reaction scares the shit out of me in a way I can't explain. My heart pounds as I step closer, ready to catch her if her legs give out. She's seconds away from crumbling, and I keep my gaze trained on her as I speak to Briggs. "She's going to stay with me until this gets figured out. Keep me updated with your progress on the case, okay? Until then, contact Olive on her cell or through me. I'll send you all of the numbers."

I hear Olive take a deep, shuddering breath behind me, and it's my cue to shove both police officers out the front door.

When I close it behind them, I turn to her, ready to take her into my arms. But Olive has straightened herself up and is striding down the hallway. She disappears for a moment, and when she returns she's holding a box of large trash bags. Her face is a mask of determination, and she whips a bag from the box and shakes it open, starting to shove trash inside.

"Olive?" My voice is quiet.

She glances up at me but doesn't pause in her task. "Yeah?"

I approach her the way I would a wounded, wild animal. The last thing I expected her to want to do is clean up this mess right now. "Are you sure you want to do this now? I mean, we can hire someone...or come back tomorrow after you've had a minute to process this."

She stares at me, her expression so blank I know she had to wipe it deliberately clean. I have years of experience with doing just that. "I can't leave my house like this, Ronin. I need to clean it up and I need to do it now."

The strength of this woman…Jesus Christ.

The only clue that she's not truly all the way okay is the very small tremor on the last couple of words. And I know that this is important to her; this is the way she's going to process and heal and function. So I grab a bag from the box and help her work through the house room by room, setting everything right again and cleaning up the flower petals that have invaded her space.

She's hyperfocused on the task, and sometimes I glance over at her to see her biting her lip while she concentrates on something especially tedious or her nose wrinkling as though the flowers disgust or disappoint her. As I'm tying up the last trash bag, she sighs and drops to the edge of the bed. Her expression is weary, her eyes slightly glazed.

Setting the bag down on the carpeted floor, I stride over to stand beside her. "Hey. It's going to be okay."

She nods mutely.

"You want to throw some things in a bag for my place?"

Finally, she slides her gaze to mine. Hers becomes steely and resolute, the expression that seems to represent the core of Olive's personality. She and Rayne are so different. I got to know her sister while Jeremy and the rest of the team protected her from the psycho ex-employer who stalked her from Phoenix, and even though both Alexander women are tough as nails, Olive wears her strength in a much different way. She's a little more subtle, more refined. She's frostier, more aloof. The loosest I've ever seen her was when she danced and played with Decker at the wedding. It allowed me to know that there's a softer side to the woman, maybe even a melted center, but it's not something she shows to outsiders.

She stands, wrapping her arms around her stomach. "Yes. I'll do that."

It's like she's startled she didn't think of it first.

I give her a nod. "I'll take the last bag downstairs and you can join me when you're ready to go."

My last glance is of her staring into her closet with a determined expression just before I walk out her bedroom door.

7

OLIVE

If I'm being honest, there were a couple times when I pictured where Ronin lives.

I haven't spent much time around the man at all, but he's not the kind of guy you can just forget about once you've met him. The intensity in those gorgeous sage-green eyes. All of that bronzed, taut skin stretched over miles of rock-hard muscles. And the way he carries himself is…gulp-worthy. He oozes power and sexiness, moving like a panther with coiled-up energy ready to strike at any moment. And now that he's basically come to my rescue, I can add "Ronin protecting me from all the scary things in my life" to my seemingly endless list of fantasies about this man.

He's not the kind of guy who fits into my very small, very planned-out comfort zone. But he's apparently the kind of guy I fantasize about.

Walking into his condo, I gaze around me in wonder because it isn't at all what I would have expected. Ronin lives near the top of a really large building. It's the kind of place with a glossy front lobby and amenities galore: fitness center, pool, rooftop deck. The unit is large and wide open, with modern fixtures and sparse decor. As soon as I walk in the front door I can see straight through to the wall of glass at the back of the living room and my attention is drawn there.

Ronin closes the front door behind us. He sets my bag down on the gray marble tile and leads me down the short hallway leading to the wide-open great room. "This is my place."

I twirl in a slow circle, my designer's eye finding points of interest at various spots in the space. The high ceilings. The mosaic tile fireplace surround. The contrasting colors of white natural stone countertops paired beside navy blue shaker cabinets in the kitchen.

"It's beautiful, Ronin."

A half smirk indicates the pleasure my compliment brings him and he lifts one shoulder in a shrug. "Thanks."

I decide to distract myself from this horrific night by focusing on the beauty of his home. "Was it a new build? Did you get to pick the finishes yourself?"

He nods and I give the room one more appreciative sweep with my gaze. Who would have thought a man like Ronin Shaw would have a good eye for design?

The whole space is done so well. Where I expect to see black or brown leather sofas and chairs, there's actually a really lovely white sectional sofa and a driftwood coffee table. I walk over to it, running my hands along the wood. "This is handcrafted."

I glance at Ronin, who's still standing in the mouth of the

entry hall and am met with his nod of confirmation. "Worked on it with Jeremy. He's got a workshop in the back of his house."

My surprised gaze is stuck on the man before me. I'm seeing him in a completely different light than I had before, and it's unnerving. Sharp tingles of interest and attraction sizzle along my skin and a very clear line of tension pulls tight between us as he stares back.

Clearing my throat, I look away and walk toward the wall of glass. It's late, and there are no city lights in sight, which lets me know that this balcony must overlook the ocean. Glancing back at Ronin, I indicate the slider. "May I?"

Crossing the room, he unlocks the door and pulls it open. I step out onto the balcony and the rush of the waves to kiss the sand gives me an instant feeling of serenity like I've never felt before.

I grew up here in Wilmington, so the beach is nothing new to me. It's never really been anything to marvel at either, in my opinion. But for the first time, here on Ronin's dark balcony, all the best parts of the sea hit me at once: the salty, fresh air, the lulling sound of ocean against shore, the enormous sense of something bigger than you making a place like this possible.

I sigh, walking up to the railing and resting my hands on top of the metal. In the dark of the night I can make out the different shades of black marking the horizon, the sea, and the sand, and a feeling of utter peace washes over me.

This isn't at all like the security I've surrounded myself with in my little suburban community with friendly neighbors and a perfectly ordered home. This isn't a white picket fence and a manicured lawn. No, this sense of home is completely different and I can't for the life of me understand how I can feel so perfectly comfortable here. It's wilder, freer, more wide-open and unpredictable.

Four things I avoid at all costs.

I close my eyes and just listen to the sea.

I feel Ronin as he steps up beside me, his presence unmistakable and almost tangible in this place especially. *His* place.

Neither of us speaks for several moments. But then his voice rumbles across the bit of distance between us and I shiver.

"Everything makes more sense out here, doesn't it?"

Opening my eyes, I turn my head and take him in. He's leaning against the railing on his forearms, his big hands clasped. His heat pulses into the air around us, warming me from the inside out. I suck in a breath and exhale slowly, trying to calm my galloping heartbeat.

"I never thought so before…but right now? Yes. I'm at peace." I swallow around the words. I'm uncomfortable, because I don't know exactly how much of that peace comes from the ocean, and how much of it comes from the man standing beside me.

He turns to face me. The scrutiny in his expression is clear. "You never thought the ocean was peaceful before?"

Shaking my head, I think about how I can explain it. "Not really. Too wild."

Ronin's head cocks to one side. "But the sea is one of the most predictable things on the planet. It might be wild, but it's also tame in that way."

"I've never thought about it like that before."

But Ronin is absolutely right.

We spend a few more minutes at peace before Ronin pushes off the railing and gestures toward the slider. "Let me show you the guest room. It's late. You must be exhausted."

Neglecting to point out that he's right—I am tired—but I don't want to be alone, I follow him back inside the condo and down the hallway that leads to the bedrooms. He opens a door on the right and enters, my bag clutched in one of his hands. Sparing a quick glance for the closed door on the right, I follow him inside and smile at the cool, calm blues that surround me. The bed is big and inviting, and I suddenly feel the need to curl up in the center of it and completely cover myself. Shield myself from the world outside while in the safety of Ronin's home.

If I have to be alone right now, I'm glad it's here.

The thought startles me enough that my eyes find Ronin, who's watching me. He's set my suitcase down on the bed, and he's evaluating me while I stare around the room.

"You thinking about what happened tonight?"

Glancing away from him, I study the floor at my feet. "I just…when I woke up this morning, this wasn't how I pictured the day ending."

Ronin folds his arms across his chest. "You're gonna be okay, Red."

Lifting my head, I see his belief in me so clearly. "How do you know that?"

He gives a small shake of his head. For a second, confusion flickers across his handsome face. "Because you've got real strength inside of you. Anyone would be stupid to underestimate that."

I swallow, looking for any sign that he didn't mean what he just said. But there's nothing but truth staring back at me. I suck in a breath, wondering if the way he see me is what's really inside, or if it's just the facade I put on. I'm only as strong as the control I hold, and right now it feels like that's slipping away.

"I'm going to let you get settled. If you need anything, Red, just holler."

He doesn't move.

Staring at his chiseled face, I'm struck by how *beautiful* he is. He's a huge, solid wall of what can only be described as everything masculine, but there's a hard beauty there just the same.

I try to put into words how I'm feeling. "Thank you, Ronin. This is…you didn't have to let me stay here. I appreciate it more than you know."

His expression holds a thousand secrets, and I can't begin to guess at any of them. "Yeah…well…I don't mind. Jeremy's like my brother. And that makes Rayne family, too."

I drop my gaze. The fact that he's helping me out of obligation to my sister and her husband shouldn't sting, but it does. It really, really does.

Ronin turns to leave, and my mouth blurts out the question before my mind can stop it. "Where's your room?"

He pauses, still facing the door. It takes a beat for him to answer me. "Right across the hall."

Right across the hall.

The thought is ridiculously comforting and insanely terrifying at the same time.

Ronin shuts the door quietly behind him, and I turn to

my suitcase. There's a bathroom adjoining this bedroom, and I can see some of what's inside through the open doorway. It's been such a long, draining night that the bathtub is calling my name.

Walking into the bathroom, I sigh in appreciation at the soothing design, light gray floor tiles making the white cabinetry and stand-alone tub sing out chorus. The sea foam wall color is just as calming as the muted blues in the bedroom, and as I stare around me in wonder I think I might just love this place. There are no knickknacks on the counter, nothing decorating either room that makes it scream out "home," but it doesn't matter. I know that this is Ronin's place and that's enough to make me feel comfortable and safe.

Leaving the hot water running in the bathtub, I head back into the bedroom to pull out some of the things I've brought with me. Hanging up a couple of outfits for work in the closet, I then pull out comfortable pajamas and new underwear before shucking off the clothes I wore to work and dinner with Ken—

Ken!

I let my head fall back against my shoulder blades and sigh. How is it that I've gone through two hours since finding out that my house has been broken into, talked with the police, and agreed to stay at another man's home, and not remembered to call the man I'd been out with earlier tonight?

If that's not a red flag then I don't know what is.

I glance at the closed bedroom door, knowing my purse is still out in the living room where I'd dropped it after seeing the view from the sliding glass doors. I contemplate throwing on clothes and going out to get it but then I shrug. What's the point? If I'd felt the need to have Ken by my side during this ordeal I would have thought to call him first. But who had I called?

Ronin.

I snort, thinking about just how much trouble I might be in when it comes to the strong, quiet ex-soldier who oozes sex appeal without even trying.

Leaving my purse where it is, I grab my pj's and head for the bathtub that's calling my name.

8

RONIN

When I walk back into the living room after leaving Olive alone for the night, all I want to do is throw my head back and roar. Or run five miles. Or put on some boxing gloves and punch the shit out of a bag until the energy racing through my veins is quieted.

Why'd I bring her here? Now that I'm out of her presence and can take a breath and think, I realize that this is going to slow down my investigation into who killed Elle. My first priority right now should be *her*, not Red.

Pain stabs me in the gut as I feel like I might be betraying my dead wife.

Leaning back against the cushions, I sigh. "I swear, Elle. I'm going to find the man who did this to you. And then he's going to take his last breath."

Maybe I could deny it before…chalk it up to curiosity or mild interest in a beautiful woman. But now that I've been in close proximity with Olive for the past two hours, and *ex-*

tremely near her for the last fifteen minutes, there's no denying shit.

There are serious fucking sparks between Olive Alexander and me. The kind you can't ignore without going insane.

All I want to do is throw her on that bed in my guest room and *have my goddamn way with her.* Get it out of my system. Make her scream my name, just for a night. I can picture how it'll feel to run my hands all over that creamy, smooth skin and then chase the trail with my tongue. Find little places to use my teeth so she gasps as I kiss the sting away. I want to peel all of those uptight business clothes off of her, inch by inch. And I could, dammit. I can see it in her eyes, this isn't just one-sided. I think that despite the cool, aloof signals she tries to put off, she wants me, too. Her eyes rake me over when she thinks I'm not looking. Her body turns toward mine when she talks to me, like she doesn't even know she's doing it. God, if I could just get my hands on her, she'd respond. My mouth waters as I picture it, and I scrub a hand over my face.

Jesus.

What's wrong with me? I just found a clue that could lead me straight to the killer I've been waiting to run into for the last seven years. And Olive Alexander wouldn't just be some woman I'd spend the night with. No, I've had plenty of those over the years. She's my best friend's sister-in-law. She can't be a one-night stand. And I'm not the kind of man who does anything halfway but, I'm too fucked-up inside…there's no way I can give Olive the kind of relationship she probably wants, and definitely deserves.

After I lost Elle, something inside me broke. Any piece of

me that was available to love someone else? That died right along with my wife. There's no coming back from that. Not for me.

Groaning, I stride to the couch and sink down onto the cushions, dropping my face into my hands. I take a deep breath and then another, trying to calm my raging thoughts and the hectic, almost violent passion ramping up inside my body.

A ringing sound forces its way into my thoughts, and I move my hands away from my face as I freeze and listen.

Glancing around the room to search for the intrusive noise, my eyes land on Olive's purse. The oversize, brown leather bag is sitting on the end table at the mouth of the entry hall. Rising from the couch, I walk toward it and grab hold, pivoting and heading for the closed guest room door.

Knocking softly, I lean my forehead against the wood and wait. No sound comes from within the room, and Olive's phone stops ringing inside the purse clutched in my hand.

She's probably asleep. And giving her the bag tonight isn't worth waking her up. But if it was me, I'd want my phone with me. Okay, maybe I'm just giving myself validation to go into her room because I want to see her again.

With a sigh, I gently push the door open and scan the dimly lit bedroom. Empty. Then, Olive's soft, off-key singing voice drifts toward me. I zero in on the bathroom door, sitting ajar, and a smirk crosses my lips as I listen to her sing her very own version of Adele's *"When We Were Young."* It's so unexpected, and it's cute as hell, and I'm drifting forward before I've given my feet permission to move. The shower's not running, but I'm not stupid enough to push open the door without knocking.

"Olive?" My knuckles meet wood again.

The singing stops. Olive's voice, slightly panicked, rises. "Ronin?"

I lift one arm overhead and grip the doorjamb. "Yeah…it's me. I have your purse. Your phone was ringing. I thought you might want it?"

A pause. "Yeah, thanks. I'm, um, in the tub. Could you leave it on the bed?"

My eyes slam shut. Instantly, an image of her body, soaking wet, bubbles clinging to her skin, blazes into my mind. My body reacts, my dick going painfully hard in my jeans, the zipper digging into me with a vengeance. *Fuck. Me.*

"Ronin?" Her voice wavers with uncertainty.

Clearing my throat, I try really hard to pull my shit together. "Uh, yeah. I'm here. I'll put it on the bed. Let me know if you need anything."

It takes every ounce of strength I have to turn around and stride out of that room, dropping the purse on the bed as I pass. Shutting the guest room door behind me, I lean against it and take a breath.

My mind in a slight panic, I try to bring Elle's face into my head to replace Olive's. When I'm able to picture my wife instead of the woman singing in the bathtub, I breathe a sigh of relief.

Having Olive in my space? It's fucking with my head, bigtime. I'll be lucky if I don't end up doing something unforgiveable before it's all over.

When Olive enters the kitchen the next morning she's in her

full work attire. Her charcoal-gray skirt smooths over her hips and my eye is drawn there first as she sashays into the room on nude heels. Then the olive-green blouse she wears pulls my gaze because she's left two buttons undone at the top and there's an expanse of creamy skin exposed above the valley of cleavage that calls out to me like a goddamn song. When I finally find her eyes I discover them locked on mine, two pools of evening sky searching my gaze with a question in them. Her hair is piled up on her head the way it normally is. She's sleek and polished and put together, because, as I now know, it's rare that anyone ever catches Olive in any other way. Last night was a huge exception to the rule, and it isn't lost on me, now that she's staying here, that I might get to see her undone more and more. A small thrill zings through my body at the thought.

"What?" I'm leaning against the counter with a mug of coffee in my hands. I got up with the sun this morning the way I always do, heading down to the fitness center for a workout.

Clothed now in nothing but black sweatpants and a smile I observe the drag and pull of her eyes as they skitter across my bare torso, almost like it's against her will.

"I…" She clears her throat. "If you're not ready I can totally drive myself, Ronin."

Sipping my coffee I refrain from rolling my eyes. "Actually, you can't. Your car is at the office. And I want to keep an eye on you until we figure out who wrecked your house last night."

Jeremy's warning about the fact that Olive might have something going on that we don't know about decks me in the gut. If she's in trouble…

No. Don't go there. You don't know anything yet. It's not like before.

She huffs out a breath, two spots of color glowing in her cheeks. The sight of her flustered and frustrated brings a smirk to my lips. I don't know why; it's a jerk move for sure. But seeing her getting wound up makes me want to see just how far I can push her.

The thought surprises me, because it's not my usual style. I'm not the guy who pushes a woman's buttons. I'm the kind of guy who finds out what makes them feel good and then leaves before anything gets complicated.

Her hands rest on her hips. "I don't know why all you ex-army men think your one job in life is to 'protect the womenfolk.' I can take care of myself, Ronin. I don't need a bodyguard."

My mind instantly spins toward the faint memory of another woman, standing with her hands on her hips, miles of dark, wild hair floating all around her. Her words were so similar to the ones Olive just uttered.

"You don't have to worry about me while you're deployed, Ronin. I can take care of myself."

But Elle's lilting tone was full of tease and tenderness. Olive's is full of sass and fire.

Shaking my head and brushing off the memory, I school my expression and push off the cabinet. "Wait here. Grab coffee. I'll be ready soon."

With that, I turn on my heel and stride to my bedroom. I don't mean to slam the door shut as hard as I do, but my muscles twitch when the door rattles in the frame. Marching into the bathroom, I jerk the handle on the shower until the water is running full blast and whirl toward the sink.

Gripping the gray marble with both hands until the pressure causes pain, I stare at my reflection.

She's right. Who the fuck are you kidding? You can't protect her...if she's in trouble, you'll fail her. Just like you failed Elle.

The words in my head mock me as I stare at my reflection. The emotion building inside my chest is almost too much for me to handle, and I clench a fist in preparation to shove it into the glass with every ounce of power I have.

Trembling, I close my eyes and take a deep breath. In through my nose and out through my mouth. Again.

Again.

When I open my eyes my heartbeat is no longer slamming through my ears. My breathing isn't ragged and heavy. My fingers have relaxed against the granite. I sigh, shoving my hands through my hair.

"She's not Elle. She's not in the kind of trouble Elle was in. I'm not going to fail her. Olive is going to be fine."

It's a mantra I'm going to have to keep repeating, keep telling myself, until I actually believe it.

Olive is *not* Elle.

Dropping my sweatpants, I step into the shower. The warm water cascades over my shoulders and down my chest, and I stand there for a minute to gather my thoughts.

Remembering the irritation on Olive's face when she basically told me she didn't need me sends a shot of annoyance through me. *Why does that bother me so much?* The last thing I need is for someone to rely on me, right? But thinking about

Olive wanting me, depending on me, *needing* me? That brings another element of interest to the table. I realize I want this woman to want me, and that realization shoots an unexpected surge of need straight to my dick.

With a groan, I lean forward until my hands meet tile and squeeze my eyes shut. Growing stiffer by the second, images of the gorgeous redhead standing in my kitchen start to roll through my mind on a loop. Unable to help myself, I take my steel-hard length in one hand and stroke. My bottom lip gets caught between my teeth as I imagine her hand gripping me tightly, her little fist working me the way I imagine she can: hard and fast. Sparks crackle in my veins, my blood heating as I jerk, my stance widening and my other hand fisting against the tiled shower wall.

It only takes a few minutes until my imagination combined with my movements brings me to the fucking edge. Hissing through my teeth as I come, the warmth of my release mixes with the heat of the water streaming down all around me and stars explode behind my eyes with the sheer force of it.

Goddamn. I can't remember the last time I exploded with this kind of force on my own. Whatever Olive Alexander is doing to me is quickly becoming undeniable, no matter how hard I'm trying to downplay it.

It's unnerving as hell. Because all I ever do is *fuck*. There're no feelings and there are no attachments. It's the only thing I'm capable of. When I lost Elle, I knew I'd never be the same. I'd never again be the kind of man who could allow a woman to worm her way into his heart, because all that's left in my chest where my heart should be is a gaping hole.

At least that's how it's been for the last seven years.

But if that's still true, then why, after all this time, is the nonexistent muscle starting to beat again when I think of Olive?

9

OLIVE

Glancing over at Ronin while he drives, our conversation in the kitchen half an hour ago plays through my mind. His abrupt behavior when he left the kitchen threw me off balance, and that's a feeling I can't stand. It was so un-Ronin-like, the quick flare of temper and the about-face from the room. I've never pegged him as the type to run from a confrontation, or to grow angry because of a few words tossed around. But the look that crossed his face after I spoke was less angry and more...*shredded*. Like the words I'd spoken about being able to take care of myself had actually cut him.

The tension between us in the car is palpable, and I turn away from his chiseled profile to stare out the window. We both live on the same side of town, and my office isn't far from his condo. The streets of Wilmington roll past in a spinning mix of quaint and coastal, and then Ronin's truck is pulling in to the small parking lot intended for our firm. Ronin cuts the truck's engine and steps out of the cab. As he heads to my side,

I scramble down from the cab and grab my laptop bag from the floor.

A look of irritation crosses his face as he stands beside me. Reaching over my head, he settles a hand on top of the passenger-side door and leans in close. "Didn't anyone ever teach you that you should wait until a man opens the door for you?"

His green eyes blaze, and they drop to my lips before focusing again on my own. Clearing my throat, I stare up at him and hitch my bag up on my shoulder. "Didn't anyone ever tell you that times have changed and a woman is never required to wait for a man?"

A muscle in his jaw twitches and he doesn't reply. We stand there, eyes locked, his body close enough to mine for me to smell his cologne and feel the unbelievable heat rising from him. My legs give a slight tremble at the same time that his pupils dilate in the never-ending sea of green.

When my phone chirps in my purse, I drop my eyes and slide out from under his arm. My voice is stiff. "Thank you. For the ride."

I don't turn back because I don't know what will happen if I do. Just as my foot hits the sidewalk to head up to the front door, Ronin's voice makes me pause.

"I'll pick you up here at five. Keep me posted if you hear anything from the police, and I'll do the same."

I nod and step onto the sidewalk.

"And, Olive…"

I pause again, but Ronin doesn't speak. Slowly, I turn. God, he's a sight, leaning against the side of his truck in his tight black T-shirt, his biceps bulging with his arms folded across his broad chest. The traitorous girl inside me shivers. "Yes?"

"The next time I want to open a door for you? Let me."

I let out a breath and turn, picking up my pace until I'm stepping inside the design firm. I hurry to my office and drop into my chair. I stare at the open doorway, wishing for the first time that our office wasn't designed as an open office.

I want an office door that I can shut right now. Badly.

Inhaling, I pull my phone out of my purse and note the e-mail icon flashing red. I click open my in-box and the breath gets stuck halfway to my lungs. My eyes grow larger with every word I read.

Hey there Olive,

Did you like my surprise? Roses were always your favorite. Why haven't you responded to my last message? Can't imagine you'd ignore me…not after everything we've been through. I'm back in town, and I want to catch up. I miss you, baby. Let's get together soon, yeah?

Love, your M.J.

My heart drops down to my feet. I'd known it the second I saw the corsage, just like the one he gave me in college, but this confirmation just makes it that much more real.

It was him…M.J. was in my house the other night.

Why did I think that hearing from him once was a fluke?

Just before I'd left for France, I'd received an e-mail similar to this one. I pull it up now with frantic fingers, my eyes scanning the words far more thoroughly than I did the first time, when all I'd wanted to do was shove it into the background.

Olive,

God, I've missed you. How have you been? I'm sure you heard how everything fell apart after you left me. But you know what, Olive? I'm a determined man. I couldn't let failing out of college because of the depression you put me in be the end of me. No, instead, I went to work for my uncle. You know the one…and now I'm ready. Ready to step back into your life, ready to show you why you were wrong all those years ago. I have money. I have power. I have everything I need to take care of you. You and me…we belong together. Always have. Always will. I'm going to show you that, Olive. And I'll keep showing you, until you believe me. No matter what it takes, you and I will be together. Forever this time.

See you soon,
Your M.J.

Reading it a second time sends a series of shivers coursing through me. I'm not even sure how M.J. got my current e-mail address. After everything that happened between us in college, I made sure to cover my tracks as much as possible.

I never wanted to hear from him again.

He was the bad boy, the kind of guy I never would have usually dated and certainly never have again. But at that time in my life, I was more vulnerable than I'd ever been before. I was hurting: deep, dark scars that still haven't completely healed.

And M.J. was there, ready to pick up the pieces and help me get back to the person I used to be.

But after a while, I realized that he was into some things that I couldn't handle. Drugs. Crime. Really serious crimes that I had no business being anywhere near. When I found out that the money he'd given me to pay for a semester of tuition that my parents couldn't afford was dirty, I told him we were done.

I thought he got the message then. He left school and I didn't hear anything else from him. Until now.

Remembering it now, I fold my arms across my chest and shudder. M.J. was unstable back then. I can only imagine what the grown-man version of him is like now. Especially since, based on the e-mail he sent, he's been plotting our reunion the entire time. I can't even imagine…my *God*.

I'm still holding the phone when Berkeley appears in the open doorway.

Without pausing, she breezes into my office and scans my face. Her expression softens.

Tucking a strand of hair over her shoulder, she focuses concerned eyes on my face.

"What's wrong?" Her question is instant.

Closing my eyes to fend off the onslaught of tears, I shake my head slightly. "I…I don't think I can work today, Berkeley. I'm going to take a few days off."

The last thing I want to do is let M.J. ruin what I have going on now. Not for a second. But if he's searching for me…my office is the first place he'll look. And after the stress of the past twenty-four hours, I don't think I can handle coming face to face with him.

I quickly fill her in on what I found when I walked into my house the previous night. Berkeley rubs my shoulder, her sweet compassion bleeding into her expression. "Just tell me how I can help."

I glance down at the floor, shame filling me up and making me feel sick. "You know the ex I told you about?"

Recognition flares in her eyes. "What about him?"

"He's been contacting me. He left town years ago...I thought he was gone for good." I suck in a breath. "But apparently...he's back."

Berkeley reaches out to rub small hands up and down my arms. "Oh, Olive."

"He wants to see me," I blurt out.

I never told anyone how I'd been so vulnerable to get involved with a guy like M.J. in the first place. And all I'd told Berkeley about him was that he was a part of my past I'd like to stay there. A bad choice from my youth.

But now...

Berkeley's brows pull together, her bottom lip disappearing between her teeth. "What are you going to do about him?"

Sighing, I retreat to my desk and lean against it. Looking back to my friend, I shrug.

"I honestly don't know what I can do."

Berkeley folds her arms across her chest and studies me. "Has he directly threatened you?"

Picking up my phone, I hand it to her. "He's much too smart for that."

It was one of the things that had driven me crazy about M.J. If he'd only used his brains for good, he could have been an incredible man. He had a father who loved him and tried so hard to keep him on a straight path. I'd tried, too. But there was nothing either of us could do to change the trajectory that M.J. had been on back then. He was determined to follow in his uncle's footsteps. And his uncle was one of the worst people I'd ever known.

Gritting my teeth, I take the phone back from her. "He wouldn't threaten me in an e-mail."

Berkeley's voice grows more serious. "Trust me on this, Olive. You should go to the police with this information."

Berkeley is gearing up for war. I can see it written all over her fierce facial expression. She wants to blaze in with both barrels smoking, and I hold up my hands to top her progression before she goes too far down that path.

"I've got this, Berkeley. The police were called when my place was broken into last night. And…Ronin is on it. He's helping me. I'm actually staying at his place right now."

The truth is that calling Ronin and pouring out the information about the e-mails M.J. sent feels as natural as breathing. Ronin hasn't been in my life very long at all, and he's already my go-to when I'm having a problem. After learning at an early age that I have to be self-reliant first and foremost, depending on someone else to help me shouldn't be easy at all. I'd depended on M.J. back in college, for the first time in a long time, and look where that had gotten me. Since then I've been on my own. But now, Ronin steps into my life like this big, badasss protector and I'm ready to let him shield me from the man I fear most.

Berkeley's eyebrows fly up toward her hairline.

"Wait...what?" Her lips curl into a small smile. "That doesn't sound like you. Did he drag you to his house kicking and screaming?"

With a roll of my eyes, I twirl my phone in my hands. "Practically. He's pretty damn bossy."

Berkeley's gaze practically twinkles, but worry still saturates her eyes. "Call him. Tell him what's going on. I'll leave you alone, but really...I want you to take all the time you need. I'll help Paisley on the boutique hotel project, and I'm sure Beth will jump in to help you on the downtown Victorian while you're out."

Sadness permeates my heart. I love both of the projects, and I don't want to give them up. I'll try to keep myself involved as much as I can while I'm out of the office. "Thank you, Berkeley. I'll try to get this resolved as quickly as possible."

She closes the distance between us and grabs me up in a tight hug. "Be safe, my friend."

As soon as she's left the office, I grab my phone and pull up Ronin's name in my contacts. The last thing I want to do is bother him at work. I know that his job is important, and that he has an entire life outside my newfound problems. Listening to the ringing while I wait to hear his voice is tedious, but as soon as his concerned voice comes across the line all the air leaves me in a *whoosh*.

"Red? You okay?"

I swallow, the movement suddenly so difficult. Just the sound of his voice makes me want to break.

And I never break.

Comfort. That's what Ronin's voice sparks inside me, and I'm not quite ready to think about why that is.

"No," I answer with a tremble in my tone. "Can you meet me at my office?"

10

RONIN

The sound of her voice on the other end of the line keeps scraping against my memory. I was just getting ready to head into a morning meeting with the NES staff when my phone rang. I asked Olive if she could sit tight at work, and when she agreed, I told her that I'd meet her as soon as my meeting ended.

My mind murky with thoughts of her and the fact that she'd just received a threatening e-mail, I take a seat at the long table in the conference room at the Night Eagle office. Leaning back in the leather chair, I rub my hand against the rough stubble on my jaw.

"What's up?" Dare Conners, fellow NES member, slides into the seat beside me.

I barely acknowledge him, because my head is too full of all things Olive and what I'm going to learn about her situation.

Grisham Abbot walks into the room with our boss—and also his future father-in-law—Jacob Owens. Taking a seat across from us, Grisham shoots both Dare and I a chin lift before leaning forward on his elbows. "Dude. You look like you're about ready to jump out of your chair. What's up?"

Dare leans in closer as Jacob welcomes an unexpected guest: Sayward Diaz.

"Something going on?" Dare speaks quietly, not wanting to alert Jacob to our conversation.

"I'm dealing with it." I don't meet either of their gazes.

Dare and Grisham are more than friends. In the time that we've all worked together at NES, they've become more like brothers. And when it comes down to it, I know that if I need them to help out with either Elle's case or whatever Olive's got going on, I'll reach out. But I don't know all the pieces moving on the board yet. I want to know exactly what I'm dealing with before I share the situation with them.

Plus, anything I do on my own time concerning Elle's case can't have anything to do with NES. I'm on my own with this, and I know it.

Grisham's shrewd eyes study me. He pushes his blond hair off his forehead. "You sure?"

I give a slight nod as I focus in on Jacob at the head of the conference table. Sayward settles in the seat beside Dare, whipping her laptop out of its bag.

"'Morning." Jacob's voice is a permanent bark.

We all know his gruffness comes from years of having been in charge of some of the strongest, most aggressive men in the world: army Rangers. As all of us served in Special Forces at some point, we're more than familiar with the nature of his leadership and we all respond to it like professionals.

"I want us to welcome Sayward back to the fold." Jacob clears his throat and glances at Sayward. Her eyes remain fixed on her laptop screen, but it's obvious she's listening.

"With Teague gone," Jacob continues, "Sayward has agreed to step up and join the team. You've all had firsthand experience with what she can do on a computer, and I don't want to let her get away. You guys good with that?"

I sit up straighter in my seat. "Brains is coming back though, Boss Man."

He meets my gaze head-on. "Yeah. I know that. And when he returns, we'll adjust. We can use Sayward on all the tech, even though Brains is our resident geek. It'll give him more time to focus on taking a more active role in missions, leading more. He'll be good with it."

I consider it. Sayward really did a kickass job on the last mission, and she wasn't a permanent member of the team then. I can only imagine what she'll be able to do after she gets to know us better and has a firm grasp on NES protocols.

"Yeah. We're good." I speak for the team, but Dare's and Grisham's nods cosign the effort.

Jacob has been accepting more and more private ops contracted by the government. We've done everything from protecting important international diplomats to bringing down illegal arms dealers in South America. Even though Jacob has a second branch of NES open in Texas, with a friend of his from the army running that branch, our Wilmington base is garnering so much work that adding more team members is inevitable. I think Sayward is just the first wave of what's to come.

"Do you have a military background, Say?" Grisham asks.

She snorts, finally looking up from her screen. "Um, no. Even basic training would be more difficult for someone like me than it is for everyone else. I wouldn't have wanted to put myself through it. I'm good at home where I'm behind a computer."

Jacob speaks up. "She received her training from the School of Hard Knocks. I did a job with her father a long time ago, though. I know Sayward is going to fit in here, gentlemen. Trust me on it."

Grisham nods. "Got it."

Sayward's hands leave the keyboard of her laptop, only to begin fiddling with the zipper on her hoodie. She focuses on Jacob and he rubs his hands together in preparation to launch into the meeting agenda.

"There's been an unusual amount of illegal activity here in Wilmington over the last few months." Jacob's voice goes even more solemn than usual. "My friends at the Wilmington Police Department have been talking about it, but we've now had an official request from the FBI's Organized Crime unit. They want us to step in, put together an op to infiltrate the Margiano crime family and bring it down. I think we're up for it. But it'll take about a month to gather intel. We'll then penetrate the organization, and then bring it down. Once Teague is back with us, we'll definitely be up to the task. Agreed?"

We all nod without a moment's hesitation. "Agreed."

Jacob continues the meeting with wrap-ups from a personal security assignment and then dismisses us. My hands were clenched in my lap the entire time, aching to pick up my phone and check to make sure Olive hadn't called or texted in the last forty-five minutes.

As the meeting ends, I flag Jacob down and pull him to the side. "I have to get out of here, Boss."

He lifts a brow. "Why?"

I'm almost bouncing on the balls of my feet, ready to head for the truck. I lower my voice further. "Jeremy asked me to keep an eye on his sister-in-law while he's gone. She's got something going down. I need to be there."

Jacob's thick, sandy brows furrow. "What can I do?"

Shaking my head, I take a step back. "I don't know yet. Maybe nothing. I'll keep you posted. Keep this between us for now?"

Jacob nods, pointing a finger at me as I take another step backward, heading for the door. "Regular updates. Got it? You don't go off-grid. Not even for an hour."

Lifting my chin in understanding, but not making any promises, I turn and head out of the conference room, down the stairs, and follow the route leading out of the NES office.

I shoot Olive a text while I head to my truck.

On my way.

Midmorning traffic in the fall is minimal, so it takes me only ten minutes to get to Olive's design firm. When I burst through the glass front doors, Berkeley is standing behind the counter, and she smiles when she looks up at me.

Walking around until she's standing in front of me, she reaches up and gives me a quick hug. I squeeze her back before holding her at arm's length and nodding my head toward Olive's office. "Hey, Berk. Olive's still here, right?"

She nods, her expression clouding. "Yeah. She's waiting for you."

I stop short in the doorway. Olive is standing by the window, her back facing me.

I pause at the sight of her, just watching. You wouldn't know at first glance that she's feeling threatened. She stands tall, poised as ever. The tendrils of hair hanging down around her slim neck are slightly curled, and I can tell that her arms are folded across her chest.

The only thing amiss—and I'm pretty sure I'm only noticing because I've studied her—is the slight hunch of her shoulders. It's like she's trying to cave in on herself…like if she curls up tight she'll be safe, protected. My chest aches at the sight, and I rub my hand absently over the spot.

Stepping in, I clear my throat. Olive turns around with a start, and when she sees it's only me, she lets out a breath.

"Hi," she whispers.

I walk right over to where she stands, stopping only inches in front of her. I didn't expect to feel so much relief at the sight of her. I knew she'd be okay, but still…

I tuck a finger under her chin, forcing her to hold my gaze. "Tell me exactly what happened."

Her phone already clutched tightly in one hand, she gives it over and pulls her lip between her teeth as I scan the e-mail. A simmer of rage begins to boil in my veins, and when I glance up at her again she looks so close to tears I want to reach through the phone and grab whoever sent that e-mail.

"Who the fuck is M.J.?" A small spark of possessiveness ignites in my chest, and I try hard not to let it spread. She's not mine. I'm only keeping an eye out for her while Jeremy's out of town.

But I can't ignore the twinge in my gut, the twist of something dark and nasty. Jealousy? I haven't felt the emotion for so long, I'm not even sure that's what it is.

"He's an ex. Someone I dated in college. He was bad news then, and his family ties are despicable. I can only imagine what he's like now. I told him back then that I never wanted to see him again. I thought ignoring him before I went to Europe would make him go away..."

She inhales, and I can see her slender throat working as she swallows.

"Wait a minute." Confusion flares. "Before Europe?"

She nods, her face flushing. "Yeah, he contacted me with an e-mail once before. Just ahead of my leaving. And then I jumped at the chance to go, get away from the thought of him tracking me down. It was stupid to ignore it, and now I'm back and..." She gestures helplessly at her phone.

It's so obvious that feeling helpless is something she's not used to. There's a fearful expression in her eyes, but it's mixed with this fierce determination, something ingrained inside of her to beat whatever odds are stacked against her no matter what.

Where does she get that kind of intensity? How'd she become so tenacious?

She squeezes her arms even tighter around herself, and the urge to take her into my arms becomes almost uncontrollable. "God, Ronin. What am I supposed to do?"

There are more words on the tip of her tongue, but she doesn't say them. There's more to this than an e-mail from an ex. He doesn't exactly threaten her, but there's something creepy about his words. And the sight of them clearly scares Olive to death.

"Why are you so scared of this guy, Olive? What am I missing here?"

She sighs, hugging her arms around her middle. "I ended things with M.J. because he became obsessive. He was controlling who I saw and when I saw them, where I went and anything else about my life he could control. When I broke up with him, he went crazy, following me, threatening anyone I spent time with. I almost took a restraining order out on him, but he suddenly disappeared and I didn't hear from him again until a few months ago."

Shit. No wonder she's scared. The thought of this dude having the nerve to even *glance* in her direction again, much less contact her? *Fury.*

I pull her to me, holding her against my chest. With a sigh, I press my lips to the top of her head. "Okay, Red. Listen to me. *You* don't do anything. You let me handle this dude. I need all the personal info on him you can remember. I'll find him, and make sure there are no more messages. Okay?"

"What if he doesn't want to leave me alone? You didn't know him back then…there was nowhere for me to turn. The night I ended things…he squeezed my arms so hard he left bruises. My roommate walked in on him losing his shit completely…she's the one who gave me the courage to break it off then and there. There was a time in my past when I felt completely helpless…I never wanted to feel like that again. And then M.J. happened." Her eyes fill. "I thought I had put that part of my life behind me, Ronin. Having him show up here now, like this. It feels like it's starting all over again. Like he wants to hurt me for hurting him."

Fuck. I've never seen her like this…didn't know it was possible. Suddenly, I want the asshole's throat in my hands more than I want my next meal. "I'll guard you, Red. Until we're sure you're safe."

Her eyes widen, on the verge of disagreeing with me. "You have a job. You don't have time to be my bodyguard. Even saying it makes me feel ridiculous."

My hands tighten on her shoulders just a little bit. Her expression becomes obstinate, and I want to roll my eyes. "Listen, woman. I know you're all independent and that's great, but this is serious. You've been threatened, your home has been breached. I'm qualified to protect you. Let me. If not me…"

I inhale, because I want it to be me. No, I *need* it to be me.

But should it be me? What if I fail? What if he gets to her? It'd be just like Elle…

Shaking my head to clear it, I drop my hands from Olive and ball them up at my sides. "If you don't want it to be me, that's okay, too. I'll call Dare or Grisham. Or we can get Jeremy and Rayne back on the first flight from Aruba."

Before I can list any more options, Olive stiffens and practically shouts, "No! Don't you dare call Jeremy and my sister. Fine. I choose you."

Lifting an eyebrow, I pull my phone out of my pocket. "You sure? Because Jeremy's number is right—"

She reaches for my phone and I lift it out of her reach. Then she actually leaps for it, and I can't help the rumble of laughter that bursts from my chest. This woman…Jesus.

"Ronin." She glares. "I said I choose you, okay? Put the damn phone away."

Sliding the phone back in my pocket, I focus on her. "And you swear to listen to me, even when you don't want to?"

Listening to her mumble something under her breath about never wanting to, I chuckle and wait.

Finally, she sighs. "Yes. I'll listen. I'll be a good girl, I promise."

The term "good girl" in reference to Olive doesn't seem far-fetched, but it does draw all kinds of dirty pictures in my mind that I can't erase.

I gesture toward her desk. "Good. Let's get out of here, then. You're riding with me. We're going to the police station. You're going to show this to the detective working on your B and E from last night. If you think it could be this M.J. dude, it'll be good to have him on their radar. We'll go from there."

11

OLIVE

The day has taken such a toll on me that I don't even bat an eyelash when, after the police station, Ronin asks me if I mind stopping at his friend's bar for an early dinner so he can check in with him.

Bars like this aren't in my comfort zone. If I'm at a bar, it's usually the kind with glossy surfaces and polished floors, where most of the people sitting on stools are sipping cosmos and martinis. In the past, before Rayne arrived back in town, I'd often been out with Berkeley and her friends. So I know the places they gravitate toward are more casual, and I'm totally fine with that. It's just that the people in my usual circles of friends dance to a very different beat, and it's difficult to decide where I fit in best.

As soon as we walk through the front doors of The Oakes, the warmth and comfort of the place seeps into my skin. It's dim, and a little worn, but it's clean, and the scent of deliciously fried food snakes around me like a cloak.

Ronin leads me to the bar, and I gaze at the handsome man standing behind it. He drops the rag he's using on the bar top and leans back, folding his arms across a broad, strong chest. The biceps, on display in a soft gray T-shirt that stretches tight across his pecs, bulge with chiseled muscles that could be cut from actual stone. Winding ink swirls over one complete arm, colorful and vibrant in a way that matches the mischievous twinkle in his green eyes.

The smirk drifting across his lips is both welcoming and taunting. I don't know who this guy is, but the dog tags around his neck inform me that he's served our country, and the immediate respect I feel for him is instant, much like when I met the men of Night Eagle Security.

I eye him warily as we sit down. The square set of the bartender's jaw, coupled with the general roughneck look of him tells me that he has a past, filled with secrets and darkness the world knows nothing about. I shudder slightly in my seat.

"Bennett Blacke," Ronin announces as he points to the bartender. "Meet my guest for the foreseeable future, Olive Alexander."

One of Bennett's thick brows lifts inquisitively. "Guest, huh? Sweetness, I'm guessing that means you're in some kinda trouble, and Ronin here stepped up to help. Not surprising, knowing him."

I can feel my face heating, surely turning crimson in the dim light of the bar. "He's…helping me out with something, yeah."

Ronin chuckles, and Bennett bursts into loud laughter. "You sound real thrilled about it."

Rolling my eyes, I rest my elbows on the bar. "Can I have a drink, please?"

It's been a day straight out of the ninth circle of hell. I needed a drink two hours ago, and now all I want to do is play catch-up.

Ronin turns to me, his eyes scanning my face. "We'll order food, too."

Waving my hand in the general direction of the swinging door at the end of the bar, I'm too tired to think anymore. "Sure. Whatever you like here is good enough for me."

Ronin's eyes widen just a tiny bit, outright shock swirling in the depths of the sage irises. "Damn. I might never hear you say that again...why didn't I get it on camera?"

I shove his shoulder, my lips curving in a smile. "Don't you dare get used to it."

He places a hand over his heart, shaking his head. "Never, Red." The corners of his eyes crinkle when he truly smiles, something I've missed in the handful of times I've been around him before this. It's endearing, this soft side to him. The playful side. Usually he seems like he's all-business, or either he's taking in everyone and everything around him in this intense way. But right now...he's lighter. More jovial. And even though I can't deny the pure, instinctual attraction I have to that other side of him, even as it drives me mad, this side of Ronin? I'm startled to find that I *like* it.

And I won't lie...every time he calls me "Red" my toes curl and my heart thumps a little more wildly in my chest.

Our eyes catch, and hold.

My phone rings, breaking the strange and unnerving spell

Ronin Shaw has temporarily placed me under with all his charm and intensity and delicious heat.

"Hello?" I'm unable to tear my gaze away from Ronin as I answer, but as soon as I hear the voice on the other end of the line my spine stiffens.

"Olive? Where are you? I've been ringing your doorbell for five minutes!" Ken's agitated voice snakes across the line.

Oh, dammit! I cringe, and Ronin leans forward slightly, his eyes scanning my face. "Oh, my God…Ken. I'm so sorry! It's been a horrible day."

I can almost see Ken's blond brows furrowing, the annoyed tick of his jaw. "So, what? You're not coming? I paid a lot for these theater tickets, Olive."

The breath I huff out blows a loose strand of my hair. "Yeah, well, I'm happy to reimburse you, Ken. I should have called."

"Yes, you should have." The quick snap of his voice lets me know that he's past irritated, well on his way to pissed-off.

An uncomfortable silence drifts across the line, and I clear my throat. *Don't worry about me, Ken. No, I'm fine. Thanks for asking.*

Ronin's still scrutinizing my every move, but the taut, lean muscles in his forearms relax.

"Again, Ken, I'm sorry." Swiveling on the stool, I place my elbow on the bar and lean into it, finally tearing my gaze away from Ronin's. "I'll call you next week to reimburse you on the ticket."

I end the call and place my phone down on the rough wood. Lifting my hands to rub gentle circles on my temple, I try to bring one of the bottles racked behind Bennett to me through telepathy.

"Kenny feeling left out?" Ronin's remark is casual, but the sharp edge to his tone makes me pause.

"We had plans tonight. I forgot." My tone is flat, because I'm beyond tired. I'm unraveling. I nod at Bennett.

"Vodka cranberry, please."

With a short nod, he turns to start preparing my drink.

"And," Ronin adds. "Go ahead and put in a sampler platter for us to share."

Back to us, Bennett's voice drifts over his shoulder. "Roger that."

I'm not even concerned enough to ask what's on the sampler platter, but as soon as Ronin says the word a loud growl emits from my stomach and I cover it with an embarrassed hand. He chuckles beside me.

"So," I say, turning in my stool so I can face him once more. "You come here often?"

His chuckle grows louder and he shakes his head at my silly line. "Matter of fact, I do. Bennett and I were both overseas, and he's a friend now. I come here sometimes after work. It's a relaxing place for me to shake off the stress of the day. "

Turning, Bennett pushes a crimson drink in a tall glass my way, and I toss him a grateful smile. He didn't skimp, and the first sip goes down nice and smooth. I watch as he slams a squat glass of golden-brown liquid in front of Ronin. He picks it up, and I watch in fascination as he swirls the glass in his hand.

Ronin has nice hands. They're big, capable, and I have a feeling those hands have done a lot of really dangerous things. His fingers are elongated and strong, his nails clean and cut, but I'd be willing to bet that if I studied his palms I'd find calluses roughing up his skin.

"And you? How was Paris?" he asks suddenly. He turns those intense green eyes on me and I find that when I look closely, I can see swirls of gray running through the irises. That's what creates the unusual color. I bet if I could stare at him at length without seeming like a complete weirdo, I'd find all kinds of little puzzle pieces that contribute to the whole picture of his gorgeousness.

"Great. I actually stayed at my client's chateau outside the city. The French countryside is absolutely beautiful."

A wistful sigh leaves me as I recall how much I loved sitting on one of the balconies and catching sight of rolling green hills peppered with wildflowers. The scene of Parisian splendor sprawling in the distance only made it all seem that much more exotic and amazing, and I couldn't get enough of it. I could have stayed there forever.

"Judging by that dreamy look on your face, you must have really loved it there." His eyes sparkle.

"I did."

He finally sips from his glass, and I wonder what kind of liquor he likes. He swallows, his throat working with the movement, and my gaze is drawn there momentarily. "Tell me about it."

"Well, not only is it stunning there, I had a friend in my client. Her name was Mrs. Dubois." The little slice of happiness I'd felt when remembering France dims as I think of dear, sweet Clara. But I won't ever forget the safety I felt in her home, especially after I was contacted by M.J. right before I headed there. Being in France—and a world away from my problems in Wilmington—seemed like heaven.

Ronin's brows pull together and his eyes are sharp. "Was?"

I take a long sip of my drink and take a deep inhale. "Was. She died two weeks before I returned to the States. We never got to finish the reno on her chateau."

He observes me, his eyes jumping all over my face as he tries to read me. "I'm sorry, Olive. You must have grown close to her?"

Nodding, I avert my gaze. "It's difficult to explain, but yes. I'm not close with my own mother, and the way Clara swept me into her home and her heart like it was nothing at all…I've never known anything like it. It sounds silly, but I felt safe there. It broke my heart to lose her and I'd only known her a few months."

I feel a strong, warm hand on mine, and when I glance down, my hand is being dwarfed by Ronin's much larger one. "At least you had the time with her you did. At least you got to feel that kind of bond."

His voice has changed. It's softer, more vulnerable than I've ever heard it. There's a sliver of rawness in it that lets me know he understands the pain I feel when I think of Mrs. Dubois. He truly understands it. And the only way someone can understand loss like that is if they've lived it themselves.

"Having it and losing it?" He clears his throat. "A thousand times better than never finding it at all."

When I look at him, his eyes aren't on me. He's staring

straight ahead, like he's maybe not all the way in this moment with me. And suddenly, more than anything, I want to know where he's drifted off to.

His hand is still warm on mine, and I squeeze gently. "Ronin..."

Bennett appears in front of us again, this time with two huge platters of food. Placing the steaming plates down in front of us, he gives a slight, comical bow. "Bon appétit."

Ronin sucks in a deep breath and releases my hand, pulling the small plates Bennett also brought closer and separating them. Putting one in front of me, he names everything on the platters. There's a variety of bar classics, from buffalo chicken wings to fried pickles, and even though I don't usually eat like this, it smells like the best thing I'll ever put in my mouth.

Digging in, we're both quiet for a few minutes while we eat. I finish my vodka cranberry and Bennett brings me another.

We're about three-quarters of the way through the meal when Bennett, who's been helping other customers seated at the bar, stiffens. The atmosphere around us changes, shifts, and a shiver runs through me in response. Ronin places his fork on his plate and wipes his mouth with a paper napkin as he eyes Bennett, and then he slowly turns in his seat to face the front door, which has just banged shut.

I whirl, too, and the sight of the man sauntering forward toward the bar sends a shot of pure fear jolting through me.

It's like fate is playing some kind of cold, cruel joke. *No...please, no.*

He's dressed casually in jeans and a plain button-down, and although his sandy brown hair is shaggy, it's not messy or greasy. His face is slightly rounded, with a pointed chin and prominent cheekbones. The dark shadow on his jaw is neat, like he's only been a day without shaving, and overall he appears pretty well put-together.

He's different, he's older. But he's still very certainly M.J.

It's his eyes that scare me most. They're icy blue and they keep moving, roving all around the bar. Searching, appraising, and I don't even want to know what he's looking for. They gloss over Ronin, then Bennett, before landing on me.

And it feels like the whole damn world stops turning.

He peruses me like a hungry wolf, and the only thing I want to do is turn and run.

Every muscle in Ronin's body goes taut, and I draw back involuntarily.

The man continues forward, pulling out a stool beside Ronin and plopping into it. Looking at me, he grins, but it's twisted and ugly. It'd be better if he just sneered.

"Well hey there, baby. Finding you here sure does save me a whole lot of work." His tone is casual, like we've never lost touch.

His words slide along my skin like the blade of a knife, and I recoil.

I can't speak. I just can't understand why he's here right now. How did he find me?

Ronin leans toward me, blocking me from M.J.'s sight.

M.J.'s grin falters just a little bit, and then his eyes narrow on Ronin. "You again, huh? What was your name?"

Ronin's words are monotone. "I'm Ronin Shaw. And if you call her baby one more time, I'm your worst fucking nightmare."

M.J. laughs. "Oh, man. Don't worry, *Olive*. I'll get to you in a minute. I have some business to attend to first."

He turns to Bennett. "Guessing my old man clued you in. I'm runnin' shit here, and you can either fall in line or move on."

The tension rolling off of Ronin is practically vibrating, but Bennett doesn't move.

"Your old man," starts Bennett. He leans forward and aims a solid glare in the newcomer's direction. "Seems to think that you're finally gonna do right by him and this business. But I have a feeling you have him snowed. You don't look out for anyone but yourself. That about right?"

M.J. cocks his head to the side, studying Bennett. "What I do is none of your business. You wanna stay here and manage this dump, go for it. But just know that you answer to me. And what I say goes."

Leaning round Ronin, M.J.'s eyes wander down from my face to my cleavage, peeking out over the undone button on my top, and his grin grows wider. I swallow down the disgust and wipe the expression from my face.

"Oh, baby…I missed you."

Ronin stiffens beside me, but I open my mouth to speak before he gets the chance.

"Did you break into my house?" My voice trembles, but I swallow and try to keep my expression hard. Showing M.J. my fear would be a mistake I don't intend to make.

His mouth tips up on a friendly smile, but I can see the sinister edge behind it. "Break in? All I did was leave you some flowers. Thought it'd be romantic."

I suck in a breath. *Romantic? It wasn't romantic at all. It was insane.*

When M.J. makes to step around him, Ronin moves, leaping off his stool and standing behind M.J. faster than I can register what's happening. One thick arm wraps around M.J.'s neck, the other pressed against his head.

"One millimeter." Ronin's voice is still strange and mechanical, but the vein throbbing on the side of his temple tells me his max temper has been reached. "That's all it'll take for me to snap your neck right now."

M.J.'s whole body has gone stiff, but he still manages a chuckle. "Pretty sure that won't go well for you, Shaw. But if you want to kill me right here in a bar full of witnesses, go right ahead."

"You don't contact her, you hear me? And if you think about busting into her place again? You're a dead man."

"The kind of money my family has? That's for real. You think she's going to want you once I get her away from whatever spell you put on her? She belongs *to me*. She always has." M.J. almost hisses the words through his teeth. And those words send a shiver skirting along my spine.

Ronin removes his arm from M.J.'s neck, only to slam him down on the bar. My hands fly to my mouth as M.J.'s face presses painfully to the wood.

His voice thick with rage, every word out of Ronin's mouth rings with an absolute truth. "Didn't you hear me, you little shit? She told you it was over a long time ago. You don't own her. And if you make another move, I'll end you. Please test me on that. I'm going to enjoy making you bleed."

"You going to let a murder go down in this place, Blacke?" M.J.'s voice is strained.

Bennett folds his arms. The glint of his dog tags catches the light as he shifts his feet and settles in a stance that dares Mick Oakes to test him. He doesn't say a word.

Finally, Ronin releases him and M.J. moves his head from side to side, adjusting the sore muscles in his neck.

He snorts. "You army assholes are so damn predictable. One for all and that bullshit. You realize I own this place, right? Might want to be nice to the hand that feeds you." M.J. gestures toward our food and drinks. Dipping his chin in Bennett's direction, he stands and walks around the bar.

"Let's take a walk to the office, Bennie boy. We've got some business to discuss."

Ronin makes to follow, but Bennett gives a sharp shake of his head. "I got this. Stay with your girl."

I'm barely able to register the fact that Bennett just called me Ronin's "girl" when he disappears behind a swinging door beside the bar right behind M.J.

Ronin lets out a string of curses on the stool beside me, frustration clearly eating him alive inside.

I can't say anything at all. Fear has rooted me not only to my stool, but also to the past. Where M.J. terrorized me all because he wanted to own me.

Ronin grinds his teeth, the sound grating across my own nerves and making me anxious "So Mick is M.J.?"

Mutely, I nod. "Why was he here?"

Cursing again, Ronin places both hands on the bar and

takes several deep breaths. Finally turning to face me, his face is a mixture of sympathy and rage. "His father, Mick Oakes Senior, is the owner of this bar. Your ex-boyfriend has just taken it over."

12

RONIN

I want Olive out of there by the time Mick returns from his meeting with Bennett, so I hustle her out of The Oakes. In the back of my mind, I want to know what he's got planned for Bennett, but in this moment, Olive is more important. Her face looks like she's just seen a ghost.

The fury, the frustration seething inside me at the fact that Mick is her ex, that she got herself mixed up with a man like him at any point in her life, threatens to take me over. I'm silent as I drive her back to my condo, and when we walk in the front door I'm ready to explode.

She drops down onto the couch, but I stalk to the kitchen and pull a beer from the fridge. Popping the top off I take a long, cool sip. Swallowing, I suck in a few deep breaths and then turn on her.

"Tell me," I growl, barely keeping the anger out of my voice. "Tell me how you hooked up with him. Tell me how it ended. Tell me everything."

When my eyes land on her, I expect to see the Olive I've known up until this point. The Olive that stands tall no matter what obstacle blocks her path. The stoic, coolly gorgeous woman who holds her head up no matter what the situation. The tough sister who handles her business and doesn't ask anybody for shit.

Instead, her face crumbles. Every last ounce of color drains from her expression and she sways slightly where she sits. Then she buries her face between her knees. When her body begins to tremble, I'm across the room in two strides and pulling her against me.

Damn keeping her at a distance, forget all the bullshit about not getting too close. She needs me, and I'm damn well going to be right here. It's an instinct, a pull from somewhere deep inside, all the way in my goddamn soul.

Olive doesn't pull away, she doesn't tense up. Hiding her face in my chest, she melts into me. Her breath comes in deep, shuddering gasps.

And at that moment, the thing I want most in the world? Is to go back in time and snap Mick Oakes's neck.

I thought this part of me was broken. The part that's able to comfort someone else, to be a soft place for another human being to land.

When it comes to work, I'm there for my brothers. I always have their back and I always will. But personally, when it involves something like this…I've been dead. For seven long years.

So when I hold Olive in my arms, when the soothing words come naturally as I whisper in her ear, I'm not even sure how

I'm managing it. Not when I thought that part of me was gone.

But this woman? She's bringing it—*me*—back to life.

"Shhh. Red, it's okay. You're safe. You're with me and he can't hurt you. I'll never let him hurt you." My lips brush her sweet-smelling hair, and I inhale until her scent is all I know.

She gasps like she can't inhale another breath, and I pull her onto my lap. Her body molds to mine and the sweet jasmine scent of her hair envelops me, sweeps into my senses like the flower is being held underneath my nose. "Hey…I've got you."

And I hold her. I hold her until she's breathing almost normally again, until she's able to lift her face from my tear-soaked shirt and meet my eyes. The expression in hers rips through me like a sharp hook to my gut.

"I…I thought he was gone from my life. I should have known better." Her dark blue eyes are full of secrets, and I want to know every single one of them.

I wait, because I've already asked the questions. Now it's up to her to tell me. To trust me. To let me in.

In the back of my mind, I picture Elle. If she's watching this from heaven, there's no way she'd be angry with me. She'd want me to help Olive. And so I push my guilt to the back burner and focus on the woman sitting in front of me.

"I met him my freshman year of college." Her voice is dull, quiet. Almost lifeless.

"He was…everything a girl is searching for when she wants a bad boy. I met him at a bar, and he was so charming, so into me, that I went home with him that night. And from that moment on, we were pretty much inseparable. I was still going to class, still making school a priority, but every other ounce of my time belonged to M.J."

I try to picture her back then. A young Olive, innocent and full of wit and fun and life.

"My friends hated him. They thought he was bad for me." Her eyes are cloudy as she remembers, going back to that time in her mind as she recollects the story for me.

"What about your family? Did they approve?" I stroke her hair, pushing it out of her eyes and behind her ears.

Her expression darkens. "What family? My parents...they were barely in my life at that point. They were never the same after Rayne got pregnant in high school. They moved away from Wilmington not long after she left for Phoenix. For the most part, I was on my own. I did tell Rayne about him much later, though."

Nodding, I force myself to keep from commenting on this. I want to know how parents could let their daughter date someone like Mick without doing everything they could to put a stop to it.

"It was a time in my life when I was extremely vulnerable. Something...happened...to me during my high school years that changed me. And to truly understand how I could have possibly ended up with someone like M.J., you'll have to know what that was first."

She takes a breath, and her whole body shakes with the effort. What the hell is happening to this woman right now? It's slowly clicking into place, the reason she's so controlled, so put together, so *on*, all the time. She has darkness in her past that she needs to keep out in order to keep on surviving. And the thought of that almost breaks me.

She continues, her voice so small that I have to lean closer just to hear it. "I was always a pretty thin kid, but my weight really skyrocketed in my last two years of high school. I was a seventy-five pounds heavier than I am now."

I try not to react, but she must sense something in me because her gaze focuses in on mine. A wry smile crosses her lips, just briefly, before it disappears. "I know. After my weight gain, I lost friends, and that sucked. But the change was somehow...freeing. I didn't have to be the girl my mom wanted me to be anymore. I didn't have to be anything for anyone...especially if I didn't want to be. I *liked* the difference. But it spiraled into a problem."

Confusion forces me to interrupt her. "Why, Red? Why did you feel like you needed to change?"

She stiffens and pushes away from me. Escaping to the farthest end of the couch, she pulls her knees tight against her chest and focuses on the opposite wall. Her voice wavers.

"I was always like a little doll for my mom to dress up. She put me in every pageant across the Southeast for as long as I can remember. I was always the girl known for being a pretty face. And one day, I got the kind of attention for that face that no young girl should ever have. I had an uncle...well, let's just say he loved my face. And the rest of me, too."

Realizing what she's saying to me, my stomach plummets. A wave of nausea rolls through me, and all I want to do is snatch her back up into the safety of my arms. But it's so very clear that she doesn't want that. She's almost in her own little zone, curled in on herself and barreling through the darkness of her past. She's getting this story out, because it needs to be told. But she doesn't want to be comforted. She just wants to get through it.

"What I really wanted to do was end it all. Just be done with it. I just wanted to fade away."

No… Christ.

"But I was never able to do it. So instead, I coped by eating. I gained the weight, stop wearing the frilly pageant dresses, and stopped doing my hair and makeup. And when I realized the effect it had on the people around me, I started to depend on food even more. I actively *tried* to become invisible, unattractive, ugly."

Trying to picture her as a scared teenage girl, who had a grown man in her life who was hurting her, my heart breaks. It fucking shatters, right there in my chest.

"What about your goddamn *parents*?"

She shakes her head, a sad smile picking up one side of her lips. "I made a mistake. I told my mom. She was pissed as hell. Not only did she not believe me, but she also accused me of craving even more attention than I was already getting."

Fury made me see red. "And your uncle…he just…continued?"

She nods. "He did, although he definitely became a lot less interested after I changed. And then…he died. Freak accident involving his motorcycle. So I was set free from my abuser, but…inside I was still such a mess."

My hands itched, because I want to pull her back into my arms so damn badly.

"I went to college, happy to escape it all even though I didn't go very far away. And that was when I met M.J. His attention flattered me, it made me feel pretty, when I never wanted to feel pretty again. I thought that after what had happened, no boy would ever want to touch me. But he did…even when I was at my heaviest. He wanted me. It didn't really dawn on me that he wanted me because I was vulnerable, because I was easy to control."

She shrugs helplessly, like if she could go back and change it, she would. "I started going to counseling, after a while. I knew that all the baggage, all the fear, all the dark, dark memories I was living with weren't healthy. At first, I didn't tell M.J. I was in counseling. I don't know why. Maybe even then, on some unconscious level, I knew I couldn't trust him with that. But as I started getting healthier, he grew more and more controlling. My counselor helped me to see that I didn't have to keep on the weight to be safe. She made me see that it wasn't my looks that contributed to my attack. It was just something awful that happened to me."

"M.J. didn't like it when the weight came off and I started dressing well and wearing makeup. When I started finding myself again. Back then, I thought he was just worried he'd lose me. I was an idiot. I got sucked into his web. He wanted me all to himself, alienated me from my new friends. He never touched me violently until the end, but he made me feel like without him I'd be nothing. I knew then that I'd never be truly healthy with someone who tried to keep me down, tried to make me believe that I was less without him."

She takes a deep breath, releasing the air like she's letting go of all the dark thoughts her story brought to light. I try to picture her back then, a strong young woman trying to overcome the shit she'd gone through. God, she must have been amazing. She still is. Maybe more so now that she's gotten through it all and come out on the other side. I knew I was attracted to her when I first saw her at the wedding. I didn't want to be, but I was. But now? Now I see that she's so much more than I ever imagined.

"And then I found out about the illegal activities he was getting involved in with his uncle."

Sitting up straighter, I eye her intently. "What kind of activities?"

Looking at me again for the first time in a while, but still drawn into herself in the corner of the couch, she shrugs. "You name it. His mom's side of the family is basically like the mob. They run Wilmington, at least the dark sides of it. They migrated south back in the 1980s, or so I heard, to start a new branch of the Margiano enterprise. They have legitimate businesses that are just a front for drug dealing, racketeering, money laundering, and God knows what else. M.J.'s dad was always a good guy, trying to keep him in line. I think he's the one who encouraged M.J. to go to college, get an education. He tried to show him that he didn't need the kind of power that came with being a Margiano."

As soon as the name she's now said twice registers, I freeze. What the hell are the chances? Fuck. *Fuck!*

I run back over the meeting with Jacob back at Night Eagle. Now we're going to need significantly less intel in order to start the organized crime op. Olive just might be able to give me inside information into the family responsible.

Standing, I begin to pace the room. "Do you know what he wants from you, Red?"

Pacing toward the kitchen counter where I left my beer, I grab it and take a long swig. Then I pace back toward the glass sliders.

Olive shrugs. Her tone is defeated. "I'm guessing he just wants me. It was probably a blow to his ego that I left him, and now I'm back in town doing fairly well for myself. I mean, he paid for a semester of my tuition back then. If it's the money he wants, I'll gladly pay it. I want no more ties to M.J. Not a single one. I got out when I found out what he was doing. When I learned he was being groomed by his uncle, Albert Margiano himself. After M.J. became violent with me I knew I couldn't take my chances with him or with his family. Like I said before, I was about to get a restraining order when he suddenly left school. I thought I was in the clear. I hadn't seen or heard from him until a few months ago."

Rolling my eyes skyward, I want to chuckle. Hell, I want to burst out in hysterical laughter. Because this is just getting better and better.

Albert Margiano is the head of the Margiano crime family. The police force knows he's guilty for crimes from money laundering to murder, but they've never been able to gather enough evidence on him to put him and his family away. It's why NES will step in on the FBI's payroll.

The last person I'd want Olive involved with is someone from that family.

Fucking Mick Oakes.

Protecting her was important before, but now it's fucking vital. And there's no way I'm going to be able to let my best friend stay on a relaxing honeymoon in Aruba when his sister-in-law is here dealing with this.

With a long sigh, I turn and face her. "We're going to have to call Jeremy and Rayne. They're going to want to know."

She leaps off the couch. "Ronin! No. I don't want my sister or my nephew anywhere near this. And if you call them, they'll all come home."

She has a point. The idea of Decker and Rayne being caught up in this shithole was disturbing. But I didn't want Olive involved in it, either. "Then I'm sending you to Aruba to stay with them."

Her face is horrified. *"On their honeymoon?"*

Narrowing my eyes, I point a finger at her. "Yes. On their honeymoon. I don't give two fucks, as long as you're safe."

Folding her arms, she straightens up and shakes her head. Color appears in her cheeks, and suddenly she's the woman I know once again. She's *my* Red. "There's no way in hell I'm going anywhere. And you don't call them, Ronin Shaw, do you hear me? I'm not running away from M.J. Oakes. Not again."

That's my girl. Fuck me, she's gorgeous. Every part of me responds to her, especially when she's wild and bossy and argumentative. That might be twisted, but it's real, and I like it.

As we stare each other down, a brand-new sense of respect blossoms in my gut for the woman standing in front of me. She's stubborn as hell, but it's damn sexy. At the same time, a foreboding sense of fear creeps into my awareness like a vine.

I don't want to lose her the way I did Elle. She's under my skin, and the thought of anything happening to her feels like a knife in the chest. But I don't want to be at the mercy of these growing feelings either, knotting me up inside and twisting my actions in a way I don't recognize.

So, it seems, either way...when it comes to Olive Alexander, I'm fucked.

13

OLIVE

That night, I lie awake in Ronin's guest room, eyes wide open, staring at the ceiling. I can't believe I saw M.J. again tonight. He's a part of my past I thought I'd put behind me.

Seeing him brought up all the feelings, the way I used to be back then. I was lost, searching, and hiding. Lost because a piece of me died every single time my uncle put his hands on me, or made me put my hands on him. Searching for someone who'd love me unconditionally, who would see the real me because I wasn't the beautiful girl I used to be. And hiding from the filth that I was sure lay inside of me because of what I'd endured.

And all those years ago, I was so certain that M.J.—Mick—filled that void.

He hadn't been all bad. Not at first. At the beginning, I'd fallen in love with him. He'd been sweet and charming. He called me his "perfect match." He'd told me he liked that I was smart and driven, yet not someone who sought attention. It made me feel like he *saw* me. Especially when I was so far from looking like the beauty queen I used to be. When we'd fallen in love, he'd always told me he'd never let me go, now that he'd found me.

I should have taken that to heart, because clearly he'd meant it.

I think that in the end his feelings for me had turned into an obsession. It became more about keeping me, because he'd been so used to having me dependent on him emotionally. He'd had me all to himself, and when I started to heal I realized that I needed more from life than just him.

I sigh. My thoughts turn to the man lying in his own bed, just across the hall. Ronin is everything Mick never was…strong, good to his core, and protective. There's really no comparison. Not that Ronin has shown any interest in anything other than making sure I'm still in one piece when his best friend returns to town.

For some reasons, the burning sensation of forming tears blurs my vision. And in the cold darkness of the bedroom, I realize that the churning, oily feeling in my stomach is fear.

I'm afraid of Mick Oakes.

I don't know what his intentions are where I'm concerned. I never paid him back for the tuition money, because at the time, I couldn't. Is that what he wants from me?

But in the bar, I saw how his eyes scraped across the length of my form, like this body still belongs to him. Back then, I gave myself over to Mick because, in my desperation, he was the only hope I could cling to. But I'm not that little girl anymore, running away from the things that hurt her.

I'm a woman, a strong, capable woman, and I will never let myself be taken in by anyone every again.

But no one told that to Mick. He could very well think that he's going to walk right back into my life.

I flop over onto my side, pulling the covers up to my chin and trying to control the quaking in my bones. It doesn't take long until discomfort forces me to flip over to my other side, my eyes searching the darkness of the room.

When I can't take lying there anymore because it feels like the walls and the ceiling are closing in on me, I climb out of bed and, clad in my silky pajama pants and matching long-sleeved shirt, pad down the hall and into the living room. A lamp burns on one of the side tables, and I walk into the kitchen to make something hot and comforting to drink.

Finding milk and cocoa mix, I pull down a mug and make quick work of fixing the drink. I take my cocoa to the couch and sink down into the cushions and flip on the TV. My thumb flicks through the channels idly while I sip until I find one of my most favorite, mind-numbing shows. I settle in and my eyes devour the scene in front of me.

I'm so zeroed in that I don't notice Ronin's entered the room until he's standing in front of the TV, and a small squeak of surprise escapes me at the sight of his huge form.

"Holy shit." I breathe. "You scared me."

My pulse races, but I'm not sure how much of that has to do with the small scare, and how much has to do with the gloriously shirtless man standing in front of me.

God in heaven. Does he do crunches while he sleeps?

Ronin's clad in low-slung black pajama pants, pooling

around his bare feet. His torso is bare and ridiculously muscular, ripples of abs going on for days. My eyes trace the lines of the tattoos swirling around his entire upper right arm, the desire to read and understand each picture there strong and intense. When I find his face, he's staring right back at me with an expression I can't begin to read.

"Red."

It's not just an acknowledgment, it's a caress, and I can feel it wrapping around my body like a blanket.

Ronin kneels down in front of me, his eyes searching my face. "Are you okay?"

Pulling the mug to my lips, and also attempting to hide from the intensity of his gaze, I nod. "I'm fine."

But my voice doesn't convey that I'm fine. It's thin and high, and doesn't sound like me at all. My hands start to tremble and I grip the mug tighter, willing them to stop.

I'm strong. I'm strong. I'm strong.

I repeat the mantra to myself, over and over again, until the mug is gently taken from my vise-grip.

Ronin puts the mug down on the end table, and then takes my hands hostage in his much larger ones. "Tell me what's wrong."

The green of his eyes swirls, and I'm lulled by them, the shaking in my hands quelled by the strength of his. "I don't want him to think about me. I don't even want to be in his orbit again. I'm not the same person I was back then."

Ronin's mouth thins as it sets in a grim line. "Then you won't be. Not sure if you've noticed, Red, but you're pretty damn strong."

Had he heard my mantra?

My eyes fall to our hands. "Yes…I am. I know."

He glances down the hall, and then back at me. "Couldn't sleep?"

"No."

Releasing me, he gets up and walks down the hall. I hear a door open and close and when he returns, his arms are laden with a cozy-looking gray chenille blanket. Pausing in front of me as I look up at him in confusion, he uses his leg to nudge my knee.

"Scoot over."

Moving sideways, Ronin sits down and stretches out behind me. Then he spreads the blanket out over his legs and wraps an arm around my waist. He tugs, and I find myself settling down in front of him while he spoons me from behind. He places the blanket over both of us, and then wraps his other arm around me.

It's like I'm trapped in the hardest, warmest, most protective, best-smelling cocoon there ever was.

At first, I'm stiff, because *what*?

Ronin's scent wafts over me, and I breathe it in like a woman deprived of air for an hour. It's partly cologne, but it's a fresh, masculine clean scent with just the tiniest hint of spice. It's amazing. His body, pressed up against mine in the most intimate way, is so hard that heat pools deep in my gut and my thighs clench together to try to fight the bubbling desire he's stirring up inside me. A kind of true desire I haven't felt in years.

His arms tighten around me, pulling me closer. "Relax,

Red." His words raise the hairs on the back of my neck, and a delicate shiver rolls through my whole body.

Taking a deep breath, I allow myself to soften against him.

"Not comfortable being touched, are you?" Ronin's voice in my ear is husky and deep, and it feels like he's reaching inside me rather than just speaking to me.

I shrug. "Not usually."

It's true that in five dates with Ken, we'd never been more intimate than a hug and a brush of lips. And for it to go any further than that, it would have needed to be planned and I would have really had to talk myself into it ahead of time. It's why the five date rule sticks in my head. It's how I mentally prepare myself. I'm not celibate by any means, but it takes a lot for me to throw caution to the wind and be close to a man. I have scars that don't show on the outside, and they prevent me from being as free as other, normal women.

"Do you want to talk about why that is, Red?"

My eyes trail over his hands as his capable fingers begin to stroke unassumingly along my forearms. It's the slightest touch. Barely a caress, really, but the way I can feel it reverberating everywhere from my neck to my toes is unsettling. I've never been touched on a level as deep as this, and I don't know what to do with the way it feels.

Shrugging again, I think about how to answer that question.

"I'm just…cautious…after everything."

There. That should satisfy his curiosity.

But Ronin doesn't quite let it go. "There's more to you than cautiousness. And that's okay…I get it. I have layers, too. Ones that go so deep I don't know if I'll ever get to the bottom of them. And I'd never expect anyone else to, either."

The sheer understanding in his tone floors me. He doesn't elaborate on his own issues, and he doesn't ask me to delve further into mine. I've never been around a man who doesn't ask for something from me, usually too much, in return for spending time with him.

Tentatively, I caress the bicep that holds me so tightly. The corded muscles jump beneath my touch, and I can feel the breath that Ronin sucks in.

"Tell me about these?" I ask, caressing the giant bird tattoo in the center.

His voice low, velvety, he answers me. "Well, this is an eagle in flight. I got it when I first joined the army."

I trace the intricate details of the tattoo, the fine lines given to each of the bird's feathers.

"And this one," he continues, indicating the three thick, black bands stretching around his arm nearer his shoulder. "Represent each time I had to pass a test to achieve something great. Army entrance, officer exam, Ranger training."

Marveling, I imagine the sheer amount of strength it took for him to achieve each of these goals.

He's silent for a moment, and I trace the bright, bold heart tattoo entwined with rope. "And this one?"

Ronin stiffens slightly. He pauses, but then when he answers, there's a cooler quality to his voice, one that I don't understand. "That represents my heart."

And that's it. That's all he says, and it surprises me how much that hurts.

We sit in silence for a few long moments, the tension swirling between us, when I finally feel his body relax against mine once again.

I haven't stiffened since we started talking. I haven't felt the need to flee from his hold, to shy away from his closeness. It's huge, at least for me. This doesn't happen. Not unless it's on my terms, and with men I can keep at a safe distance.

But something tells me there's no keeping Ronin at a distance. It should terrify me…but it doesn't. Instead, a spark of hope flickers to life inside me. Hope that this man can succeed in breaking down the walls I've built so carefully around my heart.

When a chuckle rumbles through his chest, I almost jump out of my skin and his grip on me tightens for just a moment to reassure me.

"What the hell is this?" he asks.

Focusing my attention on the television, a smile ghosts across my lips. "It's 'Behind the Scenes: Big Top.'" Reality television is an addiction for me, and the show that follows the leading players in a traveling circus behind the scenes is one of my favorites.

His laughter grows louder and I can't help myself; I chuckle right along with him.

"Red…please tell me why we're watching 'Behind the Scenes: Big Top.'" The teasing lilt in his voice makes my pulse race.

"I like it." Feeling the need to defend myself, my tone is indignant. "If I weren't an interior designer, and I was just a little bit braver, I think I'd probably be a circus performer."

Ronin's laughter fades away as he considers my words. "What act would you do?"

I can answer that question without a second thought. "I'd be a trapeze artist. Flying high, all those dangerous catches? The freedom of it? It'd be amazing."

Ronin's quiet for a moment. I think he's forgotten all about my answer when he speaks again, his words dusting across my skin once more.

"That's a circus I'd pay big money to watch, Red. Because I think I'd really enjoy seeing you look free."

14

Ronin

When I become aware the next morning, I smell her before I open my eyes. It's like I've slept in a blanket all wrapped up in peaches, and I instinctively pull her closer just so I can have more of it. In sleep, she's soft and warm and perfect, and I take a minute to just enjoy this unguarded, pliant Olive because I know the second she wakes up she'll tense up and pull away.

When I'd heard her moving around last night, I was up and out of bed before I even really thought about it. All I knew was that I didn't want her to be up alone. So I snuck out of my room, and when I saw her sitting there on my couch, all huddled up and small, something in my chest broke apart. She was scared, that much was clear, and the urge to get close to her, to comfort her, was unstoppable.

My thoughts flash to Elle, and I allow myself one minute to compare. It was a rare occurrence to wake up next to Elle, because she was such an early riser. I usually woke up to the sound of her cooking in the kitchen, or to music playing as she got an early start to cleaning up around the apartment we shared. Olive is taller, a little more slender and graceful than Elle was, so the way she fits into the curve of my own body is more compatible and I like it way more than I should. My dick, especially, responds, hardening against her ass as she sleeps.

Elle was also an open book. Every thought or feeling she ever had was written across her face, and if she was pissed it came out in a slew of Spanish curses. She was a fireball, but she melted just as readily as she sparked. Olive is so much harder to read, to understand. She's a puzzle that I can't seem to totally figure out.

But what if I really tried? If I opened up to the possibility of truly knowing Olive? If I tried to get to the bottom of her mysterious nature, would she let me in? She's been dating Ken, apparently. Has he been able to penetrate her walls?

Something inside me doubts it.

It also seems, from the tone of her conversation with Ken on the phone last night, that whatever they had is over. That thought makes me smile.

A soft, sleepy moan comes from the woman in front of me, causing the erection in my pants to become painfully aware of her closeness. I can't cover my answering groan even though I try, and the redheaded beauty goes stiff and cold in my arms.

I know she's awake, but she doesn't say anything and I just wait.

Finally, tentatively, she turns onto her back and I loosen my hold to let her. She glances over at me, finding my eyes open and staring back at her, before she quickly turns her head toward the ceiling.

"Good morning." Her voice is a sexy, throaty whisper that almost makes my eyes roll back in my head. I haven't even touched her, not really, and she's doing things to my body that I haven't felt in a long damn time.

"Hey." That's all I've got. Fucking brilliant.

"Ronin?" Her eyes remain glued on the ceiling, and there's trepidation in her tone.

"Yeah?" I turn onto my back like she is, folding my hands on my chest.

"Who's Elle?"

I freeze; every muscle in my body, including my tongue, locks up. I can't move, speak, or think.

What the fuck?

Elle isn't a secret. Jeremy knows because he had my back when I returned to finish my tour after her funeral. And my team at Night Eagle deserve to know, because they're like my brothers and we all have each other's backs every day. I don't keep secrets from them. But there's an understanding that what happened to her is in my past. I don't talk about it. I don't think about it.

Until I got the call from Detective Watson.

Now I can't stop thinking about Elle.

Olive doesn't turn toward me, but when I don't answer her question she barrels on. "I mean, it's just that you said her name a few times in your sleep. One time I woke up and thought you were talking to me, but you…weren't. And you said her name again. More than once."

Sitting up, I push the blanket onto the floor and scrub a hand over my face. I can't deal with this shit. Not now.

Maybe not ever.

Rising from the couch, I head toward the kitchen. "You want coffee?"

Olive doesn't answer and I don't wait for her response. Pulling two mugs down from the cabinet, I fill the single-cup machine with water and place a mug under the spout.

As it fills, I lean against the counter with both hands and close my eyes. Concentrating on taking deep, calming breaths, I try not to let the images of Elle bombard me, take me over.

"Ronin?" Olive's soft voice is right behind me, and I turn to face her.

"Yeah."

She stands with her arms folded, her figure slim and feminine in her silky pajamas. "I didn't mean to pry. She's someone who is important to you, that much is clear. I won't ask again. But you don't have to run from me."

Realizing that Olive is going to be hanging out with me today, because there's no way I'm going to let her go anywhere without me by her side, not with Mick running around, I meet her gaze. I don't want her thinking that there's a woman in my life right now who could walk in when she and I are lying close together like we did last night.

And fuck me...yes, I want that to happen again. And again.

She was honest with me about her past, even though it was painful for her. I can give her that same honesty.

"I'm not running, and you didn't do anything wrong. It's just...it's a tough subject for me. But...you should know."

She sucks her bottom lip between her teeth as she waits for my revelation.

"Elle is…*was* my wife. She was murdered seven years ago." The words feel like bombs every time I have to drop them.

The deep dark blue of Olive's eyes goes dim and glassy. "Oh, God. I'm so sorry, Ronin."

I dip my chin, both to accept her condolences and her genuine sadness.

I've heard it so many times before. Every time I've told someone that I lost my wife. They're always sorry. And it never makes a damn bit of difference.

But as I look into Olive's eyes, I can see the hurt there. The sadness echoes mine, and I know that she feels my agony because she's felt real pain herself. Our aches are different, but pain recognizes pain, regardless of the source.

I try to shrug it off. "It's been seven years, you know? That's a lot of time passed."

Her head tilts to the side, understanding shining in her gaze. "That's true. It's been a lot of time, but that doesn't mean the scars aren't there."

Spreading my arms wide, I laugh bitterly. "I really think I could have moved past it by now. But they never found her murderer. *I* never found him."

"It wasn't your responsibility to do that, Ronin."

"Maybe not, but as long as her murder goes unsolved, I can't move past it. I need to know why it had to be her. She was in trouble, that much was clear. But she never told me about it. I failed her." I almost choke on the last words as the familiar hook takes hold in my gut and pulls.

Turning away from Olive, I pull the filled mug from underneath the spout and start the second cup. Taking a sip of the hot black liquid, the scald as it slides down my throat feels good compared to the burning in the place my heart used to be.

Two small hands slide up my back. They leave a trail of burning skin in their wake, and my whole body stiffens. Goddamn…her touch. It's enough to make me weak, leave me wanting. When I turn around, her hands slide until her palms are pressing against my chest. I glance down at them, before looking her in the eye.

Those eyes…it's like they can see things inside me I've tried for so long to hide from. The hurt, the anger, the loss…but also the longing I have for someone to mean something to me again. The heat between us surges, pulls tight.

"I have to go into NES today. I want you to come with me." I try to keep it together, but the words are strained with the straight-up *need* rolling through my body.

Her mouth turns down at the corners as she takes a step back and I can see her defenses rise like a flag. "You don't need me tagging along after you. I'll be fine here." She goes to the refrigerator and takes out a carton of milk for her coffee. "I already told Beth I wouldn't be in, and it's not like Mick knows where you live."

Placing my now-empty mug on the counter, I lean against the granite and fold my arms across my chest. "I don't know what the hell Mick Oakes knows, and I won't leave you here alone. Please, humor me, Red."

She sighs, rolling her eyes. For the first time since we woke up, I notice how adorable she is in the morning with her hair tossed into a messy bun on top of her head and her eyes still bleary from sleep. She's more gorgeous this way…more *Olive*. There're fewer barriers she puts up between us, and I like it. I really fucking like it.

Then Elle's face pops into my head, and I remember what else I need to do today.

My voice firm, I give Olive a pointed glance. "You're coming with me."

She huffs. "Fine. God, has anyone ever told you how annoyingly bossy you are?"

Hiding a smirk, I turn away. "Be ready to leave in forty minutes."

Then I turn and walk to my bedroom, ready to take a long, cold shower.

15

RONIN

I know from the curious looks my team tosses around when I walk in the front door with Olive that the first order of business this morning will be to explain her situation to the group.

Olive has brought her work with her, so I lead her down the hallway toward our offices and set her up at my desk. Leaning against the partition that separates my workspace from Jeremy's, I assess her. She's settled in my chair, her laptop open on my desk. There's a sketchbook sitting next to it, and she has spread various swatches and samples over the place where my paperwork usually lies. Olive is casual today, in jeans, boots, and a sweater that clings to her torso. Her deep red hair is still pulled up, her sleek ponytail not showing a strand out of place.

She looks beautiful, and the sight of her sitting at my desk does something strange to me. It makes me want to see her there again and again. This is the second space of mine that she's been thrust into, and instead of making me uncomfortable, it's making me want more of her.

I clear my throat. "You gonna be okay here while I go into the morning meeting with the guys?"

An amused expression crosses her face. "Don't you mean 'the guys and Sayward'?"

Shrugging, I give her a small smile. I'd reintroduced her to Sayward as soon as we'd arrived. "Sayward is one of the guys."

Olive rolls her eyes. Every time she does that, I want to pull her to me and dare her to roll those eyes again. She's so damn sassy. "I don't know, Ronin…can I survive an hour alone at your desk? I mean, whatever will I do with myself?" Putting on an exaggerated southern accent, she fans herself and bats her long, dark lashes.

"Okay, smart-ass, easy. I was just saying, if you need anything to let me know now." I'm fighting hard against my smile.

She gestures toward her array of supplies. "I'm all good here, Ronin. Just try to forget about me and do your day, okay?"

If she thinks she's forgettable, she's seriously unaware.

Of everything.

I walk away, but I know that during the whole meeting I'm going to have the picture of her sitting at my desk stuck at the front of my mind. When I stride into the office I'm met with three sets of smug eyes.

"So," begins Dare. He settles his elbows on the conference table and leans in, like he's gearing up for the Spanish damn inquisition. "Jeremy's is gone for three days, and you're already moving in on his sister-in-law?"

Dare shakes his head like he's disappointed in me, but I can see the gleeful spark in his eye, and it's making me want to knock him out of his chair.

Grisham joins in the game. "So did it happen the night of the wedding, or did you actually wait until the next day?" His tone is serious, but his stupid laughing eyes give him away, too.

Sayward's glance darts among all of us, her confusion clearly written on her face. "Why did she need to work here today? Doesn't she have her own office?"

Even though Sayward's the one who has issues when it comes to social interaction, she's the only one who realized the problem with their idiotic teasing.

Folding my arms against my chest, I wait for my teammates to realize what Sayward just pointed out.

Grisham's expression sobers first. "What's going on?"

Behind me, Jacob Owen enters the room, closing the door behind him. "Going on with what?"

Moving out of his way, I settle in my usual seat and send irritated glances toward the other two men. If I weren't really worried about Olive and what could be going through Mick Oakes's head, I'd usually think their ridiculous teasing was funny. It's our thing to rib each other, poke each other, especially when it comes to women. And I know they didn't know, because I hadn't told them that Olive might be in trouble.

"Olive's with me because before Jeremy and Rayne left for their honeymoon, Jeremy asked me to keep an eye on her. I just found out that someone from her past is back in town, and he's bad news."

Every ounce of humor gone from his expression, Dare's critical eyes assess me. "Tell us who he is and where to find him."

I relay the story of Olive and Mick's relationship and Mick's Margiano family connection, along with what happened when we ran into him at The Oakes last night. The team listens intently until I'm finished, and then they begin firing off questions about Bennett, the bar, and the connection to Mick.

I answer it all as best I can, and when I'm finished the four other people in the room look just as concerned about Olive as I am.

"Apart from breaking into her place, which we can't actually prove he did, he hasn't actually done anything illegal. But Olive doesn't scare easily, and she's terrified of him. It was clear as day from the way she shut down when he walked into that bar. I want to make sure he doesn't come near her." Even I'm surprised at the determination in my voice, but I mean every single word.

Jacob strokes his chin, thoughtfully. "You're right about that. Keeping her with you is the best way to keep an eye on her for now. And we can't just go in, guns blazing, and take out Albert Margiano's second-in-command without tanking the whole op. In the meantime, we'll look into what Mick Oakes has been doing since she cut ties with him, and find out where he likes to hang out now. If there's anything that doesn't smell right in his recent history, we'll find it."

I nod, relief flowing through me. Having my team makes me feel a little bit better, because with all of NES on her side, I know that Olive will be safe.

My mind travels to my other problem while Jacob starts running down the details of an upcoming project. I need to find the connection between Elle's murder case and the new homicide the WPD are investigating. Not just for Elle's justice, but also for my own damn sanity. The guilt is eating me alive.

About an hour later, everyone disperses, leaving the room to train. I pull Sayward up short before she exits, and she turns to face me expectantly.

"I know you're going to look into Mick Oakes for me, and I appreciate it. Can I also ask you to look into something else?"

She studies me, and I'm not sure what she's searching for in my eyes but eventually she nods. "Name it."

I inhale, lowering my voice. "I want you to find me a list of family members, with current addresses, for a Grace Hodges. She was the victim in a recent homicide here in town."

Sayward tucks the name away and looks at me with shrewd eyes. "Why?"

I hesitate, wondering how much to say. I know how close Sayward and Jacob are, and I don't want my boss to know what I'm doing. "I have a friend who's the lead detective on the case, and I'm helping him out. Can you get me those addresses?"

She nods. "Of course."

I know that if there's information to be found, Sayward can dig it up.

"Thanks."

When I make it back to my desk, I'm forced to pause. Olive is sitting there, her sole focus on her swatches, her bottom lip sucked into her mouth. I'm hit hard with desire.

"Hey." Keeping my voice low so I don't startle her, I move into the space with her.

Her eyes dart up to meet mine, and an immediate smile crosses her lips. That smile? Stabs me right in the gut. Because it's something she didn't have to think about: it's automatic. Why do I like that so much?

"Hi. I didn't hear you come up." She leans back in the seat and eyes me as I perch a hip on the desk, glancing down at her work.

"What are you working on?"

She picks up two pieces of fabric, a printed tawny pattern and a sage green that has shiny leaf-like designs on it in the same color. "Well, I'm doing the master bedroom in this amazing old Victorian downtown. Well, Beth is doing it now, but I'm hoping to help finish up when I'm back at work. I'm going for a style that won't disrupt the classic design of the era, but modern enough to satisfy the owner."

Holding the swatches up to the light, she narrows her eyes. "Do you like these?"

I study them, noticing how well the colors fit together even though I wouldn't have known to put them side by side on my own. Then I glance down at the sketch of the room's decor, and I realize that this woman is truly talented at what she does. "It's beautiful, Red."

Her smile goes a little shy. "Thanks. I'm going to have to find a way to get these to the office this week."

"We'll make it happen."

I pull a chair to the opposite side of the desk and we work across from each other for a while. The scratching of her pencil against paper mixes with the sound of my fingers tapping against my keyboard, and to my ears it seems like a melody we're creating together. I'm leaning back in my chair, ready to ask Olive whether or not she's ready to take a break for lunch, when Sayward sticks her head around the corner.

"Swagger…I've got the information you asked for." She passes me a printed sheet of paper and grins. "Easy as pie."

Returning her smile, I thank her. "I'll let you know if I need you to find anything else for me, cool?"

"Cool." Giving Olive an awkward wave, Sayward disappears.

Olive glances at me. "She's an odd duck."

Chuckling, I shake my head. "I don't care how odd she is, she's a genius with a computer and that's what we need her for."

Olive's eyes sparkle. "She's really pretty, but I don't think she even knows it."

I absently nod, glancing down at the list of names and addresses Sayward just handed over, complete with thumbnail–size images for each of the three persons. I'd asked her to look up the other homicide victim, Grace Hodges's, surviving family members, and that's exactly what she'd given me. I'm staring at two women, one appearing to be in her twenties and one who looks to be older, and one middle-aged man.

Grace has a surviving twin sister. That's better than I could have asked for. I'm willing to bet she knows more than anyone else about what her sister might have been up to, who she might have been seeing or talking to, leading up to her murder.

"Hey."

Olive looks up at my voice. "Yeah?"

"I need to take care of something. I want you to come with me, and then we can grab lunch. Sound good?"

She places down her materials, then stands up and stretches. My eyes stray to the slash of creamy skin on display where her shirt rides up above her jeans. I can't help it; I wonder what she tastes like there.

As sweet as she smells?

"Lead the way, McBossy."

Laughing outright at her nickname, I place a hand on the small of her back and lead her out of the office.

16

OLIVE

The apartment building Ronin pulls up to is one of the smaller ones, the kind that houses only four or five units in one large brick unit.

Ronin turns to me in the front seat of his truck. "This conversation I'm about to have is related to my wife's murder. The woman inside is the sister of a recent homicide victim. The case is identical to Elle's, and I need to find the connection. I wouldn't bring you along, except that you need to be with me until we figure out what's going on with Oakes. Just hang back, stay quiet. I don't expect anything dangerous to happen, this is just an interview, but if I give you an order you need to listen. Got it?"

I'm tempted to roll my eyes at his tone, but I stop myself when I realize how serious he is. Ronin does things like this for his job, and if he needs me to be compliant, than I certainly will be. The note of authority in his voice is evident, and I know he just can't help himself.

"Why don't I just stay in the truck, then?" The last thing I want to do is impose on his investigation. I suddenly realize that I want to help Ronin, not hinder him.

Ronin immediately shakes his head. "I'd rather have eyes on you."

With a sigh, I agree. "Okay, then. Let's go."

He gestures for me to wait a moment, then climbs out of his seat and walks around the front of the truck. Opening my door, he reaches out a hand and helps me down. Then he does something he's never done before. He takes my hand.

When I glance down at our clasped hands and up at his face, he winks. The man actually *winks* at me. "Go with it. I need this woman to answer my questions, and if I give her a cover story about who I am she's less likely to slam the door in my face. You being here is actually going to make her feel more comfortable."

With the strong warmth of his hand curling around mine, and his touch doing strange things to my stomach, I don't bother to reply. I just follow him through the parking lot, up the sidewalk and stairs, and to the front door of a second-floor apartment.

When the door opens, Ronin offers the woman standing before us a bright smile that I've never seen him wear before.

Damn. That's his smile when he's actually trying to be charming?

If he did that more often, there would be women dropping their panties at his feet everywhere he went.

Who the hell am I kidding? There probably already are, with or without that megawatt grin.

"Hey there. I'm Raymond Rogers, and this is my girlfriend Jenny. We just moved in downstairs."

The woman at the door flashes a look toward me, and I try really hard to match Ronin's friendly smile.

"Anyway," he continues. "We were just wondering if you were able to get a satellite working with the tree line so close to our balconies, or if you went with cable."

God, even I'm totally charmed by Ronin. His smile, the chiseled body that's just so obvious even below his jeans and long-sleeved T-shirt, the sinewy grace that slides just above the total power he holds. It's not just charismatic, it's utterly compelling, and he's even putting me under his spell.

She takes a step backward, gesturing inside her apartment. "Why don't you guys come in? I actually do have a satellite, I'll show you the angle it hangs so that it works with the crazy tree line."

"Awesome. Thanks so much." Ronin slides past her inside the apartment, and I follow.

The woman closes the door behind us, and when we turn to face her she approaches and extends her hand. "It's nice to meet you, neighbors. I'm Lindy Hodges."

Ronin shakes her hand. When she offers it to me, I only hesitate for a second before shaking it firmly. When I glance at Ronin, the look in his eyes is reassuring. I can almost hear him telling me he'll explain this to me later.

"Can I get you all something to drink? I have…hmm." She walks into the kitchen and opens the refrigerator. With a chagrined chuckle, she turns to us. "Milk and water. I'm sorry; I wasn't expecting company."

I brush her apology aside with a hand. "Don't worry about it. We're fine."

She nods, approaching slowly. "So, you moved in downstairs? I didn't know the Framptons moved out."

I smile. "We didn't know the people who lived there before us. But yes, we just arrived today."

Lindy studies me a moment. "So do you want to see the satellite, then?"

I offer her a smooth smile. If Ronin wants to talk to her about his wife's murder, then I'm going to help him as best as I can. I ignore the stab of jealousy that pierces me when I think of Ronin's wife. He's still so obviously in pain about what happened to her. Why does that bother me so much?

"Actually, can I just use your restroom? I'll join you two in just a moment. I'm sorry, Lindy. It was a long drive here. We moved from Georgia."

Well, hell, Olive. The lies just roll right off your tongue, don't they?

Lindy gestures toward the hall. "Of course. First door on your left."

I shoot her a grateful smile, then give one to Ronin, before I venture down the hall. I hear him asking her about her satellite company as I disappear down the hallway, and I wait until I hear the sound of the sliding glass door opening and closing before slinking back down the hall to the living room.

Scanning the room, I head over to a bookcase with cubes for units. There are various knickknacks hidden in the squares, from squat, colorful vases to an assortment of picture frames. Picking up one of the photos, I stare down at a picture of

Lindy and a woman who looks exactly like her. The hair on the other woman is lighter, more of a platinum than a honey, but their features, including the clear blue eyes, are identical. There's no doubt that this is the sister Ronin was referring to.

Putting the photo back down and turning when the sliding glass door opens, I put on a bright smile as Lindy and Ronin walk back inside from the balcony. "So will it work, babe?"

His eyes flare at the fake endearment, his intent stare holding me captive from across the room. "Sure will."

Seeing me beside the bookcase, Lindy comes over. "You and your sister are such beauties."

Her smile drops, her expression going sad. "Yeah. She was."

Stepping up beside me, Ronin places an arm around me and pulls me close to him. I like the feeling of being pressed against his body way too much; the desire to settle in and get comfortable is strong.

Lindy stares at the picture, a faraway look on her face. "My twin sister died a few days ago."

Even though I already knew this to be true, the absolution of her statement sends a jolt of pain through me for her. What must it be like to lose the person you considered to be your other half?

"I'm so sorry, Lindy." Reaching out to touch the other woman's shoulder, I attempt to send consoling vibes from my hand to her. I turn and see Ronin clearing struggling with something.

"Lindy…I have to be honest with you now, I'm sorry we lied to you. And you'll figure out soon enough that we're not actually your neighbors." Ronin's tone is apologetic, but determined. "Seven years ago, I lost my wife, Elle Shaw, in the exact same way that your sister was killed. I'm here to ask you about the murder."

Stiffening, Lindy takes a step back from us and folds her arm across her chest. "Who are you?"

Letting me go, Ronin holds both hands out in front of him as if to show Lindy he means no harm. "I'm just someone who wants to find out who did this to my wife, and to your sister."

Her expression is doubtful, wary. "The cops already talked to me about this. They're looking for the murderer. Are you a cop?"

"I used to be. But I was a soldier on deployment when my wife was killed." The stark pain in Ronin's voice slices cleanly through me. "They never found her killer. I don't want that to happen to you and your sister. Now I work for a company with the means to find things the police will have a much harder time finding. We have security clearances the WPD can only dream about, and I'm highly trained. Please let me help."

Giving Lindy a sympathetic, sincere smile when she glances my way, I nod. "He's telling you the truth. My brother-in-law works for the same company, and they're seriously badass. I'm not his girlfriend, but I do care about him and I know he can help you."

Lindy's eyes flip back and forth between us. "Let me see some I.D., if you work for this security company."

Without a word, Ronin slips his wallet from his pocket and pull out a card. Handing it to Lindy, he waits while she inspects it.

With a deep sigh, Lindy heads for the couch and drops

down. Ronin tracks her with his eyes and then takes her silence as compliance, and he pulls me to the love seat adjacent
to her.

"Did your sister have any known enemies? Anyone you
think might have wanted to hurt her?" Getting straight to the
point, Ronin waits patiently for Lindy's response.

Lindy shakes her head "My sister was a nursing student. All
she ever wanted to do was help people."

"Was she dating anyone?"

The question from Ronin sounds strained. I want to ask
him why, but now isn't the time.

Lindy hesitates before answering. "Kind of, maybe? I mean,
there was a guy. I never got to meet him, though. Actually,
I don't even remember her mentioning his name, now that I
think about it."

Ronin presses on. "Was that unusual? For you not to meet
someone she was dating, I mean?"

Lindy barks out a laugh. "It was unusual for her to be dating
anyone. Grace kept to herself where men were concerned. She
got burned once in high school, and after that she never
wanted to give a guy the time of day."

I shift. *I understand that sentiment.*

"Lindy…Grace was your twin. You had to have known her
better than anyone else. Did she seem happy with this guy?"
Even though Ronin's voice is calm, there's an edge to it. I can
see that not answering him isn't usually an option for most
people.

Lindy watches him, clearly thinking hard. She finally
glances away. "She seemed…different. I can't say she was

happy. But if I asked her about it she would withdraw. She didn't want to discuss her relationship, and I didn't want to pressure her. I had no idea that I wouldn't..." Lindy chokes on the words. "That I wouldn't have the time to press her on it."

I nod with sympathy, trying to imagine what it would be like to lose my sister. The thought makes my heart clench tight. "That's understandable, Lindy. There's no way you could have known."

Lindy breaks down then. It's like my kind words were a trigger for her sadness, and she covers her face with her hands as she cries. I wrap my arms around her, and she cries into my shoulder. When her sobs subside, she wipes her face with her hands and glances up at me. "I'm sorry."

Shaking my head, I pull back. "Please, don't be."

Ronin reaches into his pocket and withdraws a card. Handing it to Lindy, he rises from the couch. "If you think of anything else, even if you don't think it can help, give me a call."

I stand up with him as Lindy reads the card. "Night Eagle Security?" she asks with a raised brow.

Ronin gives a curt nod. "Keep in touch."

When we're back in the truck, I let out a breath. "I'm sorry she didn't know anything."

Ronin stares out the windshield, his mind clearly running through the conversation we'd just had. "She knows more than she's letting on."

My eyebrows shoot skyward in surprise. "How do you know that?"

Ronin glances at me, and the expression in his eyes is akin to the ferocity of a dog with a bone. "She hesitated before answering a question. It wasn't because she didn't know the answer, it was because she was trying to decide how much she should say. Which means there's something she didn't."

Impressed, I think back to the talk with Lindy. Her reluctance to answer whether or not her sister had been seeing anyone comes to mind, and I nod. "You're right."

But frustration pours off of Ronin. "If I had her at NES, if she was a hostile witness...I could have gotten the answers I needed. But this is a different situation. I had to cut off the questioning there. I'm not an official part of this case. Walking out of there was hard, Red."

He starts the truck's big engine and touches the phone image on the dash screen. Pulling up his contacts, he presses SAYWARD.

"What's up, Swagger?"

The nickname makes me smile. It's so perfect for him, and I'm not even privy to the events that led to him earning it.

"I need you to check phone records for two women: a Grace Hodges, deceased, and a Lindy Hodges. E-mail me the information for their records when you get it. Let's go about a month back."

"This something you want done under the radar?" Sayward's tone is businesslike.

"For now."

She agrees and they end the call, Ronin still looking contemplative as he turns to me.

"You were a good partner back in there, Red."

With a small smile, I cock an eyebrow at him. "You sound surprised."

A tiny, crooked smile curves his lips, and there's a sparkle in his eyes that wasn't there before. "I guess I shouldn't be. You surprise me all the time, Olive."

When my name rolls off his tongue I can't help the shiver that rocks me.

Settling back into my seat, I grin. "Just call me Sidekick."

Ronin chuckles as he pulls out of Lindy Hodges's apartment complex. "Okay, Sidekick. Now let me buy you lunch."

17

RONIN

Olive Alexander is still a mystery to me. A sexy, gorgeous, gift-wrapped mystery that's been set in front of me, and I can't help how much I want to unwrap it.

When she told me about her uncle and what he did to her, it explained so much. It told me why she has such a hard outer shell, why she's one of the most aloof people I've ever met. Why cool and unaffected is her go-to demeanor. And why she's so goddamn tough.

Finding out the connection she has with Mick Oakes makes me crazy. I want to go back in time, find the college-aged Olive, and shake her, or take her into my arms. I want to tell her that Oakes doesn't have what she needs because…

Because what? Because I do?

That, I know, is impossible. I don't have anything to give her. Not now. Not when I'm searching for my dead-wife's killer. It's the only thing I should be thinking about right now. Not to mention that Olive deserves better. I don't have anything left. And after what she went through, Olive deserves the world.

But I can't help the fact that my eyes follow the curve of her body from top to bottom as my hand settles at the small of her back as I close the truck door behind her in the condo parking garage. And the feelings bubbling up inside me? They make me think there's possibility...like maybe I can have a future with this woman. The kind of future I never thought I'd have again. Something warm spreads across my chest, mixing with the ache that's lived there for years.

Standing next to the vehicle, Olive leans against the shiny black exterior. She looks like hope. There's a relaxed expression on her pretty-as-hell face and she's more casual than I've ever seen her. Her ponytail isn't so tight, her body is clad in jeans, and goddamn, she looks *perfect*. Her lips tilt upward in a small smile.

"So," I begin, not in a hurry to rush inside. "Was it the interview at Lindy Hodges today, the sushi lunch, or the afternoon working at my desk that put that pleased smile on your face?"

My tone is teasing, but I really do want to know.

She shrugs. "Why can't it be a combination of all of the above?"

The parking garage is quiet around us, and I naturally become completely in tune with our surroundings. It's a habit that will never die. I continually scan the area around us with my eyes, looking for anything out of the ordinary. My ears practically prick at every little sound.

"I think you feel like you have to do this alone," Olive muses as she scans my face. "Like you're the only one who can figure out what happened to your…wife."

Her words pack a punch, and I can feel them in my gut. "It's not that. It's just—"

I stop, my head whipping around. I can't put my finger on the sound I heard, but I know it doesn't belong in this parking garage. I've lived in this building long enough to have familiarized myself with everything—and something here doesn't belong.

In my chosen field, I've learned more times than I can count that trusting my instincts is key. I have them, and they serve me well. At the sound of slow footsteps approaching, I'm already ready to act. There's no one in sight yet, but I already know I don't have time to hustle Olive to the elevator standing about forty feet away. And pulling her out into the open in order to make a run for it isn't something I'm willing to do.

First, I watch. This part of the parking garage is only used for the units on my floor. There aren't many, and it isn't often that I run into someone else during the walk from my car to the elevator, or vice versa. So even though there's a chance it could be someone who lives in the building, my gut tells me it isn't.

Pulling my gun from the holster at my ankle, I push Olive behind me. She goes quiet, her muscles tensing.

"What?" Her question is barely a breath against my spine, and her fingers brush against my back as she reaches for me.

Turning my head so she'll hear me, I whisper, "Someone's coming."

I don't need to see her eyes to know that she's scared. The

way her fingers tighten their hold in my shirt is evidence enough.

And suddenly, I'm pissed. Not because someone I don't know is encroaching on my territory. But because whoever belongs to those footsteps is scaring her, and that right there is unacceptable. Olive Alexander has been through enough.

The footsteps grow closer, and I hear Olive suck in a breath. She doesn't let it out. My back teeth grind together, my gun held ready in my hand but lowered beside my thigh.

Rounding the hood of a car only feet away from us, Mick Oakes strolls to a stop as soon as we're spotted. He takes a casual stance, hands held loosely behind his back as a smirk rolls over his face.

"Hey," he says in a friendly tone. Not looking at me, he directs his greeting at Olive. "I missed you, baby."

She stiffens, and I shift to cover her more completely. "You don't talk to her, Oakes. What the hell do you want? How did you get in here?"

He shrugs, shifting on his feet. He looks like he has his shit together in a button-down and slacks, hair slicked back, but even when a snake sheds its skin, it's still a snake underneath.

His eyes flash with anger before he gets a handle on it and blinks, refocusing on me. "I didn't come for you. This is between me and the lady there. So…"

He actually gestures his head to the side, like he's dismissing me.

Laughing, when I really want to point my Sig at him and shoot, I work on getting his attention back on me. Olive, as hard as I know she's trying to fight it, trembles at my back.

"If you did enough research to discover my address, then you must know who I am by now, right? You think you can dismiss me with a head nod? Think again, prick. I asked you nicely once. That's the only time you'll get. Listen carefully: Olive doesn't want to talk to you. Leave her alone."

Taking a step closer, which has my trigger finger itching like crazy, he attempts to peer around me. I'm having none of it. "You hard of hearing?" The question comes out in a growl, because at this point I'm pretty sure Mick is stupid enough to have come here on his own. And if it comes to it, I'll take his ass down.

Mick raises his hands, spreading them wide. I'm not pacified, because even though he came here alone, he wouldn't have come unarmed. I'm guessing his piece is in his waistband, and I can calculate the amount of time it'll take him to draw it. Not faster than he'll take a bullet between the eyes. But I'd rather it didn't come to that.

Not today.

"Yeah. Know all about you, and guys like you. You think you have a say over what I do, just because you decided Olive should be the one keeping your dick warm this week?" He tosses the words at me like knives, and I can tell that that's exactly the way they hit Olive.

At the sound of her sharp intake of breath, my blood starts to burn. In any other circumstance, the asshole would have been flat on his back before he finished that sick-ass sentence, because disrespecting her like that? He needs to be taught some goddamn manners. But with Olive at my back, all I want to do is get Mick out of here so that I can make sure she's okay.

"What do you want?" My voice is deadly calm.

He jabs a finger toward Olive. "I want you to stop keeping her away from me. And I want you to stay out of my business at the bar. What I have going on there doesn't concern you. You might not know who I am, but you will. And if you keep showing up where I don't want to see you...I'll make sure you never show up anywhere again."

In the same calm voice, I ask for clarification. "That sounds like a threat. I don't take too kindly to those."

Mick glances around me to where Olive stands, and then his mouth curls into a smirk that I want to punch right off of him. "It's a promise. Don't get in my way, Shaw."

I open my mouth to respond when he speaks sharply. "Olive. Come with me now. I just want to talk to you. And then this asshole won't get hurt. You remember my uncle, don't you, baby?"

My skin prickles when he uses the word *baby* to refer to her again, and I'm about to let him know where he and his uncle can shove it when Olive steps out from behind me.

I tug her wrist, ready to pull her around to the shelter of my back, when she turns to me. "Ronin."

Staring into those sapphire eyes that have the ability to suck me in and keep me there, I try to read what she's saying with them. There's a note of finality in her stare, and my hand tightens on her wrist.

Facing Mick again, she speaks. "You'll leave Ronin out of this if I come talk to you?"

A real growl breaks free of my chest as I whip back in front of her. Refusing to turn my back on Oakes, I come at Olive

from the side. Letting go of her arm I grip her chin in my hand
to get her attention back on me. "Olive. This isn't happening.
You hear me? No. Just fucking *no*."

She blinks, and there's real desperation in her eyes. "I just
want him to go away," she whispers. "Maybe if I go with
him…let him say whatever it is he needs to say, he'll let me go
once and for all."

My stomach lurches at the thought of her leaving with him.
I'll throw her over my shoulder if I have to, but I won't let her
go. Not with him.

"*No.* He gets you alone, there's no telling what he'll do. You
don't need to do this. You need to trust *me*, Red. I will keep
you safe."

Glancing at Mick, I can see the joy on his face. He thinks
he's got Olive right where he wants her, but he doesn't know
me well enough yet.

She swipes at a tear before it can fall, and I slide my hand
to the back of her neck. Leaning down so that she has to look
me straight in the eye, I say each word succinctly. "Stay. With.
Me."

She holds my gaze, and everything that's been on my mind
today fades away. All that matters right now is her. Her safety,
her happiness, and the fact that I need her next to me.

Something passes between us then. I'm not sure what the
fuck it is, but understanding and something so much warmer
than that appear in her gaze. Her expression softens, and she
opens her mouth to speak, just as the sound of an engine roars
up behind us.

Another truck screeches to a stop beside us, this one red and raised up on lifts. The driver's-side door opens, and Bennett jumps down. Walking up to stand next to me, He faces off with Mick without glancing at either me or Olive.

With a half-frustrated, half-amused eye roll, I release Olive's neck but drop my hand to rest in hers instead. "What the hell are you doing here?"

Bennett, still staring at Mick, inclines his head in my direction. "I got your six."

Smirking, I make eye contact with Mick. "Anything else? Or are you ready to get the hell out of here now?"

Glancing from Bennett to me, Mick's expression transforms from one of elated triumph to obvious rage. He settles his eyes on Olive. "Mistake, baby. I'm comin' for you one way or another. And your boyfriend here will burn."

Bennett speaks up. "Someone's gonna burn, but it ain't gonna be Ronin." There's a promise in his tone.

With one last look at all three of us, Mick turns and walks away. When he's gone, Olive sags a little and I tighten my hold on her hand. There're words I need to have with her, but first I turn to Bennett.

"How'd you know?"

He lifts a shoulder and lifts a hand to the back of his neck. The gun he carries in a hip holster is visible when his shirt rides up. "Something he said before he ran out of the bar. He'd been holed up in the office for a few hours, but when he came out he made a beeline for the door."

"What'd he say?" I ask.

Bennett glances at Olive. "He said he'd be back later, he had to go pick up his woman. Figured that meant he'd be headed straight for you, and I wanted to make sure it worked out in your favor."

Holding out a hand, I wait for Bennett to shake it and pull him into a bro hug. "Thanks, man."

Bennett nods, turning for the truck. "It's all good. Take care of her. When Mick decides he wants something...well, he stomps his feet until he gets it. I'd hate to see Olive hurt by him."

I shove my Sig back into my holster and scowl. "That'll never happen."

Bennett nods before climbing into his truck and driving off.

As soon as he's gone, everything that just went down comes rushing back, and a surge of emotions threatens to swallow me whole. She was gonna leave with him. Maybe it was because she wanted to protect me from his family, or because she wanted him to leave her alone for good. But none of that matters, because one thing is glaringly obvious.

She didn't trust me to keep her safe.

Anger blooms like a flower.

Turning to Olive, I incline my head toward the elevator. I'm not sure how long I'll last before I explode, and I want her safe and inside my condo before the fireworks start.

18

RONIN

Olive and I are silent the whole way up to my place. I don't look at her, because I'm scared of what will happen if I do. If I hold my hands up to my face, I'm pretty damn sure they'll be shaking. During the elevator ride, I try to figure out why.

Is it because I now know that Mick Oakes has the resources to figure out where I live? Is it because he actually dared to come here and try to take Olive right out from under me? Is it because Olive is all tied up with the mob, and her past seems to keep following her around?

But, if I'm being honest with myself, I'm shaking like a motherfucking leaf because the reason I almost lost Olive tonight is because of *Olive*.

We walk into the condo and she flicks on the lights as she enters. Closing the door behind her, I toss my keys on the entry table and follow her into the living room. Olive continues to the kitchen island, placing her bag on the bar before she turns around to face me.

Our stares hold from across the room, and she brings one unsteady hand up to brush a stray lock of hair away from her face. The delicate gesture, something so simple and goddamn innocent is what finally causes something inside my chest to snap.

"Don't ever do that again." My voice is steady, belying the storm roaring to life inside of me.

Somewhere inside me, I know that starting this conversation out with those confrontational words isn't going to go well. I know that Olive won't respond to it, and that it's way too hard for a woman as strong and independent as she is not to react in anger.

But that's the wise side of me. That side of me is asleep right now, buried under the pissed-as-hell part who just came out to play.

Olive's hand snakes up to her hip, and the soft expression that crossed her face back in the garage after I asked her to stay evaporates. Now, her eyes flash with something dark and angry.

"You don't tell me what to do, Ronin. I was going to leave with him because I wanted to spare you the trouble I've been causing just by being here."

At the sound of her voice, my strides eat up the distance between us before I can stop myself and think about what I'm doing.

"I'm the one who asked you here, Red. Don't you know what I am? I'm not some pussy Oakes can push around. I'm strong enough to protect you and make sure he doesn't come near you ever again. You're just too damn stubborn to accept it." Stopping only a foot away from her, my hands curl into fists just so I won't reach out and shake her.

"Oh, yeah?" She reaches out and jabs a finger into my chest. I stare down at it, stupefied. "If you're so tough, than how come the man I *never wanted to see again* was standing just a few feet away from me? God, Ronin. Your ego is too big for this condo. There's not enough room for me and my goddamn problems."

Reeling back like she slapped me, I narrow my eyes. "He was there, but you were still safe, Olive. I'll never let anything happen to you. Not after...*fuck*. Why don't you know that?"

There's a lump the size of a grapefruit forming in my throat, and I try hard to swallow around it. Why doesn't she realize that after what happened with Elle, I'll never let anything happen to her? I'd die before I let it happen again. A woman that I'm supposed to be protecting will never be harmed.

Especially not *this* woman.

Sorrow floats across her face, reaching inside me, but she turns and storms away. My hand flies out, slapping down on the counter beside her to bar her exit. When she turns the other way, the look of desperation on her face clear, I trap her with my other arm. The sweet scent of her pours into me, and I almost lean in to catch a stronger whiff. She stares me down, no longer trying to run.

"You think I'm scared of you?" she asks. Her voice strengthens. "I'm not, Ronin. You might be bigger and stronger than me, but there's nothing you can do that could hurt me. Not after what I've been through."

I lean closer to her. Her chest rises and falls with her breaths, and the tips of her breasts graze my shirt, effectively awakening another kind of beast inside me. My dick twitches in my jeans and I'm suddenly so damn aware of every single part of her and how close she is to every single part of me.

"I. Will. Never. Hurt. You." Each word causes her to flinch, and the heat in her eyes could melt an entire candle into a pool of wax. My voice drops to a rough whisper. "I just want to keep you safe."

I'm not sure who wins the standoff. All I know is that her eyes, those melted pools of blue, grow wide, and I see that she believes me. Then that plump bottom lip disappears into her mouth. Her heat seems to expand, surrounding me with all things Olive and then *fucking hell*, I'm kissing her.

It's not gentle.

It's her lips fused against mine. Her mouth opens at the insistence of my tongue, and a soft, breathy moan slips out that I swallow whole. It's my hips rocking against hers, me pressing the hard length of my erection against her so that she knows exactly what she's doing to me right now. It's my answering groan as she sucks my tongue into her mouth.

Her fingers skate across my neck on their way into my hair, and I let go of the bar so that I can yank her up into my arms. When her legs wrap around my waist and the soft heat of her pussy meets my hard-on I almost go weak in the knees.

I'm fucking blind, lost to everything except for her. Placing her on the bar I pull my mouth away from hers long enough to trail kisses along her jaw, and down her neck. Using my tongue, I draw a line to her shoulder at the same time my hands yank the hem of her shirt up and over her head. Next, I reach for the ponytail holder keeping all that dark red hair out of my reach. After I slide it free, her locks tumble out around her shoulders and I grip a handful, gently tugging her head to the side so I can lick another path up her neck.

There're no words. We don't need any because whatever this is that's been building between us is coming to a head now and we both know it.

We both *want* it.

For a second I pull back and stare at her. Sitting on my island in her black satin bra, miles of creamy skin exposed, head tilted to the side and lips swollen from my kiss, I let my mind briefly wander to Elle.

To the moments when she might have been propped up on an island similar to this one. Waiting for me to come and get her. My stomach clenches.

But then Olive does something so totally her, that any thought of Elle disappears completely. Olive takes control. She wraps her legs around my waist again, pulling me to her and presses her hands against either side of my face. My lips land on hers again and I know that with Red, it's always going to be a battle for supremacy. She's going to want control just as surely as she wants her next breath, and it's something I've grown to understand and to crave about her.

I'm smiling against her lips, and she returns it with a grin of her own. Impatient hands reach for the button on my jeans, ripping them open and sliding the zipper down. Helping her out, I reach behind me and yank my shirt off over my head as I toe off my boots and socks. Stepping out of the pants and kicking them aside, I slide my hands down her shoulders, taking her bra straps with me. My attention is held there, to the slender curve of her arms as I reach behind her and undo the strap.

Plump, perky breasts swing free as the garment hits the counter and I zero in on the pretty pink peaks screaming for attention. I reach for them, palming the weight of her in my hands while my thumbs caress the hard, pebbled tips. Olive moans, her eyes sliding shut as she shoves her chest toward me, silently begging for more of my touch. I give it to her, leaning forward and sucking a nipple into my mouth.

She tastes as good as I imagined, when I allowed myself to fantasize about her. She's somehow sweet and tart at the same time, and I suddenly feel the need to touch her *everywhere*. Still without speaking, I reach for the button on her jeans and she leans back on her hands and lifts her hips, her heavy-lidded eyes watching my every move as I remove the pants inch by painstaking inch.

Her legs are long and lean, firm to my touch and ending in dainty red toenails that make me want to suck each one of her toes into my mouth. I've never been a foot fetish kind of guy, but every single part of Olive is just so damn pretty, I want to taste every single inch.

The only scrap of clothing left on her is a tiny, black pair of panties, and she's sexy as hell sitting on my counter in them. But I want her bare, nothing stopping me from exploring all of her. So I peel them off, watching her reaction. Her lips are parted, her eyes hooded and heavy. Tossing the panties aside, I move her legs, placing her feet up on the counter so that she's spread wide open before me.

Like a goddamn buffet.

Stepping between her legs, I wrap one hand around her waist and slide her to the edge of the island. She watches me, her breath coming fast, her hands curving into the countertop as she holds on.

Holding her gaze, I touch my index finger to her lips. Sliding it down, I follow its progress and so does Olive as it dips down between her breasts, over her flat stomach, and down between her folds. I hiss as I finger her, because she's so goddamn wet that I can't wait to taste her. Instead, I suck in a breath and sink two fingers inside her. Her eyes flutter closed as her hips tilt forward, fucking my fingers. I slip a third finger inside, watching her respond, and it's the hottest thing I've ever seen. She moves like she's made to react to me, and I'm pretty sure my other hand is making dents in the flesh of her ass I'm squeezing her so hard.

My fingers make two more pumps before I can't take it anymore. Sinking down in front of her, I let my tongue swipe a path from her inside of her knee and up her thigh before taking my first taste of the one part of her I've been waiting for.

She moans, and I almost miss it over the sound of my own approving groan. She's fucking incredible, my Red. She melts on my tongue, and the sweetness of her is almost more than I can stand. I lick her from bottom to top, and then I have to take ahold of myself in my hand because my dick is throbbing so hard I'm afraid I'm gonna explode.

I stroke myself as I lick her, and she thrusts against me with no shame. The little agitated noise she makes as I avoid contact with her clit draws a rumbling chuckle from me, and she pulls the hair on my head hard in response.

She's the hottest fucking thing I've ever seen, and she's going to ruin me.

When I finally circle her clit with my tongue, so painfully slowly, I glance up to watch her. Her eyes roll back and she drops her head, the moan that escapes her a sound of pure ecstasy. And fuck me, I'm in serious danger of exploding in my boxer-briefs. Letting go of my own hard length, I sink two fingers inside her, curling them upward to find her G-spot while my tongue flicks the heart of her over and over again.

When she clenches around my fingers, I hum against her and she comes apart around me.

"Ronin." My name falls out on a rough sigh and I can't explain the ball of emotion that gets clogged up in my chest at the sound of it. It's bigger than me, than her, than both of us together.

It's bigger than this moment.

After she comes, I expect her to be lazy and sluggish, but she pulls me toward her almost frantically. Her nails dig into my shoulders and she fumbles for the elastic band on my boxer-briefs.

I grab her hands. "Easy." Leaning toward her, I take her mouth with my own and she kisses me hungrily. Her body molds to mine and damn if I don't notice how perfectly she fits there.

Pulling back, I look into her eyes, seeing all the things I thought I'd never want again. "I'm going to fuck you on this island, and everywhere else in this house, but not tonight. Tonight I need you in my bed."

Her eyes flash with darkness and heat, and I lift her

into my arms and carry her to my bedroom. Not bothering to close the door behind us, I lay her down on my bed. Propped up on her elbows, she watches me as I strip bare, grab a strip of condoms from the nightstand, and then crawl over her.

Hovering above her, I study her. "Okay?"

One of her palms slides up, cupping my face. The room is dark, but moonlight streams in and I can see her expression clearly. There's emotion in her eyes, real emotion, and the sight of it shifts something inside of me. Out there in the front room, I wanted nothing more than to make her feel good. We were reacting, on a high from the situation we'd faced earlier in the evening. And once I touched her, I couldn't stop. The feel of her, the taste of her, was a mind-fuck the likes of which I've never experienced before.

Even with Elle.

But here, in my bed? I don't want to just please her. I want to make her feel safe. I want to make her feel owned. I want to make her *mine*.

She nods. "That was…God, Ronin. I didn't want to admit to myself that I wanted this. But I do."

There's a vulnerability in her eyes, in her voice, that I know Olive doesn't allow just anyone to see. I want to protect that openness with my life.

I kiss her, with every confusing thing that's going through my head right now, because it's the only way to convey what's happening inside of me. Maybe it's wrong, fucking a woman I'm supposed to be protecting. Maybe I shouldn't be with her, knowing that she deserves more than I can give. There's a whole lot of maybes going through my head, but I can't bring myself to care about any of them.

Sitting back on my heels, I rip open a foil packet and slide the rubber on, holding her gaze the entire time. When I fall back on top of her, I grip my cock in my fist and settle myself at her entrance.

We both moan as I slide inside.

19

OLIVE

Oh, my God.

When I woke up this morning, I never would have imagined that this is where I'd end up. Lying like this on Ronin's bed, underneath him, with his beautifully intense green eyes staring down at me while he sinks inside…whatever my imagination might have dreamed up never could have been this good.

Because it *is* good. Even though Ronin knows my story, he doesn't treat me like a broken doll he needs to fix. I really thought he would have. Instead, he handled me like a man who knew exactly what he was doing. He knew exactly where to touch me, where to hold me, how to make me explode under his tongue and hands.

I've always hated losing control. I've made sure to be in control of everything in my life up until this point, and for good reason. But with Ronin…I think I might learn to like letting go for a change.

He doesn't slide inside me inch by painstaking inch. No, Ronin Shaw does everything with full power, and he sinks into me right to the hilt. Then he stills, the look in his eyes hot enough to melt my bones.

Ronin's filling me up in a way I've never felt before. I'm deliciously stretched, and there's a growing, furious need inside of me for more. More of him, more of everything.

There was a time in my life when I thought I'd never want this again. I never wanted a man anywhere near me, much less inside me. And then when I was with Mick, everything we did was tainted by my own insecurities and the hold he had over me.

But now, with Ronin? I'm struck by how *free* I feel, even in the midst of losing control.

How is that even possible?

His fingers firm on my chin, the expression in his eyes burns but softens. "Talk to me. Are you feeling this? You're okay?"

God. Was I okay? The epic truth is *yes*. It's like he's poured some kind of salve all over the scared young woman inside of me who doesn't want anyone to get too close.

"More than okay." I breathe, trying to convey exactly what I'm feeling through my gaze.

Lust flares in his stare. "Good girl." His eyes drop to where we're joined, but he still hasn't moved.

When I can't take it anymore, I reach around him and grab the firm muscles of his ass, pulling him toward me. I need him to move.

His eyes going dark with desire, one side of his mouth tips up as he watches me. "My Red is impatient."

His Red. Oh, how I wish that were true.

With a frustrated little growl, I thrust my hips up, grinding against him. And finally, he begins to move. He pulls out of me, almost all the way, before driving back inside. The feeling is exquisite; the long, rock-hard length of him caresses me exactly where I crave it, and my eyes slide shut.

My hands slip up the broad expanse of his back, and as he pulls out and thrusts into me again, my nails find his skin and dig.

When it comes to lovemaking, I'm a "vanilla" kind of girl. I know it has to be done, and I like to get in and get it over with as quickly as possible. I don't allow anything rough, anything boisterous, anything loud, because I come from a fragile place when it comes to intimacy.

But as my nails dig into Ronin's back and I open my eyes to see the pleasure written across his face because of what I'm doing to him, a brand-new sense of power washes over me. Maybe sex doesn't have to be something I check off on a list of to-dos when dating. Maybe it can be something freeing, exhilarating, and amazing.

At least with this man, it can be.

"Red," grinds out Ronin. "The way your body wraps around mine…it's killin' me, sweetheart. I need to let go, okay?"

My muscles tense automatically, and a slight spark of fear ignites inside me. I can't help it, can't control it. My past…it haunts me and Ronin knows it.

"Hey." Ronin's big hand caresses the side of my face. "Look at me, Red."

I lift my eyes to meet his, my heartbeat racing in my chest.

"I'm not going to hurt you. I'll never hurt you. And you say the word if you want me to stop, got it?" He stares down at me, his gaze burning and sincere.

My breath, which had been coming in increasing quick little gasps, slows. I stare into his eyes and see the truth written there. I trust that truth. Ronin would never hurt me. He's been doing everything in his power to protect me.

I'm safe with him.

I nod, circling my arms up around his neck.

Holding my gaze with his, he hitches one of my legs up over his hip, sinking deeper inside me as he does. We both groan at the feeling of it, and I'm right back in this moment with him. Here and now.

I know, deep inside my soul, that Ronin won't hurt me. It's been his mission for the past few days to make sure I'm safe, and something inside of me recognizes something inside of him. I can't explain it, but I know it's true.

My toes curl as he pounds into me, the rough rhythm he finds making my insides melt. Again and again, he hits the very center of me, and I bite my lip in an attempt to stifle a scream.

"Don't." Ronin orders. "Don't ever hold back with me, Red. Let it out, dammit."

His eyes are wildfire as he scans my body, his gaze dancing from my face to my breasts, down to the place where we're joined, before starting his search all over again. It's like every time his eyes land on a spot on my body, he gets even more excited, even more turned on. And that's the hottest thing I've ever seen.

Unwrapping my hands from around his neck, he pins one

above me and inclines his head toward my free hand. Dipping his head toward mine, he murmurs in my ear and a shiver rolls through me.

"Touch yourself, Red. Make it feel good."

It's something I've never done before. I've never felt the need to pleasure myself, not even in the nights when I'm lying in bed alone. And when I'm with a man, I don't have any illusions that he's going to be able to do it for me, I just accept the fact that it's not going to happen for me. But Ronin has already given me my first orgasm tonight.

What if I'm able to help him give me my second?

The thought is intriguing, wildly appealing to all the parts of me that want control, and I tentatively allow my fingers to drift down my belly toward my heat.

He makes a deep sound of approval in his throat, his eyes simmering, as he watches me. "That's it, sweetheart. Think about how you like me to touch you, and do it for yourself."

His voice is like honey poured over almonds, or silk wrapped around a rough stone. It's the place where soft and sexy meets rough and rugged, and it's a side of Ronin that I'm naïve enough to believe only I'm getting to see.

Letting my fingers trail over my hip bones, I'm shocked at how erotic this is, at how good my own hands feel while I'm slick with the sweat Ronin's caused. I find the spot just above where he and I are fused together, my fingers brushing the soaked length of him. He shudders, and I glance up at him, surprised.

Looking down at me, he smirks. "You have no idea what you do to me, do you?"

But I can't answer him, because on their own, my fingers have found my clit and I begin to circle it gently. It's the same thing Ronin did with his tongue back on the kitchen island, and when he starts to thrust into me again the pleasure is so good I have to close my eyes against it.

"Oh, God," I moan, and I hear Ronin's answering rumble as he thrusts faster.

My breath hitches and my fingers and Ronin's rhythm seem to match it. Stars dance behind my eyes, and my hand falls away as I sink deeper into the bed. "I can't…Ronin…please."

"You're so incredible, sweetheart." He kisses me, and it's a fusion of tongue and lips and teeth and I cry out against his mouth as I fall over the edge of my own pleasure.

Pumping into me several more times, I feel Ronin's body go stiff and he grunts out his own release before falling over me. His sweat mingles with mine, the breathless sound of our gasps for air match, and I'm suddenly very, very afraid.

Not afraid of the man lying over me, but afraid of what will happen when this is over. Being with Ronin tonight changed something fundamental inside of me, and I'm terrified that I'll never go back to being the old Olive.

All I want is to be the one I am when I'm with him.

When Ronin returns to bed from the master bathroom, he slides in beside me and pulls a sheet over us. Without a word, he pulls me into his side. I rest my head against his chest, and the steady thump of his heartbeat seems to keep pace with the pulse of the blood running through my veins. I sigh.

"Talk to me," he whispers, and his fingers trail along the bare skin of my arm.

"Did we cross a line here?" I ask softly.

He chuckles. "Probably. But it's one I don't want to cross back over. Do you? Do you regret that it happened?"

I'm so sure of my answer I don't need to think about it. "No."

Ronin's deep inhalation makes my head rise and fall with his chest. "Glad to hear that, Red. Because now I'm gonna want to make love to you on every surface in my house. It'd be a shame if you weren't down with that."

A shudder ripples my body, and I peek up at him. "Is that a promise?"

He stares down at me, a sparkle in his eyes I've never seen there before. "Absolutely."

"Do you want me to go back to my room?" There's a hint of uncertainty in my voice. Just because we had sex doesn't mean that he's going to want me in his bed all night.

Ronin's arms tighten around me. "Fuck, no."

I grin into his chest. We lay there silently, letting the moon-light wash over us, and my thoughts are lazy and haphazard until Ronin speaks again.

"Listen…"

I glance at him again, startled by the seriousness in his tone. "Yeah?"

"There were some things that Oakes said tonight that I'm go-ing to have to take back to my team in the morning. We're work-ing on something, and the information I have now is going to play a vital part." There's a cautious undertone to his words.

Propping myself up on my arm, I look at him fully. "What kind of something are you working on?"

His expression shutters. "I can't tell you that."

I stare at him for a minute. My first instinct is to be hurt, angry, because after what we just did together I felt like I'd given him a piece of myself. I want him to want to share everything with me. Then again, after being at the Night Eagle office, I know that a lot of what they do there is classified, and me sleeping in his bed doesn't mean I suddenly have a security clearance. I try to rein in my anger, telling myself that even if he wanted to tell me about his work, he probably couldn't.

I sigh. "Yeah, okay. But if it has something to do with M.J., I don't have a good feeling about it."

Ronin's expression is troubled. "Neither do I. I was serious earlier, Olive. I don't ever want you to put yourself in a situation where you're alone with him. It's not an option, okay?"

His voice has gentled, like he expects a repeat of our earlier argument, but he's not going to get one from me. Not now.

Bending, I brush my lips across his. "Okay."

My stomach rumbles, and I realize for the first time that we haven't had dinner. Ronin chuckles, sitting up and pulling me out of bed with him.

"Come on, Red. Let's feed you. And then there's something else I want you to do."

"What's that?" Curious, I peer up at him.

"I want you to call Ken. And tell him you won't be seeing him again. You belong to me." His eyes, full of possession and intensity, blaze into mine just before he lowers his lips to my forehead.

Sighing, I snuggle into him. "Yes, sir."

Calling Ken is something I had planned to do anyway, but Ronin's asking me to just cements in my mind that it's the right thing to do.

And his wanting to feed me? It's such a nice, normal thing for him to say, to want to do, that a light peal of laughter bubbles out of me. With Ronin, at his place with the ocean crashing on the shore just outside, lying naked in his arms, I'm feeling something I've worked so hard to manufacture over the years.

I feel like I'm at home.

20

RONIN

After I have Olive settled at my desk the next morning, I head toward the conference room. There's an extra spring in my step this morning. It could be the fact that I woke up with a beautiful woman in my bed this morning, one who when I looked over at her my whole body went all warm and tingly. I made love to her twice under the covers of my bed last night, and the second time blew my mind just as thoroughly as the first.

There've been other women since Elle. I'm not a monk, and there were a lot of times that all I wanted was a night to forget. But that's not what's happening with Olive. At first, I just wanted to look after her for Jeremy. Then, when I realized what was going on with Mick Oakes, I wanted to keep her safe. And I still do. But now, last night I had to admit that there's feelings there. Feelings I never wanted to have, but I have them all the same. She's worked her way into my heart, and it's scary but it's happening.

I can't deny it. And I don't really want to.

I have to come to terms with what that means. Because there wasn't one time last night that I looked at Olive and wished she was Elle. Not one time. And that's never happened before. Not since I lost my wife.

So what does it all mean? How can I blend what I'm feeling for Olive with the fact that I still have a responsibility to my wife? I still need to find out who killed her; that need hasn't died. But is it something I can do with Olive by my side, or am I just risking Olive's heart in the process?

Walking through the halls of Night Eagle, I note how much busier it is now than when I first started working here. This is the main branch of two locations the security company has, with Jacob traveling between both of them depending on what we're working on at any given time. He's been bringing in more personnel as time goes by and we've been getting more government contracts and assignments as a whole. So the office is buzzing with support personnel and a few other guys with qualifications similar to mine. It's different, and hard to get used to.

As I stride into the conference room, I take a seat around the table. Everyone else is already there. Grisham and Dare both give me wide grins.

"What?" I snap as I sit.

Grisham clicks his tongue. "Well, you just walked in here looking like a very satisfied man. That have anything to do with the lovely Olive?"

Rolling my eyes, I stay silent and concentrate my attention on Jacob. He stands at the front of the room. His attention is on the touch screen on the wall, but I can see the twitch of his lips as he tried to hide his smirk.

The wise bastard is laughing at me.

"Something funny, Boss Man?" Narrowing my eyes, I watch Jacob's reaction.

Dare's chuckle pulls my attention, and I glance at him. He's close to outright laughing.

"Don't forget, Swagger." He lifts his chin. "We know what it looks like."

Leaning back in my chair, I study him. "You know what *what* looks like?"

Placing his hands flat on the table, he leans forward. "Falling for a woman you never saw coming."

Beside him, Grisham gives a firm nod.

Falling? Shit… that's not what this is. I'm feeling something, yeah. But falling?

I don't have time to think it over any further because Jacob calls our meeting to order, even though Sayward never really seems like she's paying attention to what the rest of us are saying. I know, though, that behind her computer screen she hears every single thing we say at these meetings, and that if she's called on to answer a question or lend her expertise, she'll be able to do it without a pause. The woman's a mystery to me, but she's damn good at what she does.

"Boss Man," I start. "I learned something yesterday, and I need to let the team in on it."

Jacob's sharp eyes land on me. "What's that?"

I swallow. I can anticipate their reaction before I say the

words. "Last night, after Olive and I got back to my condo, we had a visitor."

The atmosphere in the room goes thick and heavy. Every single man in the room flexes, without even being aware of it, and I meet Jacob's intense gaze steady.

"Who?" Dare's voice is low.

"Mick Oakes."

Sayward's gaze jerks up to meet mine, and I can audibly hear Grisham's teeth snap together.

"And you didn't call us?" he asks, an underlying tone of pissed-offness in his voice.

"I had it handled. And backup came in last minute." I smirk, thinking about Bennett rolling up in his big-ass truck.

"Backup?" Jacob's tone is calm but it has that crazy-alert quality only he can muster.

"Yeah. Guy by the name of Bennett Blacke. He's a buddy of mine, ex-Special Forces. He runs a bar I go to sometimes, and we've gotten to be friendly. Showed up right when I needed him."

Bennett's a badass, that's a fact. I've figured that out from the bits and pieces of information I've gathered from him in conversation.

"You know we're going to look him up, so what's his story?" The curiosity in Dare's voice is clear.

I shrug. I don't want to talk about Bennett's story. Sharing it should be up to him. And I don't even know everything. What I do know, he's told me in confidence. But I also don't want the guys to read it in black-and-white, because it could end up looking worse than if I told them myself. So I relent, with a sigh.

"He served. And did a hell of a job, doing more ops than anyone probably should have. When he retired, he came home to find his wife in bed with some prick. He went off the deep end, lost his shit. Ended up doing time for hurting the dude. Look, Bennett knows what he did was fucked-up, and I can't fault him. Hell, if I'd been able to get my hands on the man who killed Elle..."

When I trail off, the room goes deadly quiet. They all know what I'm going to say; I don't have to finish the sentence. I just want to let them know that even though Bennett and my stories are different, there's a similarity running through them that ties us together. They need to know that I trust him.

"He's a good dude. He messed up, but who hasn't? He had my back last night, and that's enough said."

The silence stretches, and Dare and Grisham exchange a glance. Sayward keeps her eyes on her laptop screen, and Jacob's critical stare burns into mine. Finally, he gives a curt nod. "We'll check him out. But let's move on. What happened with Oakes?"

As I remember the events of last night, I try really hard not to become infuriated all over again. Really damn hard. "He came for Olive. Thought he could dismiss me, get her to come with him so he could brainwash her or whatever. He wants her, and he wants her bad. I don't know why. He let her go years ago. Why come back for her now?"

Grisham strokes his chin. "That's a good question."

"I have a profiler I can get on it. Figure out what's making him tick. What else?"

A small bit of reassurance fills me, because Jacob's connections are solid. If he can get someone to figure out why Oakes is doing what he's doing, that's going to make it that much easier for me to protect Red.

"So what happened?" Dare's the calmest one in the room, which is par for the course. He's a thinker, and he's always going to listen to an entire problem, then figure out how best to make it go away.

"What happened…is that Olive was going to offer herself up to him." The tension in my voice is thick, almost strangling me. That's something I wish I could forget.

"What the fuck?" Grisham leans forward, his voice full of disbelief.

Nodding, I sigh. "The asshole threated me. Said he'd leave me be or whatever, as long as she came with him. So they could 'talk.' It was bullshit, but Olive…she was trying to protect me."

Something warm and tender flows through me, and it's such a foreign feeling that it steals my goddamn breath. She wanted to protect me.

Dare sucks in a breath. "Damn."

Those are my exact sentiments. "That's when Bennett pulled up. Rolled in like a boss, armed and ready. Oakes was pissed, but he backed off. Not before he revealed a few things."

Jacob's in recon mode, all-business. "What'd you find out?" he barks.

Leaning forward, I relay all of the information that Oakes gave me last night. It wasn't much, but it was enough to let us know that he's working for his uncle, the head of the Margiano crime family.

"There's no doubt that the Margiano family is the cause of all of the trouble happening here in Wilmington. He's our way in." Finished with my story, I settle back in my seat and focus on my boss.

Jacob is silent for a moment, thinking. Then, he starts firing orders. "Sayward, I want you to gather all the information you can find on the Margianos. Especially the patriarch. When we have that info, we'll figure out how we can send a man in to infiltrate the organization. It obviously can't be you, Swagger. Looks like you've burned that bridge."

I give him a wry smile. "Yeah. Sorry about that."

Jacob dismissed me. "We'll make it work. You're all dismissed. Kill your workouts this morning. That's an order."

We pretend to groan, but we all love working out as a part of our job in the state-of-the–art gym located at the office. The daily grind of our workout takes a lot of the edge off of what we do, but it also keeps us in the kind of shape we need to stay in so we can perform our jobs to the best of our abilities.

"You working out today, Say?" Grisham aims his question at Sayward as we all stand.

She glances up at him. "Yeah. Women have the ability to build an effective amount of muscle, and are able to use it in both defensive and offensive measures when facing an opponent. I need to work out in order to be a functioning member of this team."

She says it all in this matter-of-fact tone that pulls a grin from each of us.

"Yeah, I know, sweetheart." Grisham aims a charming grin at her, but she frowns.

"If you call me sweetheart again, I'm going to use my boxing skills to kick your ass."

Holding up both hands, Grisham backs away slowly. "Easy, there, killer. It's just an expression. I'm happily taken, I promise."

She nods. "Okay, then. See you all upstairs." Gathering her laptop, she leaves the room.

I turn to Dare and Grisham with wide eyes. "Holy shit. She's something else."

Grisham's expelled breath blows up his cheeks like a puffer fish. "Damn straight she is. I feel sorry for the bastard that falls for those killer curves and innocent look. She's like a fucking viper."

I lift my brows. "Viper? Sounds like a good field nickname for a woman like that."

We all chuckle as we leave the room. I'm not going to be the one to tell Sayward about her new nickname, but I can't wait to be on the sidelines when someone does.

When the workday is done, I glance up from my desk. I've given Olive free rein of the desk throughout the day, since she's the one who has to use it most often. Glancing up at her, I'm forced to just sit and stare for a minute. She's busy using the design software on her laptop, shifting things around in one of her projects until everything looks just so. Again, as I watch her, I'm hit with a sense of *rightness*.

She has her own office, so even if whatever this is between us turns into something real, it's not like she'll be sharing my desk on a regular basis. But it still feels like she belongs, and I'm trying hard to figure out why that is.

"Hey." My voice is softer than usual. "You about ready to quit for the day?"

She glances up at me, and when those big blue eyes lock with mine I realize just how fucked I am. Something in my gut pulls toward her, urging me to get close and stay that way. Rising from my chair, I put my arms on either side of her on the desk and lean over, inhaling as my lips brush the side of her neck.

She leans against me with a soft sigh. "God...why do you smell so good?"

I smile against her skin. I'd taken a shower earlier after my workout. "I was just thinking the same thing about you."

I run my nose along the side of her throat, and it hurts how much I want to taste her right now. The fact that anyone walking by could see us, notice how close we are, doesn't faze me. In fact, I have a strong urge to make sure everyone knows that she belongs to me.

Fuck. What the hell am I doing? She doesn't belong to me.

But could she? Somehow, the entire time I'd observed Olive in the past, noticed how beautiful she was, I knew she'd never be just another woman for me. And now that I've had her in my bed, let my hands roam over every inch of her, tasted her sweetness? I want to repeat it. Again and again.

"I want to get you home." The words come out before I can stop them.

Tilting her head back, she peers up at me. "What are you going to do with me when we get there?"

My body reacts to her; it's immediate and intense. My chuckle is dark. "Red...there's no telling. But it's probably going to be very, very dirty." I let my hands slide up her arms.

She swivels the chair, turning to face me. Her tongue darts out to lick her lips, and my eyes tract the movement. "Promise?"

The desire burning in her eyes mixes with the dark playfulness I now know is there, and I suddenly straighten. "Let's go."

The Ram eats up the road as I head back to the condo. From time to time, I glance over at Olive, sometimes catching her looking at me while I drive, and all I can do is smile. I'm not even sure where this woman came from, but suddenly she's all I can think about. It's scary, but I also kind of like it.

"Let me make you dinner tonight," she says, her voice carrying over the sound of Eric Church on the radio.

"Yeah?" I glance over at her, a little bit of teasing in my tone. "Can you cook?"

She punches me, and I laugh. Now that we've moved past the defenses we both naturally put up, it's so damn easy with her.

"It doesn't matter. You'll eat what I make, and you'll like it, *Swagger.*" She sounds sassy, but the teasing tone is there in her voice, too.

I glance over at her as I turn onto the long beach road that will take us across the Intercoastal Waterway and into Carolina Beach. "I'll definitely love what I eat tonight."

And there goes her bottom lip into her mouth, making me want to pull it between my teeth and bite down gently. With a sense of straight-up happiness, I realize that tonight, I probably will.

The autumn sun is sinking below the horizon on our right,

and the shock of red and gold reminds me of Olive's coloring. The thought makes me smile. Glancing into my rearview mirror, I frown. There's a black SUV coming up behind us, moving fast. Too fast, for the road we're on. I keep my eyes there, letting them flit back to check the road every few seconds while I watch the new vehicle's approach.

"What is it?" Olive's tone is alert. She must be reading my mind, because my gut is screaming that something about the car coming up behind us isn't right.

"Could be nothing," I mutter as my foot stays steady on the gas. It's a four-lane road, let them pass me if they think I'm driving too slowly.

The SUV rolls right up on my tail, though, and doesn't pass. The encroaching darkness outside keeps me from being able to see into the windshield of the vehicle, the bright headlights leaving me nearly blind when I try.

"Hey, Red?" Keeping my voice steady, I reach for her thigh and squeeze gently. "Do me a favor. Reach into the glove box there and grab my pistol. Put in in the console for me."

Olive doesn't hesitate. She does as I ask, and when my weapon is sitting within reach I breathe a sigh of relief.

"Someone's following us?" she asks, her voice lifting slightly higher than its usual range.

"It's okay, sweetheart." I glance into the mirror again and note that the SUV hasn't made a move. "Could just be headed to the beach same as us. When I pull off onto the turn for the condo, we'll see what happens."

She nods, and I continue driving, about halfway across the low bridge.

"Ronin," she murmurs, staring out the front windshield.

I see it, too, and my stomach drops to my feet. There's an identical SUV approaching fast from the front. Moving fast, I tap the phone icon on my dash screen and push the button for Grisham's phone. His voice comes through the speakers.

"What's up, Swagger?"

I speak at a clip. "Ghost. Might need some backup. I'm being sandwiched by two SUVs on the ICW bridge. What the *fuck*?"

I don't have time to elaborate, nor am I able to concentrate on Grisham's response. The approaching SUV makes a tight swerve, directly into our lane. I have seconds to act, and there's a choice between swerving into oncoming traffic to avoid it, or going over the bridge.

My instincts take over, my training kicks in, and I know that with a passenger in the car I can't run us into traffic at forty-five miles an hour. I jerk the steering wheel, and the metal railing gleams in the glare of my headlights.

"Ronin!" Olive's scream is the only thing I hear as the truck plunges over the side of the bridge.

21

OLIVE

The sound of metal grinding against metal as the truck slams into the guardrail twists my stomach. The split-second of free fall as we hit open air and drop twenty feet takes my breath away. And the sickening splash I hear as we hit the water in the heavy, heavy vehicle, combined with the violent jerk as my body is thrown forward, almost make me lose the contents of my stomach all over the dashboard.

"Red."

Somehow, Ronin's voice reaches me, and it sounds the same as it always does. Calm, level, even if there is an underlying note of strong urgency. "Listen to me, baby."

It's the first time he's ever called me baby, and I can't even enjoy it.

"Are you okay? Do you think anything is broken?"

I glance around me frantically, noting that we're in the water, and my stomach heaves again. "Oh, God!"

"Olive. Focus on me." Ronin grabs my hand, tugging gently.

I turn to face him, finding his green eyes blazing into mine, and I nod. In the back of my head, I know that I'm nearly hysterical, and I shake myself. *Snap the hell out of it, Olive. You're strong. You're strong. You can get through this. You just went over a bridge in a truck, and you're alive. So get the fuck over it.*

Mentally checking myself, I wince when the pain in my shoulder comes to life. "Ouch. My—my shoulder hurts."

Ronin nods, glancing down at my shoulder. "Okay. Okay, baby. Anything else?"

I want to look away from him, because we're in the water and we're sinking. I feel us lowering, and I need to see. But when I try to glance away, Ronin's voice goes sharp.

"Eyes on me, Red."

I look at him. "N-no. I don't think anything else…is hurt."

I wish I sounded strong. But I don't. I sound like I'm about to break at any second. When something cold and wet trickles over my feet, I glance down. Dread shoots an arrow through my chest. I start kicking my feet, stomping against the water, but of course that does nothing. It just keeps coming.

"Easy, Red. Listen to me. I'm going to get us out of here, I swear to you. I want you to unbuckle your seat belt." Ronin squeezes my hand, and then releases it.

I keep staring at him, refusing to look away. I'm trying so hard to ignore the water stretching up to my calves.

"Right now, Red. Do it now."

Dazed, I turn my attention to my seat belt.

"I'm going to open my door and we're going to swim out. But listen, Red, here's the catch. I'm not going to be able to do that until we're submerged."

Wait…what?

"What?" My panic rises, my voice trembling. "I don't want to drown, Ronin."

The water, colder than I would have thought it could be, splashes up over my knees. *Why is it rising so fast? Is this really happening?*

"Shhh, baby. I know. You won't. I won't let that happen. You trust me?"

Now unburdened by my seat belt, I look at him and take a calming breath. Because even though I'm in a truck sinking into the depths of the Intercoastal Waterway right now, I'm here with Ronin, and that means I can survive it.

I nod. My teeth start to chatter, and maybe part of it is because the cold Atlantic is creeping up my torso. But I'm also vaguely aware that I'm probably going into shock. Darkness is dancing at the edge of my vision, and I blink rapidly, trying to keep it at bay.

"Good girl. I have to wait until we're submerged, because the doors won't open until the pressure is equal on the inside and the outside of the truck. When I say, I'll want you to swim out through my door with me. I'll never let go of your hand, okay?"

I don't answer, because I'm still stuck on the word *submerged.*

"Olive?" Ronin's using his sharp voice again. "You know how to swim, right?"

I nod again.

"Good, baby. Good. Okay, we only have another couple of minutes. When the water covers your chin, I want you to grab the biggest breath you've ever taken, before it covers your nose and mouth, okay?"

"O-okay. I'm scared, Ronin."

I don't know if I've ever admitted such a thing out loud before. Of course there's been many times in my life that I've felt fear. Deep, dark fear that cloaks you and threatens to swallow you whole. But taking control means you have a weapon to fight it with. It's why I never let that control go. But right now, in this situation? All my control is gone. And I'm handing my life over to the man sitting beside me, trusting him to keep me safe.

Ronin, having already unbuckled his own seat belt, turns his entire body around to face me. He slides me over onto the bench seat so that I'm tucked up right next to his side. "I know you are, Red. But you're doing so damn good right now. We can do this. Okay?"

I take a few deep breaths, practicing for the big one. I try not to watch as the water rises, and for some reason my sister's face flashes into my mind.

Rayne. What if I never get to see her again?

"Now, Red. Take that breath." Ronin's strong, steady voice breaks into my thoughts.

The man is serious, unshakeable. If it weren't for his rock-solid assurance, I wouldn't be conscious right now, I'm sure.

I suck in a breath, a deep lungful of air, and hold it. My eyes wide, I try to focus on Ronin's face as he watches me intently, the water rising over my nose.

He takes both my hands in his, and I just try to focus on his touch, not on the water.

When the seawater covers the top of my head, I glance up. Bubbles froth above me as it reaches the top of the car, and then Ronin yanks one of his hands away. Not realizing someone could move so fast underwater, I watch as he pulls back on the door handle and shoves. The truck's driver's-side door wrenches open, and Ronin wastes no time reaching back for me.

My lungs are burning. Stars dance for real in front of my eyes, but I focus on Ronin as he pulls me through the interior of the car and out into the dark water. I'm immediately disoriented, not able to see a thing, but the steady tug of Ronin in front of me lets me know that he has me.

And then, my air runs out. Dismayed, I start to struggle and kick, knowing that I need to make it to the surface faster. Strong arms circle me, and my mouth bursts open even as I tell it not to. Salty water fills my mouth, and my body is shocked when, instead of air, I inhale the liquid surrounding me.

Everything goes dark.

22

OLIVE

"I swear to God, Ghost. I'm going to kill the motherfucker. The only reason he's still breathing is because I'm not leaving her here alone."

Ronin? His voice sounds like it's reaching me from at least a mile away. My eyelids are heavy, and they fight against me as I struggle to open them. *What's wrong with me?*

"We'll get him."

That's Grisham's voice. I've come to know it well, after being surrounded by the Night Eagle guys for the past few days.

Who are they talking about?

It occurs to me that I need to try harder to open my eyes.

"Yeah, but the cops can't touch him. No proof he did this. But I know he did. You should have seen his face yesterday in the parking garage."

Ronin sounds pissed. Like, really pissed. More upset than I've ever heard him, and I want nothing more than to put my arms around him.

"You called Brains, right?" Grisham's voice sounds lower, more serious now. Almost like he's unsure of how Ronin will react.

A sigh. And then Ronin's voice. "Yeah. He was fucking pissed, and rightfully so. They'll be home by morning, I'm sure. Soon as they can get a flight out of the Caribbean."

That jerks my consciousness into the here and now. I find it much easier for my lips to move than it is to open my sluggish eyelids.

"N-no." My voice sounds like I've been swallowing shredded glass. I clear it, and then try again. But nothing comes out, save for a raspy moan.

Immediately, a strong hand grasps mine. "Red? Come on, sweetheart. Come on back to me."

When I finally peel my eyes open, it's to find Ronin's green eyes staring into mine. It's that deep, mossy green, the most unusual color I've ever seen on a guy, that draws me in and makes me stay. I can't look away, even though all I want to do is let my lids fall shut again. I inhale, and the telltale aroma of hospital sterility invades my nose.

"Hey." Ronin's voice is warm and wraps around me like a hug. "Welcome back."

I blink a few times, trying to focus. "Did I hear you say…Jeremy and Rayne are coming?"

Ronin's eyes are full of regret. "I'm sorry. I had to call them. Brains never would have forgiven me if I hadn't, and Rayne would have murdered me outright."

Tears prick at my eyes. I don't have to struggle to remember what happened, now that I'm fully awake. "Your…truck."

One side of his lips tip up in a smile. Ronin leans toward me, one big hand smoothing the hair back from my face. His voice, rough and full of emotion, skates across my skin in a whisper. "You think I care about that? Seeing your big beautiful blue eyes open and focused on me, that's all I need. I'll get a new truck."

I turn toward the sound of Grisham clearing his throat. "Hey, Grisham."

He grins, his artfully styled spikes standing up all over the place, like he's run his hand through his hair a million times. "Hey there, beautiful. You scared us. The Night Eagle family is out there, just waiting for you to open those eyes. I'm going to go let them know you're awake."

He gets up to leave, and I turn startled eyes on Ronin. "They're…here? For me?"

That intense focus that's all Ronin is meant just for me right now. "You think there's anywhere else they were going to want to be after finding out what happened?"

I shift, and then immediately wish I hadn't. Ronin's forehead wrinkles with worry. "Don't move too much, baby. That shoulder's going to be sore for a while."

Groaning, I try to fight through it and battle my way into a sitting position. Ronin's eyes narrow as he watches me, but he doesn't try to stop me.

"Stubborn woman."

"I heard you talking. You think it was the Margianos that did this? You think Mick was behind it, don't you?"

He gives a simple nod, his eyes going dark with bottled-up rage.

I shake my head. "But, Ronin…he wants to *be* with me. I don't think he wants me dead. Why would he run us off the road?"

Ronin sighs, scrubbing a hand across his face as his other hand tightens on mine. "I don't know, Red. Because he's fucking crazy?"

Letting me go, he stands and paces the room. "Seems like he's getting desperate. Why is that, Olive? Is there anything else about him that you haven't told me yet? Something about the two of you I don't know?"

I watch him prowl around the room like a caged panther. I have no idea what he's getting at. "No. Why would you even think that? I've told you everything."

Ronin halts, facing me. The look of doubt on his face hurts. It really hurts, but I school my features so it's not obvious. *What's going on with him?*

"Really? Because the last time it was my job to protect a woman, I didn't know the whole story, and she ended up dead."

As soon as the words are out, he looks like he wants to suck them right back in again. But he can't.

The door to the hospital room swings open, and a nurse bustles in. I tear my gaze off of Ronin, thankful for the interruption.

"A little birdie told me you were awake," the petite, pretty woman with short sienna-brown hair says. She stops at the computer near the bed and types in a few things, before straightening and heading toward me. Wrapping a blood pressure cuff around my upper arm, she smiles and tilts her head toward Ronin. "Couldn't get this one to leave your side, not even to get checked out himself."

My eyes flit to Ronin. "Are you hurt?" Concern fills me up, even though I'm still stinging from his words.

He shakes his head, his voice cracking the air like a whip. "I'm fine."

He stands by the window, arms folded across his broad chest. I remember that we were in the water, but his clothes are dry. And then I realize that he's wearing something different from what he was, and that someone must have brought him a change of clothes.

The door squeaks open again, just a crack, and Berkeley's blond head of curls peeks around it.

"Okay if I come in?" she asks.

The nurse nods as she places the blood pressure cuff aside and sticks a thermometer in my mouth. Berkeley eyes Ronin, obviously picking up on the tension in the room, and perches in the chair at the side of the bed. She reaches for my hand, giving me a sweet smile, and lets the nurse finish checking my vitals.

"Well, you're in pretty good shape for a girl who swallowed as much water as you did," the nurse finally says. She gives me a wink. "I think you'll be just fine, but a doctor will be in soon to check on you."

I thank her, and the second she leaves the room, Berkeley turns to Ronin. "Ronin, why don't you go grab a coffee? I'll stay with Olive."

Her tone is bright and full of concern, but I know exactly what she's doing. Apparently Ronin does, too, but instead of arguing he nods. I can't say that doesn't hurt.

He gives me a long look before he leaves the room. "I'll be back in a little bit. Don't leave her alone, Berk."

She gives him a nod and a smile, and he exits. As soon as he's gone, I burst into tears.

"Oh, honey." Berkeley bypasses my hand and climbs right into my bed.

Berkeley and I have been friends and coworkers for a couple of years, but this is definitely a new level for our friendship. It's somehow not awkward at all, though, because she's seriously the warmest human being I've ever met. And I'm crying, and my sister isn't here, and I need her.

She curls up at my side and slings an arm over me. Luckily, she's on the side without a painful shoulder, and I'm just glad for her warmth and her no-strings-attached friendship.

"What happened?" she asks softly. "With Ronin, I mean."

I sniff. "I don't know, Berk. We…we've been getting close, you know?"

She pulls back, looking up at me. "How close?"

With a sigh, I give her a look that lets her know exactly how close. "Close."

She nods. "I knew it! I knew it at the wedding. I could tell by the way he kept looking at you."

"Well, apparently, he's mad at me right now. He thinks I'm not telling him everything about M.J., that I'm hiding something. But I'm not, I swear it." The words tumble out in a rush, because I'm just trying so hard to understand where Ronin is coming from right now.

Berkeley's whiskey-colored eyes are soft and sympathetic. "Has he told you about his wife?"

Pain causes my heartbeat to stutter. "Yes."

"And you must realize that he still carries all kinds of guilt for her death, right? Even though he wasn't even in the country when it happened?" Berkeley strokes my hair.

I assumed as much, yes. Ronin seems like he carries the weight of the world on his shoulders, and as hard as he's trying to find his wife's killer seven years later, I know that guilt is a big part of the force that's driving him.

"Yes."

She sighs. "I've never seen him the way he's been tonight, Olive. You know he swam to shore with you unconscious in his arms? I think he thought he was going to lose you. When we all got to the hospital and you were still unconscious, he was a freaking wreck. It looked like he was being torn apart from the inside out."

I think about that, trying to picture it. And then I try to imagine what I would have been like if the situation were reversed. If, after everything Ronin and I have been through in such a short amount of time, something had happened to him and I was helpless to fix it.

Yeah, that would have devastated me to the core.

"He was?" My voice is a whisper.

Berkeley gives a firm nod. "He was. He's obviously so invested in you. It reminds me of the way Dare was when we first got together, and especially the way he was after I was kidnapped. Afterward, I heard that he would have stopped at nothing to find me.

"And the way Grisham went after Greta when her stalker got ahold of her? He was a man possessed, I swear. That was

Ronin, tonight. Jesus, when these men fall for a woman, they fall hard. And Ronin Shaw, as I live and breathe, is falling for you."

Her words spark hope in my heart. "Do you really think so?"

She rolls her eyes. "Girl, you've lost your mind if you think otherwise. So if he's upset right now, it's because he feels helpless and he doesn't know what to do about it. The team's going to rally around him, they always do, and he'll be all right. Just bear with him, okay?"

I lay my head against her shoulder. "All right."

She grabs my hand and squeezes hard. "And if you ever scare me like that again, Olive Alexander, I'll kill you myself."

Laughter bubbles up inside me. "Okay."

We stay like that for a while, just talking about everything and nothing, and it's so casual and normal despite the ordeal I just experienced that I'm lulled back into a sleepy comfort.

When Ronin walks back into the room, hands in the pockets of his black sexy sweatpants, and his eyes immediately finding mine, Berkeley shifts and rises off the bed.

"Welp," she announces. "I'm going to grab my husband and get on out of here. Call me when they release you, Olive. Okay?"

I thank her, barely able to take my eyes off the man standing at the foot of my bed, and she leaves the room with a knowing smile on her face.

As soon as the door closes behind her, Ronin is sitting in the chair beside the bed. His hand snakes around the back of my neck, pulling me toward him with gentle insistence, and his forehead meets mine.

"I'm sorry." His voice is rough, thick with emotion. "I didn't mean to snap at you like that. If you knew how it felt, pulling your unconscious body out of the water and giving you mouth-to-mouth until the paramedics arrived..."

"You did that?" I interrupt him.

He nods, eyes downcast, forehead still touching mine. "I was fucking scared, Red. More scared than I've been since..." His voice trails away, and he doesn't have to finish the sentence for me to know he's thinking about his wife again.

"I tried," I offer. "I just couldn't hold my breath that long."

He inhales.

"But," I continue. "I'm okay now, Ronin. Thanks to you. Can you imagine what would have happened if I'd gone off that bridge by myself? You saved my life tonight. The next time that I say I don't need you, and that I can take care of myself all by myself, I want you to remind me of this moment, okay?"

He chuckles, and our breaths mingles as we stare at each other. Our lips touch, but neither of us move to deepen the kiss. We just rest there, breathing each other in.

"I don't want to lose you." Ronin's voice is nothing but a whisper.

I sigh. "Then don't lose me."

"I don't plan on it."

He kisses me then, his lips soft and gentle in a way that

they never have been before. It's a kiss that melts me, cuts me
straight to the heart.

If I'm not careful, I'm going to fall in love with this man.
And I know, without a doubt, that if that happens there will
be no looking back.

23

RONIN

When the door to Olive's hospital room creaks open, I glance up. I'm sitting in the chair beside her bed, but she's been sleeping for the past four hours or so. I keep thinking that I should sleep, too, but I can't take my eyes off her. So I've just been sitting in the chair beside her bed.

Watching over her.

Sayward steps in, and I rise from the chair, stretching my arms over my head.

"What's up?" Keeping my voice low, I glance over my shoulder at the still-sleeping Olive as I meet Sayward next to the door.

"How is she?" Sayward looks at Olive.

"They're going to release her in the morning as long as her vitals are still good." The relief in my voice is evident, and Sayward's eyes snap back to mine.

"You love her?"

I should be used to Sayward's blunt personality by now, but she still catches me by surprise sometimes.

"What? Uh…did you have something to ask me, Diaz?" Clearing my throat, I scratch my head.

Do I love her? It's a complicated question. I've known Olive for a while, but I've only gotten to *know her* over the past few days. And while I know that a traumatic experience can bring two people closer together, I can't swear that's what's happening here. I was having all kinds of feelings for Olive before we went off that bridge. All I know now, after coming so close to losing her, is that I never want it to happen again.

I don't know if that's love. It's been so long since I felt that particular emotion, that I'm really fucking hesitant to throw that word out there.

"I just wanted to let you know that I e-mailed you those phone records you asked for." She pushes her glasses up on her nose.

"Yeah? You didn't need to come all the way down here for that, Diaz."

The woman is seriously a mystery.

She shrugs. "Yeah, well. I also wanted to check in on Olive."

A grin tugs at my lips. "Yeah? You like her, too, huh?"

Sayward rolls her eyes. "Whatever. She's cool, I guess. We have nothing in common, but she's nice."

Grinning outright, I nudge her with my shoulder. "Yeah, she is. Hey, thanks for the phone records. And for checking in."

Sayward turns for the door. "No problem. Let me know if you need anything else."

"Will do."

Settling back in the chair once she's gone, I log in to my e-mail on my phone. Sure enough, the message from Sayward is there, and I open the attachment containing Lindy Hodges's phone records. She's also sent me Lindy's sister, Grace's, phone records.

As I scan them, a slow smile crosses my lips. Sayward's a fucking godsend. She's already highlighted numbers that match, and then ruled them out based on the owner of the numbers. So there are a couple of numbers that both women called frequently, and those belonged to friends. But there's one number that is unaccounted for. Using the copy-and-paste feature, I shoot Sayward a quick return e-mail, asking her to find out anything she can about the number.

After sending it, I put my phone down on my lap and let my eyes rest on Olive's pretty, sleeping form. They gave her painkillers for her shoulder, so she's out cold, and I'm glad she's resting. Flashing back on the memory of her limp, lifeless body cradled in my arms as I brought her out of the water makes me clench my jaw with latent fear. What if she *had* been alone when it happened? What if she had swallowed even more water than she did? What if, what if?

Just like that, I could have lost her. And I know now that I'm never going to be okay with that. This woman is mine to protect, even if I wasn't ready to admit it to myself before.

I'm fucking ready now.

She's still sleeping peacefully, lying on her back with a small mountain of pillows, her dark red hair spread out all over the pillow around her like a goddamn halo. The revenge-crazy beast inside my chest, the one that's lived there since the day I found out about Elle, is pushed back a little further into the background. He'll rear his ugly head sooner or later, that I know for sure, but when I look at Olive, revenge doesn't seem like the most important thing anymore.

Will I get justice for Elle? Yes. Without a doubt.

But does it have to be the only thing I care about? Hell…maybe not. And maybe if I can find her killer sooner, I can start finally putting Elle's death behind me.

Picking up my phone again, I log on to Facebook. If there's going to be information on the dead woman anywhere, it'll be here. Finding the late Grace Hodges's profile, I scan through her about facts. She was twenty-six, and although she was educated with a four-year degree, she wasn't currently working anywhere. Or, if she was, it wasn't listed on her Facebook profile. Noting that she attended school, both college and high school, locally, I move on to her photos. The folder is splattered with pictures of her and her sister. They were obviously close, but toward the end of her life there were a lot fewer photos starring the twins, and more photos with Grace and a group of people that weren't in her pictures previously.

Hmmm. Hanging out with a new crowd, Grace? What did you get yourself into?

Most of the pictures are in the setting of someplace seedy-looking. There are a few in bars or clubs, but not the kind that I'd ever take Olive to. And there are a few that look like they're in people's houses, and from the looks of Grace's face in them she's not living a happy life. I feel sorry for the woman, even though I've never met her. I don't know what could have taken her away from her sister, who obviously loved her, and into the arms of these people in the newer pictures.

And then I think about Elle. I later heard that during my last deployment she'd made some new friends. And not the good kind of friends, either. From asking around afterward I learned enough to know that she'd gotten herself into something that she hadn't known how to dig her way out of, and that she hadn't trusted me enough to tell me. Just thinking about it puts a lump the size of a boulder in my throat.

I should have been the kind of man she'd come to about that. Maybe if I hadn't been halfway across the world at the time…maybe if I'd been more present. Maybe…

I glance up when the door to the hospital room opens. Shaking my head groggily, I look around and realize I must have fallen asleep, my head resting on Olive's stomach. The steady rise and fall of her breathing was better than a damn nature sounds machine.

My eyes jerk to the door when I hear a gasp. Turning, my heart drops. Checking my phone, I see that it's just after 6:00 a.m.

Jeremy and Rayne must have taken a red-eye.

Rayne, rushing over to the bed, leans down beside me, inspecting Olive like she just needs to see for herself if her sister is okay.

"How is she?" she asks, her voice urgent and full of worry.

Pushing back and standing, I gesture toward the chair. "She's going to be okay, Rayne. Her clavicle is bruised from the impact of…the truck hitting the guardrail…but she was lucky."

She turns to me, eyes welling. "It wasn't just luck, Ronin.

She had you." Rayne turns back to her sister, and I turn to face my best friend.

He stares me down, then inclines his head toward the hallway. After the door is closed behind us, Jeremy leans against the wall, facing me. He lifts one eyebrow, before scanning me.

"You okay?"

I nod, shaking my head absently. "I'm fine. It's Olive I'm worried about."

Jeremy's eyes narrow, and he folds his arms across his chest. "Start talking."

With Jeremy Teague, I have no secrets. It's just the way we roll. We've been best friends since we met in Ranger school, and when we were assigned to the same team, we became brothers. Even if I now wanted to keep what was going on with Elle's homicide investigation from him, I couldn't. It's just not how we're made.

By the time I'm done with my story, ending with how Olive and I ended up in the ICU, he was pacing, his hands raking through his long hair.

"Fucking hell," he mutters. "I've been gone for a week, and all this has gone down?"

I spread my arms wide. "I don't know what to say, man. I did what you asked. I've been watching over her. It just turns out that what she had going on is deeper than you thought it was."

He snorts. "No shit. If I'd known...we never would have left. Rayne was a fucking basket case all the way here. I just tried to keep it together, keep her calm, for Deck's sake."

I look up, glancing around us, because I suddenly realize that his son isn't here. "Where is Decker?"

Jeremy's eyes light up the way they always do when his son is mentioned. He didn't get to spend the first eight years of the kid's life with him, but he's definitely all in as a dad now. And really proud of it.

"Called Berkeley and Dare from the airport. We dropped Decker off at their house on our way here."

Nodding, that out of the way, I return the subject back to the matter at hand. "She could have died, Brains."

Even I can hear the stark note of desperation in my voice. I'm crawling out of my skin; the only thing I want to do is hunt Mick Oakes down and make him bleed for what he had done to Olive. Even if he wasn't driving one of those SUVs, I know without a doubt that he was behind it. No matter what Olive believes.

Jeremy stops moving, facing me slowly. He searches my face, and then his jaw tightens. "No fucking way."

Raising my hands to my head, I pace away from him. When I turn back around, I look him in the eye. "It's not what you think."

Jeremy stalks toward me. All the good nature, all the brotherly worry on his face erased, he stops inches from me. The anger in his eyes is blatant.

"You slept with her?" He's almost vibrating from head to toe, his eyes blazing with fury. "I asked you to keep an eye on her, and you took that to mean 'have at my sister-in-law'?"

Raising my hands, I hold my ground. My voice is low and hard when I answer. "It's not like that. I have feelings for her."

Jeremy's eyes go wide, and he takes a step back. He says nothing as the seconds tick by, evaluating me. I know he's reading me for the truth, and that eventually, he'll figure out that I wouldn't lie to him.

Especially not about this.

Finally, he sighs. "I love you, brother...you know that. But I'm being really goddamn serious right now. You can't jerk her around. She's my fucking *family*. You've been spending time with her for less than a week."

I close my eyes briefly, and when I speak again, it's from my heart. "You think I don't know that? I know how important she is to Rayne, and to you. But now, she's damn important to me, too."

He just watches me, and then he sighs. "Fucking hell. Tell me what you need from me, Swagger."

And I know that, at least for now, that's his stamp of approval. As long as I don't fuck shit up before it's all over.

"I will. For now, I just want to be there for her, take her home when she's released."

Jeremy's tone is hopeful. "To my place? That's where Rayne will want her."

Now it's my turn for a scathing glare. "Sure, if you want us both. I'm not letting her out of my sight. Otherwise, I'm bringing her back to my place."

One corner of Jeremy's mouth kicks up in a grin. "I've never seen you like this."

I lift one shoulder in a shrug. "Never been like this before. At least, not in a very long time."

Walking up to me, Jeremy rests a hand on my shoulder. "Looks good on you."

And I'm not going to admit it to him, but I can honestly say that it feels good, too.

24

RONIN

When we walk into my condo, Olive lowers herself slowly onto the couch and laughs. "I seriously thought Rayne was going to tie me up to get me to stay at their house."

I toss the keys for the rental car onto the kitchen island and turn to face her. Jeremy and Rayne had taken us home from the hospital this morning, and Olive had stayed with Rayne while Jeremy drove me to get a rental. When I arrived at the Teague house to grab Olive, Rayne had put up a good fight.

Ultimately, I left the decision up to Olive. I know that staying with Jeremy and Rayne, with Brains there to protect her, would keep her just as safe as if she'd been staying with me. And that's all I want…is for her to be safe.

Well, fuck. No, that's not all I want. I want her to be safe, and I want her with me. Now more than ever. The thought of leaving her there and coming back to my condo alone made me feel sick and cold.

Looking at her now, all cozy on my couch like she belongs

here, sends a warm sensation floating through my chest and hot, sizzling want straight to my dick.

Fucking hell, I want her.

"Yeah, I'm pretty sure she's not gonna forgive me for this for a long time." Chuckling quietly, I move forward and sit on the coffee table in front of her. "What can I get you? Are you hurting? Do you want the pain meds they gave you?"

She's thoughtful for a second, and I can tell she's evaluating her pain level. Then she smiles, and I'm struck hard by how much I've come to want that smile in my life every day. We might not agree on everything and we may push each other's buttons. But when she smiles? It lights up all the dark corners of my world.

"I don't think I need them. I mean, there's definitely an ache, but it's manageable." Her eyes glitter with some kind of mischief I can't wait to get into with her. "Why don't you come a little closer?"

Rearing back, playful smirk in place, I hold my hands out in front of me. "Hold on there, Red. You want to get handsy with me right now? You just got out of the hospital. Jesus." Acting like I'm nothing but offended, I roll my eyes and cross my arms over my chest. All the while I'm loving it as her eyes flash with annoyance.

"You wish. I was only trying to save your ass from sitting on the hard coffee table. But, whatever. You can stay there, it doesn't make a difference to me." She turns her head slightly to the side, like she's finished with the conversation.

The hell you are, Red.

"Oh, yeah? You just want me to walk away?"

She doesn't answer, which just ramps up the competitive nature of what's about to go down.

Pushing up off the table, I cage her in with arms on either side of her against the back of the couch. I lean forward, stopping just inches from her perfect face. Still turned away, she doesn't acknowledge me at all.

The pull and drag, the give-and-take when it comes to this woman. It's so fucking exciting, and I never even knew it was something I wanted.

"So," I murmur, inches from her ear. "You'd be indifferent if I did this?"

I only have to lean for my lips to touch her neck, and I use my tongue to taste her. I feel her shiver underneath my lips, and my hands land on top of her thighs.

"Totally indifferent," she answers. But the high tone her voice has taken says otherwise, and I smile against her neck.

"And this?" Sliding my hands up, I meet the bare skin of her stomach and push upward. When my hands find the lacy material of her bra, I deftly slip the cups down and caress her with my thumbs.

That's my girl. You might be acting like you don't care, but your body tells another story.

Involuntarily, she arches into my hands, and I grip the fullness of her in my palms. Her skin is warm and smooth; she feels so fucking good I could eat her. In fact…

When I glance up at her, the stubborn expression has melted off her face, and her eyes are dark and burning with need, staring down at me.

Lifting a brow, I continue palming her breasts. "So, still not making a difference to you whether I'm here or not?"

She doesn't answer, but her eyes flash and she sucks her bottom lip between her teeth. With a smile, I lower my head below her lifted shirt and pull one tight little nipple into my mouth. I suck hard.

She moans, her hips pushing against me, and I use my teeth to nibble at her heated skin. That only excited her; I can tell by the way her fingers drift up to my hair and start tugging on the top strands.

"Ronin," she gasps.

Between nibbles, licks, and kisses, I grind out the words, "Say it. Say you want this, Red."

I can almost hear her internal struggle. She's weighing the choices: concede to me or continue her stubborn rebellion? I already know the answer though, before she even speaks.

Olive wants me just as much as I need her, and I'm going to try my damnedest to make sure it stays that way.

"Hell," she gasps. "Yes, Ronin. I want you, *now*."

"Then let's take this off." Working carefully so as not to aggravate her injured shoulder, we work together to remove her shirt. Reaching around her so she doesn't have to do it and hurt herself, I make quick work of removing the navy-blue bra.

Something I've learned about Olive? The woman doesn't skimp on underwear. She's even sexier underneath her clothes than she is when she's all dressed up. And knowing that only makes me imagine what she's got on underneath when she's fully dressed.

Pulling back slightly, I grip the edges of the soft, gray leggings she's wearing and pull them down the long length of her legs. Pausing only to remove the purple furry boots she has on, I peel them off of her completely and sit back on the coffee table to admire the beauty before me.

Son of a bitch. How had I gone this long knowing her without insisting on a taste of her? She's fucking perfect, in every way. The navy-blue underwear, tiny things with just a scrap of lace in front and a G-string in back are the next to go, even though I make a mental note to ask her to put them back on for me later. Once they're tossed aside, I lower myself to my knees in front of her.

When I look up to meet her gaze, she stares down at me with an expression in her eyes I can't read. There's lust; absolutely. There's also warmth.

But what else?

Then it hits me. There's self-doubt there, in her eyes. She tugs her bottom lip between her teeth.

"Hey," I murmur. "What's this? What's going through that pretty little head?"

Her glance darts away before it flicks back to mine. "My body...I've put it through a lot, you know? It's not perfect." She runs tentative fingers down the side of her torso. I let my gaze follow, to the faint marks that scar her soft skin.

"Stretch marks," she whispers. "From gaining and losing weight."

Dipping my head, I brush my lips gently across the marring. Before lifting my eyes to hers. "You think stretch marks turn me off? Fuck, woman. Everything about you is drop-dead gorgeous in my eyes. Imperfections? Only make you more real, more beautiful. You believe me?"

The stiff posture she had when she talked about her body relaxes and her eyes go all soft and sexy. "Yes."

Just like before, I start with a finger. This time, I start at the instep of her pretty little foot and drag it up her calf, the inside of her knee, and along her thigh. She twitches and shivers with the trail I make, her muscles flexing against me as I use the other hand to hold her steady.

When I reach the juncture between her thighs, I let my finger trail against the center of her curls.

And my eyes drift shut.

Wet. So fucking wet for me.

"Jesus, Red." My voice comes out in a low rumble. "You don't know what it does to me when I feel you like this. It just makes me want a taste."

Her cheeks flush a deep red, but her eyes grow hotter with the flame that's always burning between us. Her hands knead my shoulders, like she's telling me to hurry up.

"Be patient, sweetheart. I'm gonna taste you. But I want *you* to taste you first."

Her pupils dilate, her eyes flaring wide as I plunge my index finger deep inside her. Fascinated, I stare as I pull it slowly out again and circle it around her tight little clit, already swelling up with pleasure.

God...why is this so fucking sexy, like I've never done it before? Everything is fresh, new, and so goddamn hot.

Lifting my hand to her lips, I insert my finger into her mouth. She closes her plump lips around it and sucks, her eyes closing on a moan.

"See? You taste so fucking good."

Reaching down, I adjust myself, because watching Olive suck on my finger is almost too much for me to handle. My cock is throbbing painfully in my pants, begging me to get inside her.

Dipping my head, I lick her. *Fuck…she tastes better than the last time.*

I'm pretty sure that Olive will never be out of my system. She's going to be a permanent fixture there, and I'm surprised with how okay with that I am.

Moving my hands to hold her hips, I eat her until her muscles are trembling, until her hands are pulling at my hair frantically, until she's moaning my name over and over again. And then I stop.

Impatiently tugging me, her eyes fly open and she stares at me. Giving her a devilish smirk, I step back from her and strip down, leaving my clothes in a heap right beside hers, staring her down like she's the last meal I'll ever eat. Eventually, I'm going to bend her over this couch and pound into her from the back. But not today, after she's just been released from the hospital.

Today, I'm going to let her take control.

Sitting down beside her, I grip her waist and lift her gently onto my lap. Immediately, her soft, warm heat rubs against my throbbing dick, and my hips jerk in response. "Fuck. Don't come yet, Red. Need to be inside you first."

She nods, her eyes glazed over with lust as she rocks over me again. She rests her hands on my shoulders as I lift her hips. I slide inside, just the tip, and total ecstasy washes over me with such intensity that I almost lose my shit.

Then, I still. "Dammit. Condom."

She shakes her head, wiggling as I hold her, trying to sink all the way down on me.

"Wait, baby. I have to go get a condom."

Her eyes focus on mine, and a small smile lifts her lips. "No, you don't. Not unless you want to. I'm clean, and I've been on the pill since college."

Swallowing thickly, I'm frozen. *Do I want to?* Fuck, yes, I want to. But it's not about that. It's the fact that I've never been bare inside any woman other than my dead wife.

Olive sees my hesitation, and the disappointment in her eyes is clear. Her hurt cuts me deep, something I never want to cause her.

Fuck, fuck, fuck.

"It's not you," I start, grabbing her hand so she can't run too far. "I just never—"

Shaking her head, she smiles at me. It's a little sad, but there's no anger in her eyes. "Go grab one. I'll wait right here."

Staring at her, I'm instantly sorry that I hesitated at all. If I'm sleeping with Olive, then she's the only woman I'm sleeping with. And if she's the only one—and I have all these crazy-as-fuck feelings for her—why wouldn't I choose to be bare inside her?

Fucking hell.

No more hesitating.

Pulling her back down on top of me, careful not to jar her shoulder, I allow her to sink fully down. Her lips part on a gasp, and she's hot, wet, and tight. My three favorite things.

"I-I thought…" she stutters, her eyes fluttering shut as I gently thrust my hips upward.

"I thought, too. In fact, I was thinking way too damn much. I want this...I want you." She dips her forehead against mine, her soulful eyes burning into me.

"You do?" She gasps as I find a rhythm with my thrusts. Joining in, she bounces on top of me, and I can already feel the tightening at the base of my spine that spreads out to my legs, signaling the impending release.

"Yes. God, yes. And..." I close my eyes against the pleasure. "And Red...this thing we're doing?"

She wraps her arms around my neck and squeezes, her legs beginning to shake. "Yeah?"

"It's just me and you. Got that? While we're doing this...you're mine." I look deep into her eyes, making sure she understands exactly what I'm saying.

She nods, her fingers sliding along my slick skin, and I watch as her lip slips between her teeth.

"And you're mine?"

As I sink into her again and again, and I finally grab hold of that lip with my own teeth and suck it into my mouth, I contemplate that. And I know without a doubt that it's the truth.

"Yeah, Red. I'm yours."

25

OLIVE

Over the next week, as my shoulder heals, Ronin and I strike up an easy routine. We wake up next to each other every morning, usually naked, and I go with him to work each day. I've been checking in with Beth regularly, and chatting with Berkeley about the client she took over with Paisley, and my work is going as well as it can without me being in the office or meeting with clients. All the same, I can't wait until this situation with M.J. is resolved so that I can go back to my normal life.

But do I want to go back to my normal life?

Back to the career I love, working in my office, and being able to go wherever I want whenever I want, yes. That, I'm definitely ready for. But returning to a life where Ronin doesn't exist in my day-to-day life? I can't imagine going back.

All the men of Night Eagle, at least the ones who work on the elite special ops team with Ronin, are holed up inside the conference room at the office every morning for a long meeting. I know they're working on something new, something they're being pretty tight-lipped about, and a growing knot of worry takes up space in my chest. Ronin is great at what he does. And I'm aware that he's seriously badass, as are the rest of the guys. But I still worry about him. The thought of him walking into a situation that might end with him not coming back home to me is very real, and scary as hell.

On Friday evening, strong, muscled forearms appear on either side of me where I sit at Ronin's desk. His clean, masculine scent leaks into my senses, and his warm breath tickles my ear as he whispers, "You look so fucking sexy sitting at my desk."

My heart immediately kicks up, off to the races, and all because of a few words spoken out of Ronin Shaw's dirty mouth. I might have a silly heart, but at this point I just don't care. This man does it for me.

Leaning back against him, I sigh. "Oh, yeah? Do you want to see how sexy I'll look somewhere else? Like, say, in your bed?"

A throaty growl, and then: "Yes. *Hell, yes.*"

Someone behind us clears his throat, and Ronin straightens with a curse while I giggle softly.

"Oh, don't let me interrupt you guys. Do you want to share something with the class?" Jeremy walks around the side of the desk, perching with one hip on top while he eyes us with complete amusement.

"Not really." Ronin's clipped tone is just for show. He loves Jeremy like a brother, which has been clear to me while I've watched them this week.

"So, you ready to do this?" Jeremy folds his arms across his chest and grins.

Ronin shakes his head, and as I glance at him, he's staring at Jeremy with a death glare.

"Do what?" I ask.

Ronin turns to me, his expression immediately softening.

I love that about him. How he's so hard and can be really calculated when it comes to work or his professional life, but when he's with me he's warm, and caring, and sometimes I even catch a glimpse of what could turn into love in his eyes. I know he's not there yet, though, and maybe I'm not either, and that's okay. If he can figure out what happened to his wife, help solve her murder, then maybe he'll be able to move on. With me.

"Listen, Red."

Oh, Lord. Nothing good ever comes after "Listen, Red."

I stay silent, my brows lifted as I wait for him to continue.

"The team and I were talking, and we've been on the defensive long enough where Mick Oakes is concerned. No one has seen or heard from him since the night he confronted us in the parking garage. I can't confirm that he was in one of the SUVs that ran us off the bridge and I can't just sit here anymore, waiting to see what he's going to do next. I'm going to The Oakes tonight to find him. Bennett says there's a big party at the bar tonight. I'm hoping that Mick is taking his ownership of the bar seriously and that he'll show up." Ronin watches me carefully as he speaks, like he's waiting for some extreme reaction from me.

Which he just might get.

"And what will that accomplish?" Trying to keep my voice even, I stare him down.

Ronin's eyes narrow. "It'll give me a chance to peek into his twisted mind. The bastard tends to talk too much. Maybe he'll let something slip, like what his end game is with you or what he'll do next. I'm not sitting around while he's plotting to do something bad to you, Red. I can't do that. Don't ask me to."

My chest fills with an inflated balloon of emotion. Fear, appreciation, rage, all at the same time. "Jeremy's going with you?"

"Yup," Jeremy declares at the same time that Ronin answers, "No."

They stare at each other, resolution strong in Ronin's eyes as confusion registers in Jeremy's.

"What do you mean, 'no'?" Jeremy stands up tall, placing both hands down on the desk.

Ronin rubs his chin. "I mean, you can't come. We talked about this. It's really good right now that Oakes doesn't know who you are. If you need to blend in later on, you can. Taking you in there with me tonight will ruin any chance of that for later. I'm going to have Bennett for backup."

Jeremy rolls his eyes. "I'm your backup."

Ronin shakes his head, holding firm. "Not tonight."

Standing from my chair, I place my hands on my hips and step into Ronin's line of sight. "And what about me? Am I going to hang out at the condo by myself and just wait around as you put yourself in a dangerous situation?"

Even though I'm fine with hanging out by myself, I know for a fact that Ronin won't go for it. It's an underhanded blow, a way to hopefully make him change his mind and stay with me. M.J. is completely unpredictable. I don't want Ronin anywhere near him.

"Hell, no." Ronin's eyes flash with darkness. His voice is clipped and his tone tells me this isn't negotiable. "You're going home with Brains. He'll keep you safe for me until I'm done."

Ronin moves toward me, invading my space. Placing both hands on the sides of my face, the intensity of his green gaze deepens, and I'm held captive in his stare. "It's going to be fine. Nothing will happen to me, Red, I can promise you that."

My voice is small. "Can you?"

He nods. "I can. I'll be back for you later tonight. Try not to worry. Enjoy this time with your sister and your nephew."

Thinking about Decker does bring a little bit of calming joy to my heart. I nod, slowly. "Fine. But you be safe. And tell Bennett I'll kill him if he lets anything happen to you."

Ronin's lips twitch, tilting upward in his sexy smile. "I'll pass along the message."

Closing the difference between us, I brush my lips against his. His hand cups the back of my neck as he deepens the kiss, his tongue finding mine for the slightest touch before he pulls away.

I remember that Jeremy's watching us when I hear his amused chuckle, and I can feel my face burn.

"Oh, shut up, Jeremy."

"You lose, Aunt Olive!" Decker's voice is so delighted I can't help but grin at him.

Ruffling his hair, I put on my best "aw shucks" face. "Darn

it! You beat me every single time we play War, Decker. Tell me your secrets!"

His face goes all serious, and it's so cute I just want to pinch his cheeks.

"My dad says it's all about strategy," he says solemnly. "I have to make sure I'm one step ahead of you the whole time, or I don't have a prayer."

I manage to restrain the laugh that really wants to burst out of my mouth. "Oh, I see. Well, your dad seems to know a lot about these things."

He grins, pride lighting up his beautiful green eyes, the exact same eyes he shares with his father. "He does. My dad saves the world."

Jeremy glances up from his position at the kitchen island. He swallows, and his eyes go soft.

My heart squeezes, causing my chest to constrict almost painfully. Thoughts of Ronin flit through my mind, and I try hard to close them out because if I start thinking and worrying about him now, I'll never stop.

"He is, Decker. You're right about that." I swallow hard, and at the kitchen island, Rayne looks up sharply.

"Hey, Deck!" she calls. "I think it's time to go put on your pajamas, brush your teeth, and get ready for bed."

Tossing down the cards, he hops up. "C'mon, Night!"

Jeremy's huge Cane Corso dog hops to his feet and lets out a short, agreeable bark. I smile at the pair as they bound toward the stairs and disappear into the second floor of the historical, downtown Wilmington home that Jeremy restored himself, and that he and Rayne now share with their son.

Jeremy slides off his stool and clears his throat. "I'm gonna go supervise that situation." He leans in to kiss my sister's lips, then winks as he walks past me on his way to the stairs.

Knowing that my sister wants to talk, I wander into the kitchen and sit down at a stool at the island. We've already had dinner, delicious shredded beef tacos courtesy of Jeremy, since Rayne doesn't cook, and Rayne is putting the last of the dishes into the dishwasher.

"What's going on with you?" she asks as she loads a dinner plate into the washer. "I heard something in your voice there when you were talking to Decker."

Drumming my nails on the counter, I avoid all eye contact with my sister. "It's nothing."

Slamming the dishwasher close, she places both hands down on the island and leans toward me. "Sure it's not. We can stay here all night, Olive. Tell me what this is between you and Ronin."

I suck in a breath and jump down from the barstool. Pacing the length of the kitchen, I pause and look at my sister. "Shit, Rayne. I think I'm in love with him."

The revelation is almost as much of a shock to me as it is to Rayne. We stare at each other a moment, my hands frozen down by my sides, her face still with shock and disbelief.

"You…you *love* him?" Rayne leans heavily on the counter as she eyes me with utter disbelief.

Dammit, do I? I'd just blurted it out, but hell, what do I know about love? At one point I'd thought I loved M.J., and look how that turned out? I've spent the last few years making it a point to avoid the entire emotion, because I honestly thought, after my horrible past with both my uncle and then with M.J., that I wouldn't be able to feel any kind of real emotion with someone.

But with Ronin, as hard as I tried to avoid it, I simply couldn't. Our connection was too strong, he was too much for me to handle while simultaneously being exactly what I needed.

"I love him." I say it again, testing the words out for the first time. "I love him, Rayne."

Her eyes go all soft and gooey, while at the same time keeping a hint of concern in their navy-blue depths. "How?"

I shrug, giving her a sheepish smile. "It happened without my permission. I'm pretty sure without his, too. I don't even know if he feels the same way I do. I mean, I know he feels *something.* But he's trying to solve his wife's murder, and there's a lot on his plate. I think he originally just took me on as an obligation to you and Jeremy."

Her mouth turns down at the corners. "I've gotten to know Ronin pretty well, Olive. And there's nothing he does just out of obligation. If he does something at all, it's with his whole heart, his whole being. He's protecting you because *he wants to.* Maybe at first, he told himself it was for some obligatory reason to help out a friend. But now? No way. I saw him at the hospital. He feels the exact same way you do."

Shaking my head slowly, I plop my chin into my hands. "And now he's over at The Oakes, looking for M.J. Trying to protect me. When I got that first e-mail from M.J. I just knew, in my gut, that he was back in my life. And now…now everything is so out of control. Ronin really believes that he's the one who ran us off the road."

Rayne's gaze is steady as she stares into mine. "God, Olive. I'm so sorry you have to go through this. But trust Ronin. Let him try to keep you safe, okay?"

My eyes pull to the ceiling as I attempt to keep tears at bay. "In my brain, I know he can handle this. But everything inside of me is screaming to keep those two apart. I don't want to lose him, Rayne."

And I realize that I'm scared to death. Of losing Ronin before I'm even able to tell him how I feel for him.

26

RONIN

When I walk into The Oakes, the first thing I notice is how empty the place is. It's never totally busy, but there are always people linking the bar, waiting for drinks or a conversation, and you can always find couples or single people eating and drinking at the high-top tables. Tonight, though? The bars' been reserved for the large party coming in later, and right now it's totally empty.

Bennett moves around the bar when he sees me walk in, hands stuffed in his jeans pockets. He ducks his head low when we're only half a foot apart. "You sure you want to do this?"

Imitating his casual stance, I give one nod. "Damn sure."

He tilts his head to the side. "You got guys outside?"

I answer him with a smirk. "I've got one guy outside, my teammate Grisham Abbott. If I need him to sneak up in here, he's the best one for that. We call him Ghost for a reason. He also helped me plan this little meeting in a pinch this week.

But other than him, I've got one genius little hacker out there, a woman we call Viper."

Bennett chuckles. "Don't think I'd want to meet her unless I'm packing."

"She's dangerous, but not in that way. She's on the communications tonight, making sure everything goes smoothly with the camera Teague fitted me with. She'll make sure she and the rest of the guys back at HQ can hear and see everything going on here tonight. We might get lucky, might not have to insert ourselves into the Margiano family organization at all."

Bennett's mouth curls with disgust. "Still can't believe Mick mixed his father's business up in all that bullshit. Mick Senior ran this place clean for thirty years, despite his brother-in-law's bullying to let him have a piece of it. All the bastard wanted was another place to clean his dirty money, another back room to make his filthy deals. Now he'll have it."

I didn't lie to Olive earlier, I just couldn't include the part about Night Eagle performing an operation. Jeremy, as much as he wanted to have my six tonight, was needed to stay with Olive. I needed him to make sure she was safe while I'm dealing with Mick. If I have any doubt that she's okay, I won't be able to do my job. And the truth is, this thing with Mick Oakes is about more than what he's done to my Red. Hopefully tonight we can take him and his uncle's organization down in one fell swoop, and I'm determined to get it done.

Bennett slaps my back and then turns, mumbling under his breath, "I'm going to have to find a new place to work once this shit is all over."

I follow him and pull out a barstool. I know in my gut that at some point, Mick will show up here.

Ordering club soda in a Scotch glass, I sit and sip the drink slowly, keeping my eyes and ears open as I do.

"Been turning people away tonight," Bennett says. "As casually as I can. I even called and canceled on the party. Not that I told Oakes that. I don't need innocents in here when shit goes down."

I nod. "Good plan."

"Your girl safe tonight?" Bennett's eyes go sympathetic. "And how's she healing up?"

My girl. Maybe I haven't said the words aloud to anyone else yet but damn if it doesn't feel really good twisting around in my brain. I told her she was mine, didn't I?

"She's good. And she's with Teague tonight. He's her brother-in-law, and the only one I trust to keep her safe."

Bennett lifts his chin in understanding and wipes down a spot on the bar.

I'd say it takes about half an hour for the bastard to stroll in through the back door like he owns the place. Bennett goes stiff, because he knows Mick Oakes actually *does* own it, or might as well, and my blood immediately starts to burn, thinking about what could have happened to Olive when Mick forced us off the bridge.

Mick stops short when he sees me, like he's not expecting me to be here. Rising from the barstool and trying to relax my fingers from the fists they automatically formed, my lips thin out into a scowl. "You look surprised to see me."

One hand goes behind his back, where I know he keeps his

gun inside his waistband. He always needs his security blanket. *Fucking pussy.* My scowl turns upward into a knowing smirk.

Once he's reassured that his gun is in place, he steps forward with a cautious expression. "No, not really. But it doesn't matter, either way. I am surprised you didn't bring your whore with you."

The word *whore* in reference to Olive nearly makes me lose my shit. She's not that, she never has been. And this man, the one who once said he cared about her, who apparently wants her back, isn't worthy to breathe the same air she does. And he won't, not ever again. "She prefers not to be anywhere near you, Oakes. Especially after what you did."

He leans against the end of the bar, and I can see the anger flash in his eyes before he responds. "What I did? I don't know what you're talking about. I did hear that you and the lady were in an unfortunate traffic accident last week, though. She okay?"

He seems almost genuine in asking if Olive is okay, which is complete bullshit. "Let's not play games here, all right? We both know you had a part in that accident. And you know what? If it was just me, I wouldn't waste my time on you. But this is about *her*, and I'm not going to let you hurt her again."

He pushes off the bar and crosses over to me. "You're just a temporary distraction for her. She doesn't belong to you, Shaw."

I lift my chin. Olive does belong to me, but not in the way he thinks. He thinks of her as something material to possess. I think of her as something precious to protect. She belongs to me because she wants to. Not because I'm forcing her to stay.

But Mick Oakes won't understand that, so I don't bother to tell him.

"If you want her so bad, why would you put a hit out on her?" My tone is even, but all I really want to do is wipe the stupid expression off his face.

Mick's face fills with rage. "I didn't. I wouldn't. Is that what she thinks?"

I'm filled with confusion, but I merely quirk a brow. "Isn't that what you did?"

Mick glances behind him, like someone could be watching, before turning back to me and licking his lips. "I didn't. I don't want to hurt her. That shit doesn't even make sense."

Stepping closer, my eyes narrow and my jaw clenches so tight my back teeth snap together. "Then who would?"

Mick goes rigid. His eyes wild, he rolls them toward the ceiling like he's trying to solve some kind of puzzle.

When he finally speaks, it's like someone tosses a bucket of ice-cold water all over me.

"Dead girls don't talk," he whispers.

I move before I have a plan, shoving barstools out of my way and flying at him like a fucking rocket. Grabbing his collar, I shove him up against the dull wooden bar. Drawing my gun, I cock it and press the cold metal against his temple. My voice goes low and very, very dangerous.

"What the fuck did you just say?"

27

OLIVE

From upstairs, we hear a series of loud thumps and then the sound of hysterical laughter.

Rayne's eyes roll upward. "Seriously. They can't get a simple bedtime task done without losing their minds."

Grinning, I tip my head toward the stairs. "Should we go check on them?"

As we walk past the front door, I eye the keypad on the wall beside it. Earlier, I watched as Rayne put in the four-digit code: her and Decker's birthday numerals.

Following Rayne upstairs, I would normally smile at the sound of Decker's and Jeremy's raucous laughter, mixed in with Night's joyful barks. This house, this family my sister treasures, is special and happy. I can almost taste the memories being made here. From the dreamy look in Rayne's eyes, it's clear how much she loves them.

But right now, all I can think about is Ronin and how I can get to him. He might not need me right now, but I sure as hell need to be with him.

Rayne turns to me. "Should we get into our pajamas and then go down and watch a movie?"

Another time, big sister. I smile and nod. "Sure. Let me just use the restroom first."

As soon as the bathroom door is closed behind me, I fling open the cabinet and search the contents. I haven't thought this through, but I know I need to get out of this house. I love my sister and Jeremy so much for wanting to protect me, but I know in my heart that I should be with Ronin. There's a deep feeling of dread lining my belly, something that started the second he walked away from me and has only been growing stronger since. If M.J. wants me, he already knows he has to get through Ronin to do that.

Ronin needs me. I need to protect him this time.

My eyes land on a pair of nail scissors, and I yank them out of the cabinet. Holding them in my fist, I dig the blade into the palm of my hand and drag it across my skin.

A thin line of blood appears, compete with the bite of pain that signals my freedom. Opening the bathroom door, I call out, "Hey, Rayne?"

She appears in her bedroom doorway. "Yeah?"

Holding out my hand, I'm satisfied to see the blood oozing from the shallow wound. "Where's your first aid stuff?"

Her eyes widen. "You cut yourself?"

Nodding, I try to appear sheepish. "Yeah. I just need to clean it up and put a bandage on, though. No big deal."

She tilts her head, looking at my hand. But I know my sister, and she hates the sight of blood. She averts her eyes, and triumph swells inside me. "Downstairs in the kitchen cabinet above the desk."

Nodding, I walk past her and head down the stairs. I won't have much of a head start, but it'll be enough.

As soon as I walk into the kitchen I pause only long enough to pull the dishtowel off the counter for my bleeding hand, grab the keys to Rayne's SUV and enter the alarm code into the keypad by the garage door. Also muting the system so that the door opening doesn't cause a chiming sound. I'm quickly out of the house and into the garage.

My heart thrums, beating like a wild bird caged, as I start the ignition and press the button on the visor to open the garage door. And then I'm backing out of the garage and racing down the street, the engine revving in my effort to get to Ronin as fast as I can.

28

RONIN

Oakes struggles against my hold, but I'm hanging on to his collar with a vise grip, leaving him pinned against the wall like a fly caught in a web. I shove the gun even harder against his sweaty skin. Bennett casually moves to the end of the bar, leaning against it and folding his arms like he doesn't have a care in the world. But I know that if I looked at him, I'd see the intense scrutiny in his eyes as he assessed the situation.

"*Say it again.*" My teeth grind together as I stare into Mick Oakes's dark eyes. My insides tremble like jelly, but my hand is steady as my finger inches toward the trigger.

He swallows. "I said, *dead girls don't talk.* It's my uncle's motto. He doesn't trust women, never has. Not since his wife tried to take what she knew about his business to the cops. He ended up killing the cop she confided in right before he killed her."

My grip tightens, and he winces as the muzzle digs into his flesh. I suck in breaths like I'm running out of oxygen, because it feels like I am. I stare at Oakes for a second longer, then I release him and pace away.

Bennett, still behind the bar, keeps pace with me. "Talk to me, Shaw."

I holster my gun. Lifting my hands, they rake through my hair over and over again. The only way Oakes could know that line, was if…if his uncle was the one responsible for Elle's murder. Whether he killed her himself or had someone else do it…it doesn't matter.

I watched Mick while he spoke. The rage simmering in my stomach wasn't enough to kill every instinct I ever learned as a trained interrogator. The man didn't have a single tell that would have signaled he was lying. He's tense, and he's scared because he's a coward piece of shit, but he's telling the fucking truth.

Finally. I know who murdered Elle.

Turning to Bennett, I look him directly in the eye. "His uncle killed my wife."

Bennett's eyes go wide, and then he drops his head back to stare at the ceiling. "Jesus *fuck.*"

"Hey." Oakes's voice is sharp. "What the hell are you talking about?"

I turn slowly to face him. "About seven years ago, did you know a woman by the name of Elle Shaw?"

Oakes's face goes pale.

I take a step closer, the rage inside me boiling to a dangerous level. "Tell me what you know."

Oakes sinks onto a barstool. "She…I was introduced to her through a friend of a friend. Apparently, she'd racked up a shitload of debt that she didn't want her husband to find out about."

I close my eyes briefly. "What kind of debt?"

Mick Oakes looked at me warily. "Credit cards. She said it was bad. I offered her a job with one of our family businesses, told her she could work for us to help pay the debt. She worked on the books, in addition to her regular bookkeeping job. But she came across some numbers she shouldn't have seen and got it in her head that she could pay off her debt in one fell swoop if she received a big payout from my uncle."

I close my eyes. *God, Elle…why? Why would you get yourself into that shit? You should have come to me.* "She demanded a payoff."

Mick nodded. "Yeah. My uncle…he didn't play games like that. She paid for it."

Stopping, I turn and slam my hands down on the bar. "You motherfucking *bastard*! You should have told her to go to her *husband*!"

My long strides eat up the distance so that I can look Oakes in the eye. "Did you sleep with her?"

He shakes his head immediately. "No. No, I didn't. She wasn't down for that, and I was all wrapped up in Olive at the time. Still am."

Was I supposed to believe him? Like he was some stand-up guy who wouldn't emotionally abuse his girlfriend? I can't even process all of this right now. I knew Elle had debt. So he seems to be telling the truth about that at least. I found out about the extent of her debt after she died but I never knew why. Was she lonely while I was gone? She was apparently afraid to talk to me about it and decided to get another job behind my back.

Goddammit. What kind of husband must I have been? The kind whose wife couldn't trust him with her own financial stress? And now she's gone. I'm never going to be able to ask her about it, never going to be able to reconcile with the fact that I wasn't there for her when she needed me. I wasn't there to stop her from getting involved with the fucking Margiano family.

What am I supposed to *do* with this?

My cell phone buzzes in my pocket, and I think about ignoring it until I remember that my team is listening in on this conversation. Yanking it out of my pocket, my answer is clipped. "Yeah."

"Swagger." Grisham's voice is a mixture of sympathy and urgency. "Olive just pulled up in Rayne's SUV. Want us to grab her, or do you want—" He's interrupted by the sound of squealing tires, which I can hear over the phone and coming from directly outside the bar. "What the fuck?"

Grisham's curse ends in a shout, and I end the phone call and sprint to the front door, gesturing for Bennett to stay with Oakes. My heart thumping wildly, I throw open the door of the bar and burst into the night. Just in time to see a black SUV nearly tip on two wheels as it peels out of the parking lot.

Grisham is out of the truck, weapon drawn, staring at the vehicle as it speeds off into the night.

Glancing around the otherwise empty lot, I spot Sayward sitting in the passenger seat of the NES vehicle she and Ghost rode here in, and I see Rayne's SUV parked a few feet away. But I don't see Olive anywhere.

Grisham turns, and his face says everything I don't want to know.

"What the hell just happened, Ghost?" I bite out the words, silently pleading with him to tell me something other than what I'm thinking.

God, no. No. Please, no.

Grisham's response is grim. "Had to have been Margiano's guys. They took her. We can follow, but they've got a pretty good head start. Might not find them."

Shaking my head, I glance toward the bar. "No. I have a better idea. Meet me back at NES."

When I storm back into the bar, I go straight for Oakes and this time, I grab him by the throat. Squeezing until his eyes bulge, I make sure each word is said slowly enough for him to understand.

"Where. Did. They. Take. Her?"

I can't tell if his eyes are wide from fear, or if it's because I'm slowly squeezing the life out of him. But I won't get an answer if I don't loosen my grip, so I let go and throw him backward. He stumbles back and then reaches for his gun.

"I wouldn't do that."

When I glance at Bennett, he's already holding his pistol, aimed at Oakes's head. "Keep it holstered, Mick. I've wanted to shoot you for too long…don't give me a reason."

Mick swallows, fury flashing in his eyes. Then he turns to me. "What are you talking about?"

His phone buzzes. He ignores it, focusing on me, but I dip my head toward his pocket. "Take that."

Eyeing me with suspicion, he pulls it out and reads the text. Then he curses and shoves the phone back in his pocket. "I gotta go."

I run through all the scenarios in my head but I know I have to let him go. It will be our best bet to find Olive. But letting him walk out of this bar is going to be one of the hardest things I've done in a long time.

Turning on his heel Mick is out, gone through the back exit, before I glance up at Bennett.

"Start talking," he says.

When I tell him what happened in the parking lot, and the plan I have for letting Mick go, his eyes burn with rage. "I'll close this bar down. And then I'm coming with you."

I nod.

When Bennett goes to the office in the back of the bar and returns with a heavy-looking duffle bag slung on his shoulder, I glance at him, impatience bleeding out of me. "You leaving town?"

He shrugs, heading for the front door. "We might need this. Trust me."

Not sure what that means, I let it go. Bennett could be carrying a dead body in that bag and it wouldn't mean shit to me right now. All I want is to find my girl and bring her home.

I need to get to her. *Now.*

Bennett and I run out to the parking lot and we ride in silence as we speed to the NES offices.

I have so many thoughts running through my head. I've just learned the identity of the man responsible for my wife's death. And at some point, I'm going to have to deal with that.

I'm going to have to grieve for Elle all over again, and I'm going to have to come to terms with the fact that the one thing I've been searching for the last seven years of my life has been found. I never thought far enough ahead to say what I'd possibly do when the investigation was finally closed.

But now? Now I have something real and true to live for. Something I never thought I'd find again. And maybe I haven't found it *again*. Maybe I've found it for the first time, because, what I'm finally accepting, is that what I have with Olive is completely different from what I had with Elle.

Once we pull up to the NES offices Bennett's quiet as I use my hand to open the front door, and he mutely takes in the surroundings of the office as we head straight for the conference room.

When we walk in, everyone is already assembled. I look to Grisham. "You get it?"

"I did. Tracker is on Oakes's car, and as soon as he stops driving we'll have a location."

Jeremy speaks up. "I'm sorry, man. As soon as we realized she'd left, I went after her. I called the guys, and they told me what had happened."

I shake my head. "Not your fault. She's stubborn as hell. Now I just want to bring her stubborn ass back home safe and sound. I need you all to help me do that."

Jacob speaks up. "You know we will. Almost every man at this table has been where you are right now, and it's always come out in our favor. That won't change tonight."

I nod, thankful and ready to go after her. "Thanks."

Jeremy points to the screen situated in front of Sayward. "See this blip on Viper's screen?"

Sayward stiffens at the nickname, but then she relaxes and a tiny smile curves her lips upward. Then her eyes stray to Bennett, and they stay there.

"Oh, shit. Sorry, man. Everyone, this is Bennett Blacke. The guy I told you about. Bennett, this is the team. Can we do intros later?"

Bennett gives the room a lift of his chin, pulling his bag up higher on his shoulder.

Jeremy glances at it. "What you got in there?"

Bennett's lips twitch. "Tools."

I lean in, looking more closely at Sayward's laptop. "That the tracker?"

Jeremy nods. "Yeah. Real tiny, I just got them in last week. Ghost stuck it to the bottom of his muffler, the asshole will never be the wiser."

Sayward speaks up, finally bringing her eyes back to the screen. "He keeps making all of these roundabout turns, going in circles sometimes. I think he thinks you're following him." She snorts.

"Then he thinks I'm a fucking amateur." I watch the blip on the screen.

"What's the plan when he stops?" Dare asks seriously. He looks to Grisham and Jacob, but I speak up.

"Then Viper tells me the location, and I go get her." The decision has already been made in my head, the plan already final.

Both Ghost and Boss Man shake their heads simultaneously.

"Hell, no," Grisham says. "This is Olive, and her life is on the line. Do you really want to just run in there half-cocked?"

"Ronin." Jacob's voice is commanding, and I'd usually listen when he speaks, but this isn't the woman he loves. She's mine, and I know what I'm capable of. I go to refute Jacob but he says, "There will be a plan. You will follow it. Now listen to what Grisham has to say."

Every eye in the room turns to Grisham. Bennett relaxes against a wall, watching this all go down. Deep down, I know that when it comes down to it, he'll have my back. He's not a member of this team, and his loyalty lies with me.

"Talk. But when that beeping stops, I'm out."

Jeremy puts a hand on my shoulder, trying to calm me. But I can't be calmed. Not until Olive is beside me again.

"When he finally gets to wherever he's going, Sayward will find all the information on the location that she can. We'll scout from the outside, figure out the best way to enter. We're also going to need to assess how many people are inside, both innocent and enemy."

I'm already shaking my head. "You don't understand. These people, they're the worst kind. Didn't you hear what I found out tonight?"

Jacob gives me a look that's somehow empathetic and scathing. "Why didn't we know that you'd been investigating your wife's murder?"

I fold my arms across my chest. "Why did you think I was investigating anything?"

His lip quirks. "Because I know you, son. We all do. Sayward looked up that line that tipped you off, 'Dead Girls Don't

Talk.' She connected it to the other case that the police are currently investigating. They told you about the new case, didn't they?"

Jeremy stiffens beside me. "How long?"

I push away from the table and stand. "None of you can possibly understand this." I look at each one of them in turn. "Have any of you ever been married, and then that person was murdered while you were too far away to do anything about it? Have you?"

Dare's voice is quiet. "No. But we're your brothers, Swagger. We have your back no matter what. We'd be there, for whatever you needed."

I turn to look at Jeremy, because I know he's probably the most hurt by my omission. "I didn't want to drag you into it. I needed to see this through on my own."

He stares me down for a minute, and then he lets out a heavy sigh. "I can't fault you, Swagger. I don't know what you went through. When I thought I might lose Rayne and Deck, I about lost my shit. You actually did lose someone. Can't say I wouldn't have done the same thing if I'd been given the opportunity to find a killer."

The rest of the room murmurs their agreement, and finally, Jacob nods.

I take a deep breath.

"Oh," mutters Sayward. "Here we go."

The blipping dot on her screen has stopped moving. Her fingers fly over the keys as she searches for the location.

I slam a palm down on the table. My patience has run out. Olive is out there...alone with these bastards. "These people are basically the goddamn mob. Organized crime, keeping it in the family. The patriarch? He *murders women* who he thinks are screwing with his business. You heard that, right? It happened to Elle. There's no fucking way I'll let it happen to Olive."

"I've got explosives."

Everyone in the room turns toward the sound of Bennett's voice.

He lifts one shoulder in a shrug. "In my bag. It's kind of what I do...blowing shit up is my specialty. So it's a way in, and it gives us the element of surprise. I should be able to get you in there, and Ronin can make sure he gets Olive out."

Grisham steps forward, his face contorted into amused disgust. "So, let me get this straight. You want us to *blast* our way into a cold location, without knowing what's waiting on the other side?"

Bennett meets his gaze head-on. "Yep."

Grisham turns to Jacob. "This dude is crazy."

I stand up beside Bennett, hope and determination mixing inside of me. "Crazy might be what saves Olive's life."

29

OLIVE

I hardly know how it happened.

One minute, I was climbing out of Rayne's SUV and had taken one step toward The Oakes' front door. And the next minute, I was startled by the sound of screeching tires and I was being dragged into another car that was sweeping out of the parking lot.

Gasping to catch my breath, I look at the two large men sitting on either side of me. "What is this?"

Neither of them acknowledge me, but the driver of the car glances in the rearview mirror.

May panic rises up in my throat, but I swallow it down and raise my voice.

"Hey!" I glare at him. "Who are you people? This is kidnapping!"

He looks back at the road, like I've said nothing at all.

Assessing my situation, trying to think around the fearful chaos exploding in my head, I fidget, testing how securely the men beside me will hold me. Can I fight?

"Don't." The man driving the car speaks. He has a northern accent, maybe New York or New Jersey, and he shakes his head when his eyes meet mine in the mirror again. "We have instructions. We're supposed to kill you only if you become a problem."

My blood chills, and I look down at my hands. Taking a deep breath, I hold my head high again and look out the windows. But it's nighttime, and the dark tint keeps me from being able to see my surroundings. I have no idea where we're going, and that scares me most. I left my phone and my purse in Rayne's car.

I've been scared before. Hell, there was a time in my life where fear ruled my days and nights until it was all I could think about. It changed me, ruined me. With a deep breath, I realize that even though I can't control this situation, I can control my reaction to it.

And I refuse to let anyone make me live in fear again.

"Who am I going to see at the end of this little trip?" I ask, my voice steadier than I feel on the inside. "M.J.?"

A snort comes from the man beside me, and I jump because it startles me.

Turning to him with my eyes narrowed, I take him in. Tall, dark features, extremely built beneath his bulky coat and black jeans. Basically, I have no chance of overpowering him, and I'm not stupid enough to try.

"What?" I ask.

"Mick's the reason you're coming with us. He's not smart enough to do what needs to be done, so he'll learn."

Oh, no. If I'm not dealing with M.J. when this ride is over, that means...

Panic flares bright and hot. "No!" I lunge for the door handle, encountering a solid wall of muscle before I can move barely an inch. "Let me out!"

The driver chuckles. "Sit tight, sweetheart. We'll be there in a minute."

Slumping back against the seat, I try to think of a way out of this. But I know there isn't one.

When the vehicle rolls to a stop, I'm pulled from the backseat and led into the dark. We're parked in front of some sort of distribution center. If my biggest fears are true, and I'm dealing with Wilmington's resident crime family, then this building probably houses holdings for one of the many Margiano businesses. I'm led inside, and after the darkness of the night, the bright fluorescent lighting hurts my eyes.

My three bulky captors and I walk through a warehouse space filled with brown cardboard boxes, stacked in columns on the concrete floor and layered two stories high on metal shelving units. Glancing around me, I can't tell what's in the boxes and I know it doesn't matter.

They lead me to the back of the building, where a long table and benches are set up behind a partition. It looks like a break area for workers, but I haven't seen any workers yet. Maybe it's the time of night, but more likely is that the head of the Margiano crime family wanted the place to himself tonight.

Shuddering, I try not to wonder why he wants an audience with me. Not knowing is probably better.

But in reality, I'm about to find out very soon what he wants, and I already know it's not going to be good.

"Sit," one of the men says, pushing my shoulder down onto

the end of a bench. Wincing in pain, I comply, sitting up straight and folding my hands on the table in front of me. Every single muscle I have is tensed and coiled, ready for fight or flight. Whichever one will serve me best at any given moment.

Two of the men walk away, leaving me with one eagle-eyed guard standing against a shelf a few feet away. He doesn't look at me, instead keeping his eyes trained at a point behind my shoulder. He seems bored with the whole situation, like this is just another night for him. When for me, my whole world has just been turned upside down.

I close my eyes against the sudden sting of tears. I was *seconds* away from being in Ronin's arms. At the thought, my eyes fly back open again.

Ronin! *They wouldn't have hurt him, would they?*

Of course they would have. But Ronin was safe inside the bar. I saw his car when I pulled up. He has to be okay.

And if he's okay, that means Jeremy and Rayne are going to tell him that I left their house, and he'll be looking for me.

The thought sends warmth running through my veins and straight to my heart. If the NES knows I'm missing, then I probably won't be missing for long.

But, if Albert Margiano's message is short and sweet, the fact that the special ops team is searching for me won't matter at all.

The man against the wall suddenly stands a little bit taller, and the air around me practically sizzles with tension.

"It's been a long time, Miss Alexander."

Albert Margiano himself walks into my line of vision and perches on the bench across from me. He has to fold his tall, lean body nearly in half to fit, but once he's sitting he appears completely at ease. Fit for a man I imagine must be in his sixties by now, his lined face is actually pretty handsome. He carries himself like a man with power, and platinum sparkles in his ear, on his wrist, and against several fingers.

I assess him, working hard to conceal my fear, swallowing around the enormous lump that's formed in my throat.

The first time I met him was in college when M.J. and I were dating. M.J. had said that his uncle insisted on meeting the girl he chose to spend so much time around, and not knowing exactly who his uncle was, I'd agreed. He was an imposing figure then, and now that I know so much more about him, he's absolutely terrifying.

"It has." I remain reserved, cautious. "You could have just asked to see me."

His expression turns amused. "Oh? And you would have obliged?"

I don't answer, and he chuckles. "I didn't think so."

"What do you want? Is this about the money that M.J. used to pay for my tuition all those years ago? Because I'll gladly pay that back. We haven't been in touch for years, or I would have already."

Margiano waves a hand. "This isn't about money. Although I realize you've made quite a name for yourself with your career in design. It's about something much more important."

I stare at him. "What's more important to you than money?"

His mouth curves into a grin. The sight of it clamps an icy fist of fear around my heart.

"Power. And to remain powerful, every king needs an heir. An heir that places ambition and business above all else. My heir is currently too wrapped up in a woman who doesn't want him. A woman who gave his name to the police after he stupidly left her flowers."

I inhale and let the breath out slowly. Focusing on my breaths is difficult, but I try it again. Inhale. Exhale.

Inhale.

Exhale.

Finally, I speak, but my voice is thin, like the air on a mountaintop. "Please. Let me go home."

Margiano leans forward, his dark eyes now cold and calculating. There's not a trace of amusement left. The lines of his face that can turn his expression into a smile are now almost cruel. There's a reason this man is feared by the darkest, filthiest people in the city.

"I can't do that." The words are like napalm, inciting my heartbeat to catch fire.

"Yes, you can, Uncle." M.J. strolls onto the scene, his tone calm but his eyes angry. "Olive isn't yours to command. She belongs to me."

30

OLIVE

"I don't belong to anyone." I can't help the words. I tried to keep them in, but they flew out of my mouth anyway. "Just let me pay you the money I owe and let me go. I'll recant my statement about the flowers...tell them I was wrong."

M.J. doesn't look at me. Instead, he keeps his eyes trained on his uncle. "This isn't about money or the cops, baby. And you don't owe me anything but a chance to show you that you belong with me."

I bite my lip. "Look, M.J...."

Albert Margiano gestures in my direction, leaning back on the bench and staring his nephew down. "You see? She doesn't want you."

Anger chases hurt across M.J.'s expression. "You don't know what she wants. And this is between me and her. She's not like the others, Uncle."

Albert sighs, dropping his head as if he's exhausted. After a moment, he picks it up again and stands. Crossing to where M.J. stands, he places both hands on his nephew's shoulders and looks deep into his eyes. "She's a woman. She can't be trusted. All this time, you've been fixated on a woman. It's weak, M.J. I've shown you time and time again that they can't be trusted. They're not equals, they're playthings. You're stronger than this. I trust you to be smarter than this. You are not a child anymore, Mick."

M.J. snorts. "Then you should stop treating me like one. Let me have more responsibility. Take a backseat."

Albert tilts his head to the side. "If you truly want that, if you think you're ready, then you need to prove it to me."

M.J.'s eyebrows lift. "I haven't been proving myself to you for years? I even moved back north for a few years, smoothing things over between our business partners."

Albert withdraws his hands and walks a few paces away before turning to face his nephew. "Yes, and you did a good job. When you returned, you added another business to our holdings with the bar, and that was also a gain. I am proud of you. But this?"

He gestures toward me with a frown. "Is a problem."

M.J.'s eyes flash. "Uncle—"

"Kill her."

M.J. stops talking, and silence stretches across the room. I've been staring between them, my gaze bouncing back and forth like a pinball. But at Margiano's last words, I freeze. Even my muscles, flexing to flee this situation, are shocked into stillness.

My eyes land on Mick's, whose gaze is locked on his uncle's.

"That's not going to happen."

Margiano's calculating stare doesn't falter, but he shrugs as if he's carefree. "Then I'll have to do it for you."

M.J. scoffs at this, throwing a hand up flippantly. "You don't do your own dirty work."

Margiano moves faster than I'd expect him to be able to, getting in Mick's face. "You think that's because I can't? Kid, I've been doing dirty work since before you were even a thought in someone's mind. If I don't do 'dirty work,' it's because I've earned the right not to. You have not yet earned that right. And if you cannot do this task, I will do it for you, just like I tried to do when I planned her assassination on the bridge. One way or another, this bitch is going to die. And we'll pin it on Shaw. That fucker's been looking for his wife's killer for years, and I want him off my back for good. Two birds…one big, effective stone."

M.J. seems to sag. He glances at me, meeting my gaze for the first time. For a second, I can see the boy that I used to glimpse back when we were together all those years ago. Sometimes he could be sweet, attentive, and caring. Those times were few and far between. But I can see that boy there now.

The pain is his eyes is evident, but in that instant I know that his hands are tied.

There's nothing that M.J. can do for me now, as much as he wants to.

"Fine." Tearing his gaze away from mine, he straightens and his expression goes dead. The sight of the light leaving his eyes scares me more than anything else has tonight.

Because it means the timer I've been counting on since three men grabbed me in The Oakes parking lot has just run out.

M.J.'s words hold no emotion. "I'll do it."

31

RONIN

Six pairs of eyes scan the low-slung warehouse building Brains's tracking device drew us to. Sayward remained behind at the office, but the rest of my team is with me on this, even the Boss Man.

"One level, two entrances," Grisham muses, his arms folded across his chest. He bounces on his feet, the artificial foot on his left side just as ready for action as the right. Even a roadside bomb couldn't take Grisham Abbot out. "What do you have to help us track heat signatures, Brains?"

Jeremy kneels down beside the XXL Suburban, an NES official vehicle, digging through his bag of tricks. Bennett keeps his duffle close to his side, ready to move at a word.

"Thermal-imaging camera." He holds the device up, but to me it just looks like a regular fucking digital camera. "Be right back. Can I get a hand, Wheels?"

Dare nods, and the two job off to make a lap around the building.

While we wait, I pace. "Boss Man, I gotta get in there. I can stand around like this. Time is running out for Olive."

My voice breaks on the last words, and I swallow thickly to dissolve the emotion. I don't get emotional on missions. I need to keep my head on straight, keep my mind on the op and the op alone.

Otherwise, I'll fuck this up. And that's not an option.

"I promised her." The words fall out of my mouth so quietly, but Ghost still glances over at me with a sharp look.

"Promised her what?"

"I promised her I'd keep her safe. That I wouldn't let anyone hurt her." I stop pacing, and run my hands through my hair.

Ghost is shaking his head, his facial expression pissed. "It's not your fucking fault she's in there. You had her covered. Blame the assholes who took her. Blame Margiano. Blame Oakes. Don't blame yourself."

"I'm going to kill him." My tone is even, measured, and deadly serious.

Boss Man interrupts. "You're not going in there. We won't let you."

It takes Wheels and Brains exactly four minutes to round the building and gather imaging data, but it feels like it has taken four hours. When they return, Brains sends the images to Sayward, who can break down the data on her computer.

That takes another two minutes, but when her voice comes through our coms with the information we need, it's a relief.

"Okay, guys. You've got a group of four standing near the front door, no heat images in the middle of the building, and four in the back. The smallest heat signature is the one I'm guessing belongs to Olive, but it's only a guess."

I freeze. "Is she in the front or the back?"

Sayward doesn't pause. "The back."

Ghost speaks. "Okay, so I'm going to assume the four in front are guarding the door, and the three in back are holding her captive."

"Oakes will be in back with her. And I'm guessing that means the other signature in the back belongs to Albert Margiano himself. He seems to take a personal interest in killing women."

The team around me all nod their heads, in complete agreement.

Bennett speaks up. "OK. We'll bomb the front door as a distraction. And a lucky bonus could be taking out some of the guards in front with the explosion. The building being on one level is good; there's not much chance of bringing down the ceiling all the way in the back if the explosion I create is small and localized enough."

Grisham turns to face Jacob. "You really gonna let this guy blow some shit up?"

Boss Man is evaluating Bennett, really looking at him closely. I can see the older man's intense blue eyes picking him apart, summing him up, deciding if we can use him or not. After a minute, he nods. "Let's go with that plan. Cause a diversion, we'll split up. At the cue, two of us will enter quietly at the back while the other four take out the guards at the front."

Grisham takes over, looking at each of us in turn. "Brains and Swagger, you're at the back. The rest of us will go in at the front. The only mission at this point is to get in, grab Olive, and get out. We can take Margiano out later, especially now that Olive is going to be able to testify to the fact that she was kidnapped with an intent to kill. He'll go down."

Nodding, my heartbeat hammering against my rib cage, I rub my hands together. "Let's do it."

"Lock and load, boys," says Grisham. "Get it done."

Hurrying around to the back of the warehouse with Brains on my heels, I draw my Sig and when we've arrived at the warehouse's back entrance I take up a position on one side of the door while Brains stations himself on the other.

"We've got this," he says quietly. "We'll bring her home."

I nod. "We'd fucking better."

Jeremy slyly grins. "So this Bennett dude likes blowing shit up? Where'd you find him?"

"He's a good guy. He doesn't have to be here, but he's doing it for me. I'm going to owe him after this, but he's the kind of guy I won't mind owing a favor."

Jeremy nods his understanding. "Roger that."

Bennett's voice comes over the com. "Here we go. Three, two, one…"

The sound of the explosion rips through both our communications and the cold, dark night. The sky lightens, and I shoot the lock on the thin metal door. Kicking it in, Jeremy and I enter fast and low. Making our way through the warehouse space quickly, we turn this way and that to make sure there's no one hiding among the aisles of boxes. With the sound of raised voices, we follow along until my breath catches when my Red comes into view.

She's just on the other side of the metal shelf I'm looking through, and she looks terrified. Tearing my eyes off of her, I take into account the fact that Mick Oakes is holding her from behind, and he has a gun in his hand. He's holding the muzzle against Olive's head.

"Hurry up, you stupid idiot!" Albert is shouting. He takes on quick glance toward the front of the building. "Do it now!"

Stepping out from behind the edge of the shelf, I aim the Sig at Mick's head. "You don't want to do shit, Mick, besides put down your weapon and let Olive go."

Her big blue eyes go wide when she sees me, instantly filling with tears. "Ronin," she whispers.

"Yeah, sweetheart. I'm right here. You're gonna be okay." I lock my eyes with hers, making sure she stays with me and stays calm.

I'm proud of my girl. I know she's scared to death, but she's holding it together. She sucks in a breath, and I turn my attention back to Mick.

"Let her go. If I understand you correctly, this isn't what you want. You want her standing next to you while you lead the family business into the future, right? Can't have her if she's dead." Planting my feet, I put a tiny bit of pressure on the trigger. I will fucking murder him if I get the chance to, but I don't want to have to shoot with Olive standing there.

Still concealed behind the shelf, Brains's low voice comes over the com in my ear. "Wheels. We need a sharpshooter back here. Oakes has a gun against Olive's temple."

The fury inside me centers in my stomach, but a trickle of fear makes its way into my heart.

I could lose her. This could be it, I could lose her at the hands of this animal, and I haven't even gotten to tell her that I love her. Fuck, I'm so in love with her.

The realization hits me with a force I'm not expecting, and my hands tighten their grip on my gun.

"Put it down, Oakes." I growl the words. "She's not going to die today."

Mick's eyes are dead, but I can see his fear in the tremble of his hands. Whether he's scared of me or his uncle I'm not sure.

Margiano moves then, and he's fucking spry for an old man. He makes a grab for Mick's gun, and the gunshot rings out before I can blink. Margiano goes down.

It wasn't my shot.

Oakes's hands fly up, and Olive rushes toward me. Moving my Sig to my left hand, I catch her with my right, and whip her back around the huge, metal shelf.

Olive grips my neck so tightly it hurts, but I don't give two fucks how hard she squeezes me. Over the sound of her sobs, I speak urgently into her ear.

"Are you hurt, Red? Shot?" I want to give her a full checkup, but she won't let go.

Her head shakes, and somehow her grip gets even tighter. "No. No. Oh, my God. Ronin…"

Brains's voice echoes in my earpiece. "Margiano is down, but breathing. I've got Oakes. Get Olive to the Suburban, Swagger."

But Boss Man's voice barks a new order. "Everyone get to the Suburban. Cops will be here in five. Oakes comes with us."

Holstering my weapon, I lift a shaking Olive into my arms,

and nothing has ever felt as good as her heat and warmth against me. She buries her head in my neck, and I stroke her hair as I carry her out of the building.

"Fucking hell, baby. I thought...I'm so damn glad you're okay."

She takes a shuddering breath and lifts her head. Her eyes glittering in the darkness, she stares so deep into me, I think she can probably see my soul.

"You came for me."

My response is immediate. "I will always come for you."

With a sniffle, she curls into me, and I carry her into the night.

32

OLIVE

Ronin carries me into the condo. It's like he's afraid to let me walk. When we returned to NES, he told the guys he would debrief in the morning and plucked me into his arms from the Suburban, placing me in his rental car. When we arrived in the condo's parking garage, he scooped me into his arms again and carried me to the elevator, not putting me down once we were inside.

As soon as we enter the condo, I stroke the back of his head until he looks at me. "I'm okay, Ronin. You can put me down now."

His thick eyebrows pull together as he searches my face, like he's still looking for any sign that I've been hurt in some way. Finally, he sets me down on my feet but circles his arms around my waist.

"Thank you." The words fall out of my mouth before I can think about it, but he deserves my gratitude. He deserves so much more than my gratitude.

He shakes his head, cupping the side of my face with one big hand. His thumb brushing across my cheekbone, he stares into my eyes, and I fall right into the depths of his. "Never thank me. I promised you I'd keep you safe, and that promise was almost broken tonight. They never should have gotten their hands on you."

My cheeks burn, because I know that part of it is my fault "I shouldn't have left Rayne and Jeremy's."

Still stroking my cheek, his body heat keeping me safe and warm, Ronin doesn't break our stare. "Why did you?"

"I just felt like…like I didn't want you to deal with M.J. without me. Deal with M.J. *for* me. There was this sour feeling in the very bottom of my stomach…I couldn't explain it. I had to get to you…I suddenly felt like I needed to be with you more than anything. God, Ronin…I don't know if it was instinct or what but I just had this feeling you were in danger."

Glancing down, I'm kind of ashamed of myself. I created so much trouble. If I'd just stayed the course he wouldn't have had to come rescue me.

"Red, look at me." His voice firm, Ronin's other hand cups the back of my neck.

I glance back up into his eyes, and they're so full. Of whatever emotions he's feeling, they're written right there in his eyes.

"When I found out that you were just feet away from me and taken away, I was fucking terrified. I knew I was going to go after you, but Red? NES was always going to go after the Margiano family. And I'd just found out that Albert Margiano is the man responsible for Elle's murder. I was going after him regardless. But getting to you was my priority. I'm so goddamn sorry you got mixed up in all of it."

I gasp, one hand flying up to my mouth. My fingers tremble. "Oh, my God. Oh, my *God*. I'm so sorry, Ronin." It was M.J.'s uncle the whole time…the man Ronin had been looking for? Shivers of revulsion, sadness, rage, roll through my body in waves of emotion.

"Oakes said something that had me making the connection. So when I found out they'd taken you…shit, Red. I knew I didn't have much time to get to you. And there was so much I still haven't said."

Hope blooms inside my heart. "What haven't you said?"

Ronin steps in closer, his broad, hard chest, touching mine, our breaths mingling in the sliver of space between us. "For so long, I thought the only thing I had to live for was making sure that Elle's killer was brought down. I wanted that person dead. I could have done it tonight, you know? I could have killed Margiano, he was right there."

I start to shake my head, to tell him that he wouldn't have done that, but the dark look that crosses his expression stops me. And, deep down, I know that Ronin could have been capable of that. And I would have understood if he'd taken that road. He's fought this battle for seven years, blaming himself for not being there for his wife when she needed him.

"But I couldn't focus on that. Not when you were there, and that bastard was holding a gun to your head. The only thing I could think about, the only thing I could see, was *you*."

Something inside me melts, going all soft and gooey, and I know with every fiber of my being that I belong to this man.

"Margiano's gonna be brought to justice, and I'm damn glad, but now there's something in my life that overshadows that desire for revenge. Do you know what that something is, Red?"

His lips touch mine, and a rocket goes off inside my body. Every single muscle tenses, urging me to get closer to him, and my arms wind around his neck. Breathless, I shake my head.

He kisses me. His mouth crushes mine, his tongue delving inside my mouth and stroking mine, once, twice, three times, I turn into a puddle in his arms, melting against him, but just as I'm ready to climb up his body, he pulls back just slightly. I almost moan from the loss of his kiss.

"You," he whispers. "It's you, Red. I love you."

Desperate need overtakes me then, and a wicked impatience I've only ever felt with Ronin. "Show me."

His hands drop to my waist and he picks me up like I weigh nothing, and I wrap my legs around his waist. My lips find his again, and I'm vaguely aware that we're walking but I don't care where we're going. I only care that I'm with him.

Placing me down on the bed in the guest room, he steps back and points at me. "Stay there. But be naked when I get back."

I roll my eyes. "You may love me, but you're still McBossy."

Tilting his head to the side, he chuckles while scanning me from head to toe. "You'll like it. I'll be back in two minutes. No clothes, Red."

I salute him.

He turns, but instead of leaving the room, he goes into the

guest bath and closes the door. Within minutes, I can hear the sound of water running in the bathtub.

My curiosity is begging me to go and listen at the door, but instead I strip out of my clothes. Now that Ronin isn't directly in front of me, I'm actually dying to get out of them. I'm pretty sure I'll never wear this particular outfit again. In fact, I might burn it. I want the stink of the warehouse off of me, right along with the recollection of what happened tonight.

I want to surround myself in Ronin until the memory fades.

When the door swings open again, I'm perched on the edge of the bed, my legs crossed in front of me, totally bare just like Ronin asked.

I'm all ready to open my mouth to let him know that I'm only out of my clothes because I wanted to be, but it slams shut again when I catch sight of all the miles of hard, bronze muscle laid out before me. Ronin folds his arms and leans against the doorjamb, completely naked. His green eyes, deep and dark with want, scan me, touching me in every place he's about to touch with his hands. I'm eating up the vision of him at the same time, and all the words disappear from my head as my mouth goes dry.

"Good girl." His voice is nothing but a low, sexy rumble, and the intensity of his stare heats me up from the inside out.

Ronin holds out a hand, and I rise off the bed like a puppet on a string. His puppet. I know that I'd do absolutely anything he asked right now, and I'd be so happy doing it. Instead of being terrified by that thought, I'm aroused by it. Being the center of Ronin Shaw's attention leads to only good things. Very good things.

My eyes bounce around the bathroom as we enter, growing wider and more astounded everywhere I look. The tub is filled and with a thick layer of bubbles floating on top. Lit candles are littered across the countertop and in the wide corners of the Jacuzzi tub. When I look at Ronin, the flickering light catches in Ronin's eyes as he drags me closer to him.

"This is…" My voice trails off as I glance around the bathroom again.

He helps me into the tub, and follows behind me. We both settle into opposite corners, and he pulls my bare feet up onto his thick, hard thighs under the water.

Leaning back, his gaze is dark and hooded. "I've been thinking about this since the first night you stayed here. I was on the other side of that door, but as soon as I heard you singing and realized you were in this big bathtub all alone, it was all I could do not to join you then."

The hot water siphons away all the ugliness of the night, and I lean back and sigh, unable to take my eyes off the man across from me. He's so beautiful it hurts, and he just told me he loves me.

He loves me.

Suddenly finding space and distance between us far too much, I crawl across the soapy tub until I'm straddling his lap. My thighs fit perfectly on either side of his, and my arms slide around his neck. His nostrils flare, and he leans forward to take my bottom lip between his teeth.

I sigh and grind down on him, my clit landing on his impressive, hard length. We both groan and he thrusts his hips up to meet mine, my arms tightening around his neck as I try to draw him closer.

"You love me," I gasp as he reaches up to pull the band from my hair. When it tumbles out around my shoulders, Ronin buries his hands and tilts my head, kissing me deep and hard and long.

When he pulls away, I'm gasping for breath and grinding down on his cock with all I'm worth. Ronin's mouth leaves mine only to bite down on my shoulder, and I toss my head back.

"I fucking love you. What do you want, Red?" His words are a low growl against my skin.

I lift my hips and whimper. He positions himself at my entrance, and I sink down on him. The delicious fullness, the stretching that the hard length of his cock gives me, makes me groan and bury my head against his wet shoulder.

He thrusts up hard, and I cry out because it's the most pleasurable pain I've ever felt. Before Ronin, I didn't even know the two words could coexist.

Cradling my face in his hands, he stares at me while he thrusts, over and over again, and the thread of love that's slowly woven between us grows so thick the emotion of it all is hard to bear.

"I love you, Ronin." I'm deliberate with these words. I want him to know that they're true, that I feel them all the way down to my soul.

And that no matter what happens from here on out, I'm his.

Epilogue

RONIN

"How do I look?"

Olive twirls in a slow circle in front of me, showing off her costume. I take her in, my eyes feasting on the gold, shimmering dress hugging tightly to every single one of her curves. It's short, much shorter than anything Olive would normally wear out, and I'm already getting off on a fantasy of pulling off the stilettos and running my tongue all the way up her legs later tonight.

In fact...I stalk toward her, yanking her closer to me so she can feel just how much I want her right now. My hands snake up the backs of her thighs. My fingers gloss over the garter holster on her left leg and the toy gun stuck inside it.

"You look so fucking sexy," I murmur, staring into her eyes. "I don't want to go to the Halloween party anymore."

She swallows, leaning into me, gazing right back into my stare like she's on exactly the same page. "Jeremy and Rayne will kill us if we don't show."

I lean down and run my nose along the shell of her ear before tugging the lobe between my teeth. I seem to have a biting fetish where Olive is concerned. It's something I never knew I liked, but she always tastes good enough to eat.

"Don't care."

She moans and arches into me. "Ronin..."

Finding strength I really wish she didn't have, she pushes away from me and takes a step back. Holding up a finger, she smiles. "Later."

Scanning me, she licks her lips. "I might not be able to wait until we get home, though. You're the sexiest James Bond I've ever seen."

I smooth a hand over my dark suit, my fingers glossing over my real (unloaded) pistol situated in my hip holster. "And there's no Bond Girl out there more stunning than you."

She holds out her hand. "Shall we?"

We exit the condo and ride the elevator down to the parking garage. *Our* condo, because the day after everything went down at Margiano's distribution center, she officially moved in with me. Her house in the suburbs is on the market, and having her with me every day on a permanent basis feels like the best decision I ever made.

Almost.

Yesterday was the arraignment for Albert Margiano. Mick is testifying against his uncle, in exchange for a lesser sentence. I think he regretted the fact that his uncle went after Olive solely because Mick wanted her. But if he ever gets out of prison and attempts to contact Olive...well, that's a bridge I'll cross if I ever get there. Just because Mick isn't the cold-blooded murderer I thought he was, he was still an abusive asshole to Olive, and I'll never let him near her.

I'm confident that nothing will end well for Mick.

It was satisfying as hell, watching the D.A. tell a judge everything that bastard has done, and sitting in the courtroom with Olive by my side as I watched the judge deliver the news that Elle's killer will stand trial not only for her murder, but also for the murder of Grace Hodges and a whole host of other crimes, a deep sense of rightness filled me, and I knew that I was set free from everything that's plagued me for years. The Margiano crime family's been cut off at the head, and we all know what happens to snakes when the head is separated.

They die.

The streets of Wilmington, North Carolina, will be that much safer for it.

After court was over, Lindy Hodges admitted that she knew Grace had gotten in bed with Margiano's crew, but she was too scared to tell us, fearing retaliation from the Margianos. Olive and I both hugged her, letting her know that we understood her doubts and that we were happy she no longer had to live with that fear.

Unlocking the doors of my new Ram, I lift Olive inside and round the front to climb in on the driver's side.

"You realize that I've never in my adult life dressed up for Halloween, right?" I ask her as I start the ignition.

She shrugs. "I haven't either. But Jeremy and Rayne made a compelling case."

I snort, pulling out of the parking garage and heading for

the downtown home that my best friend shares with his wife. "If, 'Dress up for our party or be shamed for the entire next year' counts as compelling, everything I thought was true in the world no longer is."

She looks at me, brows lifted. "Even though I make a stunning Bond Girl?"

Reaching over, I grab her hand and lift it to my lips. "Not that. That's definitely the truth."

Every day I'm still trying to figure out how I got so damn lucky. If Jeremy hadn't asked me to watch over Olive while he went on his honeymoon, I don't like to think about what would have happened. She might not have turned to me when she needed help. She might not be the center of my world the way she is now. There are way too many "might not's" that I don't want to think about.

I'm just thankful we made it out on the other side as the new Ronin and Olive, together no matter what.

When we walk into the Teague house, the party is in full swing. Decker runs up to us as we close the front door, and I take one look at him dressed as a Storm Trooper and Night in a doggie R2D2 costume and lose it.

But then my stomach clenches and my heart expands when Olive drops to her knees beside the little boy and takes him into her arms. "You and Night win the best costume award," she announces, hugging him tight.

He pulls back and gestures toward the big stone fireplace in the center of the great room, where Jeremy and Rayne are standing with Berkeley, Dare, and their friends from Lone Sands, Drake and Mea Sullivan. Olive's neighbor from her old neighborhood, Macy, is here with her husband and her son. "Wait till you see Mom and Dad."

For Decker, I don't roll my eyes, but Jeremy is truly in his element. Olive squeezes my hand, and when I glance down at her that bottom lip is squeezed tightly between her teeth as she tries to stifle a laugh.

Jeremy is in full costume as Anakin Skywalker, and Rayne, tucked into his side, is dressed as Padmé Amidala.

"Oh, my God," whispers Olive. "I just can't with their little family cuteness."

Leading Olive by the hand, I walk with her over to Jeremy and Rayne. Olive places a hand on Rayne's stomach, and both sisters look down at the tiny bump protruding there.

"I still can't believe it," whispers Olive as the sisters exchange a look that only they can understand.

My hand goes to the back of her neck, squeezing gently as I swallow hard against the emotion threatening to choke me alive. When Olive looks up at me, there's something in her eyes that I'm thanking God for every day.

Trust. Deep and never-ending. It' something I'm never going to take for granted, and one day in a future not so far away Olive is going to be the one with the bump.

This is the woman I'm going to spend the rest of my days with. Start forever with. And I can't fucking wait to see her pregnant with *my* baby.

Pulling her toward me, I drop a kiss on her forehead and then lead her into the party to join our friends.

My palms sweat as I take another sip of the bourbon meant to calm me. Jeremy stares me down from where he stands in the kitchen, his hands folded across his chest and a smirk on his face.

"What the fuck are you waiting for?"

"The right time," I growl, setting the glass down on the island.

Jeremy spreads his arms wide. "Everyone she loves is here in this house. It's been the right time all night."

I nod, pacing away from him. When I turn around again, I bounce on my toes like a fighter getting ready to head into the ring. "You're right. I gotta do it now before I lose my goddamn mind."

Jeremy nods. "Thank God. Rayne's taking Deck up to bed soon, and he'll be pissed if he misses this."

I shove Jeremy's shoulder as I pass him, and zero in on Olive as I walk back into the great room. She's sitting in a chair by the front window, talking to Grisham's fiancée, Greta, and she looks so relaxed and happy that I just pause for a minute to take her in.

Until I feel Jeremy's index finger digging into my spine.

"Do it, asshole," he hisses in my ear. "Or I'll shoot you."

Rolling my eyes, I don't bother to turn around. "That's your finger, Brains."

"Sentiment's still true," he assures me.

I'm not the kind of guy who stands in front of a roomful of people and makes a pretty speech. Olive knows this about me. So she won't fault me if I screw this up.

I hope.

Holding her in my focus, I stride over to her and stop when

I reach her chair. She glances up at me, pausing in her conversation with Greta, and her eyes light up.

God, I love this woman.

"That, right there." Her eyebrows furrow in confusion as I drop to my knee.

Greta gasps, her hands flying to her mouth, but Olive's eyes well with tears as she holds my gaze in hers. She doesn't move a muscle, her eyes burning into mine.

"That's my whole reason for being, Red. When your eyes light up just because I'm around? It's not just the best damn feeling in the world. It's the driving force of my day. Every day."

A single tear rolls down my girl's face, and I want so badly to reach up and brush it away. But first, I need to ask her the most important question of my life.

"Will you let me keep making you happy to see me, every single day, for the rest of our lives? Will you marry me, Olive Alexander?"

Olive's face breaks into a beautiful smile, dimples and all, and I take a breath for the first time since entering the great room.

"Yes," she says simply.

My heart pounding, I reach into my pocket and pull out the simple, platinum engagement ring. A solitaire, pear-shaped diamond sits on top, sparkling and perfect, exactly the same way my future wife does.

After I slip it onto her finger, she slides off the chair and right into my arms.

"I love you so much," she whispers fiercely in my ear.

Greta's voice pipes up. "If you two get married before Grisham and I do, I'm going to kill someone."

The room erupts in laughter, and then applause, and through it all I hold on to the woman who saved me from a lifetime of loneliness and revenge.

She's the best fucking promise I ever made.

Don't miss Bennett and Sayward's story.
Please read on for a preview of the next book
in the Rescue Ops series,

Mine to Save.

BENNETT

I never wanted this shit.

Taking the time to add the lemon on the edge of the glass just like the coed requested, I slide the tumbler across the scuffed wooden bar toward her. I give the chick the fake-ass smile I've perfected in the past few years. She giggles, fluttering all kinds of long, dark lashes at me while simultaneously pushing her big, fake tits together in front of my face.

My dick doesn't even twitch. I'm so far removed from this type of flirtation it's almost funny. As soon as she slips a wad of folded-up bills into the tip jar I turn away and lift a brow at the next paying customer.

And the night continues.

I wash glasses. I make drinks. I watch as the town's idiots get drunker and make more bad decisions.

And all I can think about is, maybe bartending was the perfect job for me when I was fresh out of the joint. But now?

After what I experienced over the past few weeks, I realize how motherfucking *bored* I am.

My fingers twitch, itching to *do something*. Really do something. My brain flashes back to the night I helped my buddy, Ronin Shaw, rescue his woman from a mob boss. The explosives. It had been awhile since I'd made something go boom, but that shit was like riding a bike. Once I started, the rest was smooth sailing.

After I pour the remaining drops from the last bottle of SoCo into a tumbler and pass it to a grizzled old man, I stride down the length of the space behind the bar.

"Be right back. Headed to the stockroom," I mutter to the other bartender, a recent hire named Kandie who gives me then a nod and a smile in response.

I slide past Kandie, which is difficult because her ample ass cheeks take up more than half the space behind the bar, and she cuts her gaze toward me.

"You tryin' to cop a feel, B?" she asks with a smirk.

I would abso-fucking-lutely be trying to do just that, because Kandie is as hot as they come. Sexy hourglass figure wrapped up in tight clothing that leaves just the right amount to the imagination. I know she sexes it up more than necessary on the nights she works here, dropping the neckline on her tops and squeezing into the slimmest jeans possible, and it works for her. The girl cleans up in tips from the college-aged crowd who's been frequenting The Oakes for the past month, and there's no shame in her game. There are nights she takes home more than I do, and I just laugh while I watch her count her tips. Her brown skin is smooth, and the miles of waves in her thick black hair puddle around her tits tonight, even though she changes her hair up weekly.

But Kandie made it very clear when I hired her that not only does she not sleep with coworkers, I wouldn't be on her list even if she did. She doesn't swing my way.

Bumping her hip with mine, I hit her with the Bennett Blacke charm. The fact that she's immune to it doesn't stop me one bit. "Fuck yes, I am. Gotta get my touches in when your hands are full of booze, or else you'll punch the shit outta me."

She laughs, deep and throaty, and I can see the dude she's pouring the house draft for visibly swallow as he stares at her. She purses deep red lips at me and blows a fake kiss. "Kiss this ass, B."

"As soon as you'll let me," I toss over my shoulder as I push through the swinging door toward the back hall and the stock-room.

I pass by the open office door on the way there, and then I backtrack a few steps and pause in the doorway.

"Mickey? Didn't expect to see you here tonight." Leaning against the doorjamb, I fold my arms across my chest.

Mickey Oakes, the bar's owner and a longtime friend, glances up from the scattered piles of paperwork on the desk. I've been working hard as hell trying to get the books back to their pristine condition after Mickey's organized crime-bound son, Mick, rolled into the place two months ago and fucked shit up.

Mickey swipes a hand across his forehead. "You done good work here, boy. Can't tell ya how much I 'preciate it."

Mickey always sounds like he's got a wad of chewing tobacco in his mouth, even though he dropped the habit over a decade ago.

I grunt in response. I've only been doing what needed to be done. I'm not gonna let him thank me for it. He hired me to do a job, at a time in my life when no one else would. He was there for me while I got my life together, picked up the pieces from everything I'd smashed to hell.

Shaking my head, I push myself off the wall. "How you been feeling?"

As if on cue, a hacking cough starts in his chest and it doesn't let up until his weathered face is almost purple and he's wheezing to catch his breath.

Cursing, I rush back out into the bar and grab a glass of water. Bringing it back to him in the small, cluttered office, I watch as he takes a sip, the coughs dying down slowly.

There's a grapefruit-sized lump in my throat that I try like hell to choke down.

I never knew my own father, but I'm guessing that the way Mickey treats me is the way someone's old man would treat him. He tried right up until he couldn't anymore to build a good relationship with his own son, but that weasel screwed it up more times than I can count. If I had a father like Mickey...well, I'd appreciate him. That's for damn sure.

Looking at me with a worn and exhausted half-smile, he thuds his chest with a fist. "Been better."

Clearing my throat, my words are more of a grunt than a reply. "Then what the hell are you doing here? You should be home. Resting up."

After another gut-splitting round of coughing, Mickey

gulps more of the water and winces like he's in pain. "I got emphysema, son. Goes right along with the cancer eatin' away at my lungs. Ain't no amount a restin' gonna help. Wanna make sure I help you get these books straight after my fool son done messed it all up."

Then he glares at me, but his lips twitch in his attempt to hide a smile. "I don't need no babysitter. Ain't you got customers to wait on behind my bar?"

I wave my hand at him, my stomach knotted up with worry, and continue to the stockroom.

What's that old man gonna do with this place?

Running a bar was never in my grand life plan. Shit, I never even had a grand life plan. Claw my way out of the rural, backwoods town where I was raised in the low country of South Carolina, be the best soldier I could while I was in the army, and that was about it. That was as far as I got before it all went to hell.

When I almost ruined my whole life within two minutes of blind rage.

I pull liquor bottles down off the shelf and place them in a crate, which I haul back out to the bar. After I shelve them and toss the crate under the counter, I scan the bar area and note that I have new, familiar arrivals.

Sitting at a couple of high-top tables just behind the row of stools are a group of faces I never expected to see.

My buddy Ronin Shaw wears his usual too-intense expression on his face. The man always looks like he's carrying the weight of the fucking world on his shoulders, and I've told him on more than one occasion that he needs to lighten up.

He's seated beside his boss at Night Eagle Security, Jacob Owen. My gaze skates over Jacob toward Jeremy Teague, his long hair pulled back into a bun at the back of his head. Sliding over to the table beside them, my eyes land on two more NES team members, Grisham Abbott and Dare Conners before finally settling on *her*.

Sayward Diaz.

The woman they call *Viper*.

I can't help it when my eyes travel from the exotic features of her face straight to the hint of cleavage visible above the vee of her T-shirt. She might think she's hiding the luscious curves hidden underneath her uniform of jeans and a zipped-up hoodie, but there's no running away from how sexy she is. When I force my gaze back up to her face, it's to find her looking at me with irritation-filled hazel eyes. She shifts, her nose twitching with a show of disinterest as her sensuous, full lips roll between her teeth. Her long, dark hair is pulled into a messy bun and she's not wearing any makeup, but who the hell cares with a face like that?

When a woman looks this fucking perfect without even trying, she's a danger to society. I've also seen what she can do when she's sitting behind her computer, so the Viper tag? I get it. She's straight-up nasty with her tech. No one can hide.

"Two Coronas with limes please." I don't even notice as the barely legal girl bats her lashes and slides her credit card across the counter. "And I wouldn't mind if you wrote your number on the back of that receipt."

"What the hell are they doing here?" I mutter aloud as I pull two Coronas from the fridge and stick a lime into neck of each. I grab the girl's credit card and swipe it, offering her a distracted grin as I slide the white slip of paper back for her to sign.

"I'm off the menu, baby girl, but if you keep comin' into this bar I might be persuaded to change my mind."

I don't bring home women from the bar. It's a choice. The last thing I need is some chick hanging around for weeks afterward, searching for a repeat performance that won't ever happen.

I'll flirt with them until the cows come home, though, because it's what they want, and they pay nicely for a little attention.

The girl bites her lip and grabs the beers, making sure to lean over the bar as she does so. I look, because I'm not blind, but then I glance at Kandie when she elbows my side.

"You know that bunch?" She inclines her head toward the Night Eagle team, and I nod.

"Yeah, I do. Just not sure what they're doing here. Didn't expect to see most of them again anytime soon."

When Ronin's woman was taken from the parking lot of this bar by Wilmington's most notorious organized crime family, I got involved. Not only because he's my friend and he needed me, but also because Mickey's son, Mick, was at the center of the bullshit and I took personal exception to the fact that he'd dared to do it all on my turf. I backed Ronin up, worked some of my magic with explosives, and helped rescue Olive safe and sound.

I knew there were a few members of the NES team that didn't like my past or my attitude.

Doesn't matter to me. They can all go fuck themselves, because I don't answer to anyone. Not anymore.

"Well they're a pretty bunch." When I glance at Kandie, her dark brown eyes are locked and loaded on the two high-top tables. "Especially little Miss Converse Sneakers over there. That nerdy vibe she's got goin' on works for her."

Kandie watches Sayward, and I follow her gaze without meaning to. My cock stiffens in my jeans, growing uncomfortable as hell, and I turn toward the wall so I can adjust myself without looking like an asshole.

Kandie chuckles. "Looks like I'm not the only one who noticed."

With a sigh, I'm getting ready to face the music and find out what the NES crew wants with me, when a commotion at the end of the bar pulls my attention. I turn that way just in time to see one dude's fist slam into another one's face.

And then the bar erupts in absolute fucking madness.

About the Author

Diana Gardin is a wife of one and a mom of two. Writing is her second full-time job to that, and she loves it! Diana writes contemporary romance in the Young Adult and New Adult categories. She's also a former elementary school teacher. She loves steak, sugar cookies, and Coke and hates working out.

Learn more at:
  DianaGardin.com
  Twitter: @DianalynnGardin
  Facebook.com/AuthorDianaGardin